Tony Peake was born in South Africa. After graduating from Rhodes University, he moved to London, where he worked under Charles Marowitz as production manager at the Open Space Theatre. A spell on Ibiza, teaching English, History and Drama, was followed by a return to London and jobs modelling, acting and film distribution. He is now a literary agent. As a short story writer, he has contributed to *Winter's Tales* and his work is due to appear in the *Penguin Book of Contemporary South African Stories*. He has recently edited an anthology of stories on the theme of seduction for Serpent's Tail. A SUMMER TIDE is his first novel and he is currently working on his second.

TONY PEAKE

A Summer Tide

An *Abacus* Book

First published in Great Britain by Abacus in 1993
This edition published in 1994

Copyright © Tony Peake 1993

The moral right of the author has been asserted.

A CIP catalogue record for this book is
available from the British Library.

ISBN 0 349 10553 7

Printed in England by Clays Ltd, St Ives plc

Abacus
A Division of
Little, Brown and Company (UK) Limited
Brettenham House
Lancaster Place
London WC2E 7EN

I owe this book to many people. To my mother and father, to Peter, to my agent Jennifer Kavanagh, to everyone at Little, Brown, and to the many friends and colleagues (they know who they are) who have, over the years, given me their support and encouragement. Also, of course, to the island, without which the story of Lucy Hamilton would not have found its setting.

Scorzo

*L*ast night I dreamt about Benedict. It was on the island and it was late afternoon. There was no sun, just a grudging sort of light that seemed to have been thrown at the world like a bucket of slops, causing the grey of the sky to run into the grey of the sea, and the grey of the sea to bleed, via the grey of the mud-flats, into the land. I was on my afternoon walk, following the swell of the sea wall round the edge of the island, looking neither at the land nor the sea, but at the precise and familiar rhythms of my feet, utterly alone in the seeping grey silence of my world – until, as I passed the creek, I became aware of someone watching me.

I looked up and there, leaning against the hull of Norman's *Sprite*, was a man. The sea wall isn't more than a dozen yards from the huddle of boats at the head of the creek, but for some reason I couldn't make out his features. I just knew he was watching me; knew, too, that it was useless trying to continue my walk until I'd discovered who he was.

I tried to come slowly off the wall, but once I'd begun my descent it tipped me, as it always did, into a run that immediately brought the shadowy figure into focus.

'Benedict!' I gasped.

'Of course,' he replied. 'Who else?' And shooting out an arm, he pulled me towards him and kissed me – not long, or very hard even, but on the lips, fully, like a lover. After which, very slowly, he ran the back of his hand down the side of my cheek: assessing and dismissing me in a single gesture.

I extended a tentative finger to trace, in return, the outline of his jaw, but as my finger made contact with his flesh, he frowned, and with his frown came a shift in the light, a sudden darkening, making me shiver. I glanced up at the sky. 'Let's go,' I was about to say – except that when I looked down again, he was no longer there.

It woke me immediately, of course, the poignancy of this

encounter, leaving me washed up on Andre's narrow attic bed, rigid as a corpse. For what felt like an eternity I lay there without moving, my eyes fixed on the sloping eave above me, until, unable to focus any longer on the beams that delineated and dissected the ceiling, I sat up, and throwing back the sheet, slipped out of bed and padded to the window.

Although it was after midnight, it was hot still in the mews; noisy too. The suffocating closeness of the summer night lay on London like a curse against which, in place of bones, people in every street seemed to be throwing parties. There was laughter from the house at the end of the mews, music from over the rooftops, and two blocks away, from the Earls Court Road, the oddly sea-like sound of the traffic as it surged against the lights.

I could hardly credit the irony of it. All through his time on the island, and afterwards, when he'd vanished and I was sick with worry over what might have become of him, he'd never, not once, played a part in my dreams. Then, if I'd dreamt at all, it had been of Charles or Andre or Ralph. The men who stood between us. Never Benedict. Yet now, when Andre's account of what had happened should have laid him to rest, he'd come back to haunt me.

I tried making light of it. Squeezing my eyes shut, I attempted to picture myself as Charles might have done: a middle-aged princess, her sleep-dishevelled hair as startled as her thoughts, trapped at her window by a prince who never was, never could be.

But it was useless. The moment I closed my eyes, London dematerialised, the traffic became the tide, the laughter from across the mews the crying of gulls, and I was back in the shadow of Norman's *Sprite*, looking wildly round for a sign, any sign, of the man who, first with his appearance, then his disappearance, had so unsettled our lives, our island.

Alla Prima

Our island, I call it, when it isn't ours at all. We merely cohabit there, Charles and I, at Andre's pleasure; resident guests, not unlike the countless favourites (crusaders, courtiers, lovers) who, when the island belonged to the crown, were slipped this bauble of land in return for services rendered – until, in the 1850s, it passed from the nobility into the hands of a yeoman farmer and became, as it had been in Roman times, a farm again.

It's not very big, the island, perhaps a mile square – and only at high tide is it wholly an island. At low tide, when the water empties from the upper reaches of the estuary, it is nothing more than a long, low swelling on the mud-flats, a polyp in the river mouth, tethered there by means of the causeway that snakes from its southernmost tip to the caravan park opposite.

I like it best when it's an island. Charles says it's because I'm anti-social, but it isn't that at all; it's simply that I don't particularly care for this part of England. Meldwich, our mainland market town, is pretty enough: a picturesque muddle of Georgian and clapboard houses and a harbour cluttered with boats. But Meldwich is an exception. The rest of the county is dank and flat and cheerless, a dispiriting compromise of country and suburb which, as it approaches the sea, peters out in a caravan park: final proof, if proof were needed, that the land has run out of ideas for making itself interesting.

It stretches as far as the eye can see, this caravan park, replicating, plot after plot, circumscribed segments of leisure which make you gasp with relief when, past the last line of caravans, you come to the signs saying 'Private', and cresting the sea wall, are suddenly on the causeway where the only distractions are the birds picking daintily in the mud, or in

7

the sky, a sly arrangement of gulls: pointers to another, less predictable world.

Once on the island, the road runs along the edge of the top two fields (usually planted with wheat), past the creek on the left (where Andre keeps his yacht, Norman his *Sprite* and Jorgen a dinghy), before turning sharply to the right towards the centre of the island and the village.

We call it the village, though like the island itself, it barely merits the name. There are no shops, no pub, no church, just three houses, the green and the ruins of the Institute, a home for alcoholics put up by a previous owner at the turn of the century.

The first of the houses, on your left as you enter the village and known as the Chase, is a somewhat self-important, Edwardian construction, all mullioned windows and mock-Tudor beams. It is rented on an annual basis by the Landies, a couple from London whose presence on the island is generally as insubstantial as the hope that brought them here: that their daughter Harriet would grow up to love the countryside.

Beyond the Chase, and surrounded by the clean, white lines of a picket fence, is the Lilacs; a one-storied, wooden cottage inhabited on a more permanent basis, and more disconcertingly too, by Jorgen, a tabloid journalist from Denmark who both through his work and his hobby – photography – is uncomfortably adept at exposure. He came to England in the early seventies to cover the story of a local woman who chopped her lover, Iscariot-like, into thirty pieces before flushing him down the loo. He stayed because he found, to his delight, that far from being a rarity, stories like this are two a penny along this coast. In Denmark he had to ferret for copy; here all he needs is a subscription to the local papers – thus freeing time for his secondary, more subtle form of inquisition, the camera.

Across the road from the Lilacs is the old farmhouse, dark heart and hub of the village. Built in the 1700s, its bitumen-blackened clapboard façade, offset by four white windows, two in the steeply angled roof, two on either side of the plain white door, has stood testament to over two hundred years of island life, whilst its cosy, low-ceilinged interior has played host to countless occupants, the most recent being Norman, the island manager, a lugubrious individual who, gun permanently at the ready, oversees the farming of the land, repairs the houses, keeps down the rabbit population and stocks the spinneys with pheasants so that Andre and his city friends can, when the season permits, play at being landed gentry.

And finally, on the left as you leave the village, is the ruined Institute, a derelict approximation of its former, four-storey self, all gaping holes where once there were windows, doors, the roof; holes through which, at night, the wind roams like a ghost, keening the past.

On leaving the village, the road runs for five or six hundred yards between an avenue of chestnuts before emerging onto the edge of a large, untidy lawn which descends on the one side to the beach and, at the other, is brought short by the manor house, a large, square building flanked by two enormous bay windows and topped by a forbidding configuration of turrets and chimney pots. An uneasy mix of the suburban and the seigniorial, its pebble-dashed façade and mock-Tudor beams somehow at odds with its size and situation, the manor house is not a particularly handsome or likeable building. Indeed, the fashion is to deride it: golf-course Gothic, Charles calls it. But for all its shortcomings, and especially when viewed from the beach, one can't help but be awed by the way in which it commands this side of the island.

Or I can't. And it's not because I like the house. I don't. Even though we've lived in it for five years now, I've never felt entirely at home here. In fact, Charles and I use only the minimum of rooms: the kitchen, pantry and living-room on the ground floor, a bedroom and bathroom each on the first floor, and then – as Charles' studio – the attic with its enormous skylight and spectacular views across the estuary. The rest of the rooms (the bay-windowed billiard-room, the dining-room and library, the old study, the sewing-room, the myriad bedrooms on the first and second floors) we leave closed: cold, damp and, in many cases, with what's left of the original Edwardian furniture still shrouded in sheets.

The only thing I cherish, if that's the right word, about our makeshift home is what it keeps hidden at the rear: the old orchard, where, weather permitting, I spend most of my time, either reading in the shade of one of the apple trees, or else simply sitting on the rim of the old fish-pond, from whose empty concrete bowl, cracked and discoloured by years of exposure to the elements, the orchard radiates in an untidy profusion of weeds, old flower-beds and tangled fruit trees to the high wall that surrounds and protects it from the worst of the wind and the scrutiny of strangers.

And that, more or less, is the extent of the island. The only other building of any consequence is the cavernous grain shed behind the manor house; the only other field the East Meadow, at whose tip, set into the sea wall courtesy of the Second World War, is a concrete bunker from whose roof you can see to the very limit and sentinel of our world: megalithic Broadwake, the nuclear power station whose massive towers mark the point at which the river opens into the sea.

The island is owned, as I say, by Andre, and has been for seven years now. Before that it was the property of a chemicals company, and before that, going backwards in time, of Mr Benson, the industrialist; the War Office; and the aptly initialled Arthur Augustus Mudd, leading light of the temperance movement.

Arthur Augustus, or so the story goes, was so ashamed of the way in which his family had made its money – the production of a bottle much favoured by turn of the century brewers – that he resolved to devote himself to the rehabilitation of alcoholics. His first step was to find an isolated spot where these unfortunates, the lure of the pub removed, could reasonably be expected to go cold turkey. Then, having found the island, he proceeded to build the manor house, where he and his housekeeper would live; the Chase and the Lilacs for his staff; and finally, for the alcoholics, the keystone of his crusade, the Institute.

It was a project that never got off the ground. No sooner had the first batch of alcoholics arrived on the island than the fishermen of Meldwich, ever eager to earn a little extra, began, for a fee, to ferry barrels of beer into the creek, where, on the pretext of an invigorating walk along the sea wall, the alcoholics would gather to undo whatever good their unwelcome saviour had done them.

With the coming of the First World War, the island was requisitioned by the War Office and used as a base from which to test the first submarines – minute metal cylinders, no more than a few metres long, into which you couldn't have squeezed a crew of more than two. There is a photograph in the billiard-room of ten or twenty of them on the beach by the pier, lined up like cigar cases on the pebbles – and behind the manor house, empty now and overgrown with weeds, is what looks like a mammoth paddling pool, but was in fact the tank where the submarines were tested.

When the war ended, the island was returned to Arthur Augustus, who, thoroughly discouraged by his inability to redeem the English, decided to go somewhere where the natives were more appreciative of his example: Papua New Guinea I think it was, or Borneo. So he sold the island to Mr Benson, who planted the avenue of chestnuts, laid out the orchard and turned the East Meadow into an airstrip so he could commute between the island and his factory in Leeds.

The other thing Mr Benson did, throughout the twenties and thirties, was to throw a succession of fabled parties to which the guests were either flown in his private plane or brought by coach. I'm sure not all of the parties can have been as fabulous as the locals maintain, but according to legend there were always two bands, one in the hall, one in a marquee on the lawn, always fairy lights or candles in the orchard, vast tables of food in the dining-room, a phalanx of waiters, and never less than a hundred guests, the more high-spirited of whom would, in high summer and when they'd danced enough, gather in giggling groups beyond the square of light thrown by the french windows onto the grass, strip off their clothes and run, naked and laughing, into the sea.

The locals did not approve of these parties – not because of the behaviour they engendered, but because of how that behaviour was fuelled. With the Institute closed, and Mr Benson supplying his guests with drink direct from Fortnum and Mason, the fishermen of Meldwich were out of pocket.

All of which came, from the locals' point of view, to a
suitably retributive end when, in 1938, and with his wife on
board, Mr Benson crashed his plane into the estuary, killing
the pair of them. The search for their bodies, which were
never recovered, made headlines in the local paper and
there was a lavish memorial service to which, again by the
coachload, everyone came. Very few local tears, however,
were shed at the passing of the Bensons, and there was much
self-satisfied talk of how the island would always turn against
those who abused it.

Or this, at any rate, is what Norman tells me. I don't have
that much contact with the locals. They are not a welcoming
lot, besides which I don't often leave the island; but Norman,
bless him, spends as many of his evenings as the tide will
allow in the Jolly Sailor beyond the caravan park, where, over
the years, he has heard just about everything there is to hear
about the island and its history.

After Mr Benson came the chemicals company, who
bought the island by auction from the Benson estate and ran
it as a tax loss, doing absolutely nothing to it, just letting it
slide into ruin. No one lived in the manor house during
those years, nor in any of the houses in the village except the
farmhouse, which was occupied by a succession of farm
managers – each, according to Norman, less able and less
interested in the island than the last. Until, seven years ago,
the chemicals company decided to let the island go and
Andre snapped it up: unlikely, unfathomable Andre, he of
the sleek designer suits and cockney jargon who, although he
is barely thirty and comes from a council estate in Bow, runs
one of London's most influential art galleries and, in
addition to the island, owns an ocean-going yacht, a plot of
land in Barbados and a five-storey house in Earls Court.

Rumour envelops Andre, its subtle smell, heady as the
aftershave he favours (sweet, corrupt, corrupting), tagging
him wherever he goes. There's the story that as a schoolboy
boxer he floored none other than Rob Bowley in a two round
contest, which is how he's supposed to have come by his
broken nose. On leaving school they say he worked in a
clothing factory off the Mile End Road, supplying cheap

versions of the designer labels to the High Street. This certainly makes sense, for he's a meticulous dresser – though it's only for his next incarnation, as a model, that there's any proof: a pile of old magazines in a bedroom at the manor house, in each of which, somewhere, sometimes in colour, sometimes in black and white, sometimes large, sometimes small, is his impatient, hungry face, topped by its shock of spiky hair. It's as a model, most probably, that he learnt how to modulate his boxer's belligerence into his present brusque charm, that and the equally useful trick of selling people what they don't necessarily want; though these are abilities he could have acquired anywhere along the path from Bow to Mayfair and his final metamorphosis into the owner of the Charn Gallery in South Audley Street, on whose walls hang works by Warhol, Hockney, Bacon, Freud – and Charles.

People say he made this last leg of his journey through the offices of a rich and influential lover. Some, not knowing Andre well, cite a woman. Others, knowing him better, guess at a man. Still others, their eyes on the island, the yacht, Barbados, the ready availability of cocaine in Andre's circle and the rather sinister men with whom he consorts, put it down to drug smuggling. Charles is of this school. 'But of course,' he says, 'how else? It's so easy for him. An ounce of cocaine in the frame of a painting, a kilo of heroin in the base of a statue. What could be neater? Or more appropriate?' Here he smiles. 'Art and drugs. They're of a piece, remember. Mood altering, both.'

What do I think? To be honest, I don't know. Nor do I particularly want to know. Since Andre is so crucial to Charles and me, so central to our existence, his income in effect ours, I prefer to ignore the genesis of his money and pretend he bought the yacht and the island not as the tools of some nefarious trade, but simply because it's only here that he can be alone, be himself – even though he visits so rarely and treats the island as casually as he does the young men with whom, when he does come, he likes to amuse himself.

Not many people are aware of Andre's sexuality – not because he makes a secret of it, simply because of the way in

which he practises it. I know, for example, that only a few of
his boys are taken to the house in Earls Court, or included in
any way in Andre's London life. It's not that he's ashamed of
them, or of how he feels about them. It's just that there isn't
much room, in Andre's London life, for anything as periph-
eral as sex – which is what, for Andre, sex seems to be: a
distinct, discrete activity, to be practised at set times and in a
set way.

About once every six weeks he will ring Norman (who has
the only phone on the island) to announce he's coming
down for the weekend. He will then arrive on the Friday tide
with a young man in tow; always, it seems, the same young
man, an East-ender, a rougher, cheaper version of himself,
the tightly muscled body packed into faded jeans and a
tattered bomber jacket as opposed to Andre's tailored
trousers and linen shirts, and without the social graces, sullen
where Andre seems merely thoughtful, inarticulate where
Andre is simply quiet – and who, once Saturday dawns, and
under Andre's leadership, will throw himself with silent self-
absorption at everything the island has to offer: windsurfing,
sailing, jogging, shooting, snooker. He will exchange very few
words with Andre in the course of these activities, will
scarcely seem to acknowledge his host's existence, except
that he won't do a thing that Andre hasn't instigated, won't
go anywhere without his leader, so that by the end of the day,
when we have drunk too much, it will seem that there are two
Andres at the table, two Andres playing music in the living-
room, two Andres going up to bed. And it's always the same,
the pattern of each visit identical, down to the tiniest detail,
the only variable being the boy's name: Andy one month,
Mark the next, then Bob, Ted, George . . . Until we come to
Benedict. Which is where the pattern breaks. Where I come
into the picture.

It's funny, using that word: picture. You've no idea how
much I wish that, like Charles, I could reach for a brush and,
with a few deft strokes, sketch in Andre, his boys, the island,
Charles and myself – standing, perhaps, in a familial group
in front of the manor house, Andre in the centre, Charles
and I at his side, and the boys, like the children they are,

grouped athletically about our feet. But I have no ability with a brush, I must rely on words – clumsy things, at the best of times; slippery, too.

Like the words of the art critic, I forget his name, who said of Andre at the fraught and fateful exhibition that started it all: 'He's not to be trusted, our Mr Charn. Not trusted an inch.'

It was five years ago and we were caught uneasily in a corner of the Broadmere Gallery, the art critic, Charles and I, at a joint exhibition of half a dozen of the Broadmere's artists.

Charles had always exhibited at the Broadmere, ever since leaving St Martin's, and had always considered himself lucky to be numbered among their artists. They weren't, as galleries went, particularly fashionable, but they were reliable and had always managed to sell Charles' landscapes as quickly as he painted them. Or at least, they had until a few years previously, when, for some reason, sales of Charles' work had begun to slump, causing the gallery, when arranging the next exhibition, to deny Charles his usual one-man show and lump him in with five of their lesser known artists, painters whose work had yet to 'break through'.

Reason enough in itself, you might say, for Charles to be in a dangerous mood. Richard, who ran the gallery, certainly seemed to think so. He'd been hovering nervously in the vicinity of Charles all evening, keeping a watchful eye on his intake of alcohol and reporting faithfully on the least bit of interest shown in Charles' six landscapes. But what Richard couldn't know, what no one knew, was that there was another, more unsettling reason for Charles to have taken as little care as he had with his dress – habitually Bohemian, that night his rumpled shirt and baggy jacket looked as if he'd slept in them, his thinning curls as if they'd never known the discipline of a comb – another, more deep-seated cause for the speed with which he was downing the gallery's plonk: his recent discovery that two months previously I'd foolishly allowed Bobby Alton, estranged husband of our next-door neighbour and Charles' most constant drinking companion, into my bed.

I should have known, of course, when I did it, that Bobby

Alton was no different to any of Charles' acolytes – interested in me only to the extent that I was a conduit to Charles – and therefore bound to give the game away, to let slip that now he was closer to Charles than Charles would ever have thought possible. But desperation makes one do desperate things, especially the desperation engendered by twenty years of marriage to the most perfect man on earth.

As proof of which the perversely magnanimous Charles, in cool defiance of the hurt I knew he was feeling, always chose, when referring to the incident, to make light of it – as indeed, obliquely, he was doing now.

'You critics,' he was saying. 'Why rummage through the artist's life for the key to his work? Why, indeed, look for a key at all? What makes you think anything anyone does is ever understandable? I mean, if my wife was unfaithful to me' – here he lifted his glass to his lips and fixed me over its rim with a disconcertingly playful look – 'say a friend of mine hinted he'd been to bed with her, do you think I'd suddenly start painting differently?'

The critic, a skeletal young man with dandruff, all skin and bone and a rim of white, like frost, on the collar of his suit, bared his teeth in a tight, uncertain grin. 'But isn't that what we all want, artist and critic alike? To make sense of things?'

Charles allowed himself a smirk. 'What the critic wants,' he said, 'most usually, is someone's skin.'

'Oh come, now!' The critic was fussed. 'That's a little obvious, no? Not to say unkind.'

I felt the moment had come to interrupt. Any more of this, and not only would the artist dig his own grave by alienating the critic utterly, but the artist's wife might very well burst into tears. I cleared my throat and was about to suggest we go in search of food, when all of a sudden this young, sleek-suited individual with the angular, uneven face of a boxer appeared from behind us and said: 'Mr Hamilton? Have you got a minute?'

'I'm sorry?' Charles switched his gaze from the critic to the stranger. 'I don't think . . .'; but before he could get any further, the stranger had slipped an arm around his waist and steered him away.

The critic watched the two of them vanish round the side of an amorphous, Moore-like sculpture, a speculative look on his face, then turned his attention to me. I could tell he was puzzling over the significance of Charles' remark about unfaithful wives, and to forestall any unwelcome queries, I said quickly: 'Who on earth is that?'

As I hoped it would, my question interrupted his line of thought, causing him to fumble in his pocket, withdraw a small black book, and licking a finger, begin leafing through it. I saw to my surprise that it contained column upon column of photographs, all cut from newspapers or magazines and neatly pasted to the page.

'I thought so.' The critic's finger came to rest against a small black and white head shot. 'Andre Charn.'

'Andre Charn?' The name didn't mean anything to me.

The critic frowned. 'Surely you've heard of Andre Charn?'

'I'm afraid not.'

'The Charn Gallery? South Audley Street?'

'Sorry.'

'It's the most up and coming gallery in London. All the exciting new talent. And a lot of the biggies, too. Bacon. Freud.'

'But he looks so young!'

The critic consulted his bizarre little book. 'Twenty-eight, to be precise.' He returned the book to his pocket. 'Mind you, no one knows exactly how he came by his money.' He lowered his voice. 'Some say it was Warhol.'

'Warhol?'

'That they were lovers.'

I could hardly believe what I was hearing, nor why this target of such extravagant rumour should be interested in my husband.

'What on earth can he want with Charles?'

The critic shrugged. 'Who knows? But I'd tell him to be careful, if I were you. He's not to be trusted, our Mr Charn. Not trusted an inch.' Then, shooting a hand through his hair and dislodging a fresh shower of dandruff, he muttered a quick: 'Now, if you'll excuse me', and darted off.

I looked to where, partially hidden by the Moore-like sculpture (Woman with Child), Charles and this Andre character were huddled in conversation. Charles had his head cocked to one side, as he always did when concentrating, and the younger man, behaving like the older of the two, had an arm on his shoulder, shielding his quarry from intrusion. I wondered briefly whether I should attempt to join them, but quite apart from the barrier Andre had made with his arm, I didn't trust either Charles or myself to be part of the same conversation. There were too many shoals on which to run foul. The black, bleak thought of which – and not just the recent hazard that was Bobby, but all those other, more permanent sandbanks, my second visit to the doctor, Charles' reaction to the visit, the abortion and our inability to speak cleanly about these things – caused the surge of tears I'd earlier held in check to mount a second, more successful attack.

I looked despairingly about me at the gallery, where absolutely everything, not just the paintings and sculptures, but the people too, was on display: the paintings and sculptures thrown into focus by the lighting, the people by their clothes and jewels, the way they moved or laughed. They seemed so certain and secure, these people, so fully formed. Whereas I, inconsequential I, in surrendering too young – too completely, too – to marriage, had somehow lost all sense of myself, except when glimpsed in the eyes of a man.

'You must excuse me.'

Dabbing hastily with my tissue at any lingering evidence of tears, I turned to find myself confronted by the sharp, almost brutish configuration of Andre's face.

'The name's Andre. Andre Charn.' He was smiling, but despite the practised smoothness of his smile I had the distinct (though not unpleasant) sensation that I was being subjected to a thorough scrutiny. 'A great admirer of your husband – though seeing you in the flesh, I can't understand why he doesn't use you in all his paintings. He couldn't wish for a more beautiful muse.'

I felt myself blushing. 'Model,' I said. 'Model, not muse.'

Andre shrugged. 'Whatever. He has a discerning eye.'

It was like a test: a test that I nearly failed. I saw in his remark, and in his assessive, admiring eyes, my own face mirrored there, and felt first a familiar, instinctive quickening. Forty-one last birthday, and so what if my husband despised me? There'd always be other eyes in which to play at being Lucy. In tandem with which spurt of silly, spurious pride in my looks came, thankfully, the awareness that it was, of course, precisely the speed with which I was prone to lose myself in the regard of others that had been my undoing. Bobby Alton, for example, telling me in the corner of the pub whilst Charles went to refill our glasses, that my mouth made him think of summer pudding.

I bowed my head, cutting myself off from my reflection, and murmured automatically: 'You certainly know how to flatter a woman.'

He took my hand, and with a courtly flourish, kissed it.

'I can't wait for our dinner next week.'

Then, with a brief nod at Charles, he turned briskly away and began, like a surgical instrument, to cut through the crowd, slicing into conversational groups only to have them miraculously heal again in his wake. I looked enquiringly at Charles, who was in the process of perching his empty glass on the ample bosom of Woman with Child.

'I'll explain all,' he said, slipping his arm through mine, 'over a plate of Franco's best.'

And following Andre's lead, he began to steer me towards the door.

'But what about the exhibition?' I asked. 'You can't leave now. Didn't Richard want you to do some interview?'

'Fuck Richard,' said Charles, 'and fuck the interview. In fact, fuck the Broadmere.'

We were almost at the door. Out of the corner of my eye I saw Richard detaching himself from a group of men with notebooks and cameras, but before he could get to us, we were on the pavement and Charles was flagging down a taxi.

'Well?' I demanded once we were ensconced in the back of the cab.

Charles put a finger to my lips. 'Wait until Franco's.'

And so it was in an alcove of a restaurant off the King's Road,

over langoustine and a bottle of Chablis, and with my earlier
unhappiness held firmly in check by the glitter of excitement
in Charles' eyes, that I heard how Andre had offered Charles a
contract with his gallery: a monthly retainer plus sixty per cent
from the sale of any of Charles' pictures.

'It's fantastic,' said Charles. 'Unbelievable. A retainer plus
a percentage. Unheard of.'

'And the Broadmere?'

Charles scowled. 'I've finished with the Broadmere. Or
rather, they've finished with me. A joint exhibition. I ask
you!' He bit into a prawn. 'He, on the other hand, doesn't
mind what I paint. Andre, I mean. In fact he'd like me to
experiment. Push the boat out. Try different things. I don't
have to keep painting what's expected of me. And let's face
it . . .' He dropped the remains of his prawn onto his side
plate and picked up another. 'I've been in a rut this last
couple of years.'

I tried to ignore the unsettling echo in his words of what
he'd said earlier to the critic: 'I mean, if my wife was
unfaithful to me, say a friend of mine hinted he'd been to
bed with her, do you think I'd suddenly start painting
differently?'

'You're going to do it, then?'

'I'd be mad not to.'

'And this dinner next week?'

'He's having lunch with me tomorrow because there's
something else he wants to ask, something that involves the
two of us, and then, if that's okay, he says we'll both want to
have dinner with him next week.'

I thought of the critic and his enigmatic warning.

'What is there that could possibly involve both of us?'

Charles shrugged. 'God knows.'

I shivered. 'Had you ever heard of him? Before tonight, I
mean?'

'I'd heard of the gallery, of course. Who hasn't?'

'But him?'

Charles shook his head. 'Not a lot, no.'

'That weird little critic we were talking to . . .'

'Yes?'

'He said . . .'

'What?'

Charles had been in the act of lighting a cigarette, and now, as he looked up at me, the match flared against his face in such a way that the years seemed to fall off him. He looked twenty again, keen again – his eyes quite literally ablaze with excitement.

'Nothing,' I said. 'I don't think he knew what he was talking about.'

Charles chuckled. 'He certainly didn't know what shampoo to use.' He blew out the match, and leaning back in his chair, drew deeply on his cigarette. His eyes had lost none of their glow, and his voice was surprisingly tender when he added, as a coda: 'So, my one and only – what do you say to a liqueur?'

And later that night, back at the hotel, and after polishing off the cognacs in the mini bar, he surprised me again by taking my face in his hands and running a caressive finger the length of my jaw: 'Andre's right. I don't use you enough.'

Although my first reaction was to flinch from his touch, I forced myself to stay where I was and to meet his gaze.

'Even though . . .' I began.

'Even though,' he said quickly.

I felt for his hands and took them away from my face.

'It's over,' I said. 'It wasn't important and now it's over. I was confused, that's all. Lonely too. Ever since . . .'

'I know,' he said, putting a finger to my lips. 'You don't have to explain.'

'Why punish me then?'

'Punish you?' He sounded shocked. 'Good God, it isn't you I'm punishing.' He turned away, returning me, with the sight of his back, to that night in the pub when Bobby – his eyes, like mine, on Charles' back at the bar – had pursued his culinary courtship. 'All the fruits of the summer pressed into one.'

'No,' Charles was saying, 'it's myself I blame. Not you. And certainly not Bobby.' Although I couldn't see the expression in his eyes, I could tell from the tone of his voice that he was reverting to his old, ironic self. 'I mean, who can possibly blame Bobby? You're an exceedingly beautiful woman, after all.'

'Beautiful but dumb.'

He turned to look at me.

'Did I say that?'

'It's what people think. All your arty friends. Even this Andre. You heard him.'

'I heard him paying you a compliment.'

'Perhaps,' I said, turning away myself, 'I could do with fewer compliments.'

Compliments, I was thinking bitterly, although meant to make you feel better about yourself, often leave you bettered by the person making them.

What lunch the next day revealed was that in addition to joining the gallery, Andre was also offering us the use of a house on an island he owned – and to which, if we liked, he could take us the weekend after next.

'It's funny,' said Charles when he returned, expansive, from the lunch, his arms full of further celebratory extravagances: a bottle of champagne and an enormous bunch of flowers. 'It's almost as if he knew we were finished with Cornwall.'

'Are we?' It was the first I'd heard of it.

'Oh,' he said, 'I think so. Don't you?' And handing me the bunch of flowers – so large that I had to cradle them in my arms like a baby – he began to open the champagne.

I laid my surrogate baby on the dressing-table and said softly: 'I told you last night. He was lonely, me too, it only happened the once. There really . . .'

But Charles affected not to hear me. 'And anyway,' he continued, 'it's rent free. He wants someone in the house. He uses it for the odd weekend, but it's enormous apparently, you could get lost in it, and for the rest of the time, well, it just stands empty. We'd be doing him a favour. Aren't I a clever fish?'

I forsook the flowers and crossed to the window.

'Of course,' I said. 'A most clever fish.'

For now I thought about it, Charles was undoubtedly right.

As long as we remained unable to speak about Bobby Alton
– that and, more tellingly, my visit to the doctor – then yes,
we were finished with Cornwall, and Cornwall with us.

But all the same, it was unnerving how accurately Andre
had gauged our needs, how presciently he had caught us at
a time when the slightest promise of change and stability
would have reeled us in.

I tried to tackle him about it – Andre, I mean – in the
course of that first weekend on the island. I should, I
suppose, have felt only relief that he'd given Charles and me
the opportunity, however half-hearted, of putting Bobby
Alton behind us, of swapping one coast of England for
another – but it continued to bother me, in the days leading
up to the weekend, that he should have stepped so neatly
into our lives. And when, on the island, he offered no further
explanation as to why he should be giving us the house, nor
why – unless you count a couple of perfunctory references to
the excellence of Charles' work – he should be promising
Charles such an extraordinary deal; and when, more oddly
still, in the course of the walk he and I took together on the
Sunday morning, it became clear that what little interest he
did evidence in the two of us was directed not so much at
Charles as at me, my suspicions deepened.

We'd made a circuit of the island, and were on our way
back to the house when, pausing by the tank where, many
years before, though I didn't know this then, those primitive
submarines had been tested, and cutting short the idealised
account of my marriage to Charles which, under the pressure
of his questions, I'd been telling backwards – from rural bliss
in Cornwall to the early excitements of London – I fixed him
with a look as inquisitional as his and demanded: 'But why
are you asking me all this?'

He looked surprised. 'Isn't it natural? To want to know
about my guests?'

'Charles, yes, and Charles' work. I can see that you'd want
to know about that. But Charles and me. That's something
else.'

The secret smile that seemed to be his speciality flickered
briefly about his lips.

'All part of the picture, no?'

I bent down and pulled a blade of grass from the concrete rim of the tank, then made a circle with it in the air.

'I find it hard to accept, I suppose, that you should be offering us all this. It really is . . .'

'Very generous of me?' He was still shielding behind his smile. 'I like being generous. Especially when it's deserved.' He pulled up a blade of grass himself, and tapping me on the shoulder with it went on in almost the same breath. 'But you still haven't told me how you and Charles met.'

I realised it was useless trying to prise any more information out of him, so, surrendering myself to the inevitable, I continued my retroactive and idealised saga: from the party in Fulham to our first, breathless meeting under the station clock.

'Goodness,' he said when I'd finished. 'Quite a fairy tale.'

I shrugged. 'I suppose.'

'And tell me.' He'd pulled up a second blade of grass on which, thoughtfully, he'd begun to chew. 'Have you always been so vulnerable?'

'How do you mean vulnerable?'

'To men.'

'Well,' I said, taken aback by the acuteness of his observation, 'when someone sweeps you off your feet like that – and I was very young, remember . . .'

'Yes?' He was hot on the heels of my words.

Again I shrugged. 'I wasn't used to such attention, that's all. Such kindness.'

For some reason this made him laugh, and throwing his blade of grass into the empty tank, where it blended instantly with the natural detritus – weeds, brambles and rotting leaves – that carpeted the concrete floor, he said enigmatically: 'The kindness of strangers.'

'A bad thing?'

'It didn't help Blanche.'

'Blanche?'

'Du Bois. Tennessee Williams. *A Streetcar Named Desire.* "I have always depended on the kindness of strangers".'

Although he imparted the information with staccato

impersonality, presenting the facts without embellishment or explanation, I was nevertheless left with the feeling that somehow I was being admonished, warned even, though whether about myself or the strangers, I couldn't be sure.

'So what about you? You're a stranger, after all. Almost. Do you mean we shouldn't be accepting your offer?'

He placed a placatory hand on my shoulder. 'Good heavens, no. I'm different. I ask very little of people. To be themselves, that's all. But you' – and here he began to guide me back to the house – 'you, I think, are different.'

It gave me considerable pause, this strange conversation, so full of innuendo and proscription; and it impelled me, later that morning, when Andre finally gave his full attention to Charles and showed him round the house, into a careful reassessment of the sanitised story he'd wheedled out of me. Usually I dwell very little on the past, but in the wake of Andre's unsettling remark about the kindness of strangers, I found myself picking over every moment of my marriage, dissecting it for the clues it might contain to the present. Though because I couldn't be sure what it was I made of my discoveries that morning, I can only tell the story as it happened: more fully, certainly, than I'd told it to Andre, but still not fully enough.

If anyone had said to me, when I finished school and began going up to London to do a secretarial course, that within a year I'd be married to a painter called Charles Hamilton and living in Cornwall, I would have said they were mad. I was hungry for change and excitement, of course, but not – or so I thought then – at the hands of a man. All I wanted was to finish my secretarial course, get a job in London, and thus escape the strictures and stuffiness of home-life in Midhurst: the interminable bridge and golf, the endless Saturday shopping and the brisk Sunday walks.

Don't get me wrong. I wasn't rebellious. I wasn't angry or disaffected. Quite the reverse. I was a model of good behaviour. 'A credit to you, Marjorie,' my mother's friends would say, as if I were a chit that could be redeemed, cashed in. Which was exactly what frightened me. My own passivity. My innate obedience. I'd been so thoroughly drilled, by my naval commander of a father and my Midhurst mother, in the importance of not rocking the boat, of putting others first, of doing what I was told, I just knew that unless I got away, I would always do precisely what my parents wanted, would end up married to someone of their choosing and living down the road in one of the new developments on the edge of town, dividing my days between coffee mornings with my mother and waving goodbye to my husband and father when they went golfing together. It wasn't a prospect that appealed to me. I wasn't overly ambitious, but I did want a modicum of fun before I settled down – and when I did settle down I wanted it to be with someone of my own choosing. I didn't expect my life to be spectacular, but, ever the believer in fairy tales, I wanted it to be my own.

I hadn't been doing the secretarial course long – two weeks at most – when, one Friday evening as I fought through the crowds at Waterloo to catch my train, I bumped into, or was bumped into by, quite the most arresting man I'd ever seen. It wasn't just his looks, the subtle, shifting green of his eyes, a nose that ran cunningly counter to the perfection of his other features, his soft, seductive lips and his neat cap of curly blond hair, it was his entire manner: the careless way he was dressed (in baggy corduroys and a large, rather shapeless jumper with holes at the elbows), and the cheeky way he smiled at me as he stepped back and said: 'Sorry. Did I hurt you?'

The young men with whom I consorted in Midhurst, who drove up like chauffeurs in their fathers' cars to take me to the dinner dance at the golf-club on a Saturday night, or to a film in Haslemere, were altogether stiffer. They would never, in a thousand years, have smiled like this at a woman. A baring of the teeth was all they would have managed; nothing as easy, as warm, as this stranger's flamboyant, cocky grin.

'No, no,' I said, wanting to smile back at him and hating myself for blushing instead. 'My fault entirely. I wasn't looking where I was going.'

'I'm afraid I was,' said the man. 'I just couldn't stop myself. In time, I mean.'

Which only caused my blush to deepen.

'Please,' he said quickly. 'Don't look like that. I didn't mean to upset you.'

He hadn't upset me, though, just disconcerted me and – which was worse – made me hate myself for not accepting his flattery with more grace. But there was no way of extinguishing my blush, no chance of going back and running the encounter again. All I could do was hug my books more tightly to my chest and, with a muttered: 'I'm going to miss my train', duck past him and dash for the safety of the barrier.

I would like to say I thought no more about him, that the coming weekend with its twin high-points (a visit to the cinema with Gerald, golf with John) banished him from my thoughts. But it didn't. His image stayed in my mind, making itself at home there, allowing me to become familiar with it, to realise more fully just how much, and how enticingly, it differed from the norm. For there had been something pagan, something pixie-like and androgynous about the man. He was beautiful rather than handsome, ethereal and Pan-like where men like Gerald and John were solid, tangible and down to earth. He intrigued me, and I found myself wishing I would bump into him again. This time, I told myself, I wouldn't be so gauche. This time (the nag of a current thought, this, not one from the past) I wouldn't be so suspicious of his kindness.

Imagine my surprise, then, and initial delight when, the following Friday, I did see him again, leaning against the wall underneath the big clock, arms folded, his eyes – or so it seemed – zeroing in on me through the crowd. I stopped in my tracks, met his gaze, was preparing a shy smile, when abruptly, angrily almost, he turned and stalked away; as if the last thing he wanted was to speak to me.

Now I was rattled, unnerved – and even more so when, twice in the week that followed, three times the week after, I saw him again, leaning casually against the wall under the clock, watching me make for my train.

Or was he? Perhaps he was just waiting for a friend. Perhaps he hadn't seen me at all. Perhaps I'd only imagined our eyes meeting that first time. But no, I was sure they had. And now I was frightened. Only the month before, a young secretary had been found strangled alongside the line, certain of what the papers called her 'under garments' missing. Suddenly the unusualness of my stranger's looks became sinister. I shivered when I remembered the almost indecent voluptuousness of his lips – and I stopped looking out for him, I kept my head down as I ran for the train, my eyes glued to my shoes.

Until, in the fourth week and just feet away from the barrier, I collided with him again.

This time I didn't blush, I didn't smile: fear made me challenge him.

'What do you want?'

He had a large, flat parcel in his hands, which he extended with a smile. 'To give you this.'

I gawped at the parcel, totally at a loss for speech.

'A present,' he said.

And before I could utter a word, he leant the parcel against my legs and, with a funny little bow, backed into the crowd.

I just stood there, amazed, and then – because I couldn't have moved without the parcel falling over – snatched it up and ran for the train.

There wasn't an inch of space in the crowded compartment in which to open the parcel and inspect it. I had to sit with it clamped tantalisingly between my knees all the way to Haslemere, wondering wildly if it was indeed, as I'd guessed, a painting, and if so, then of what.

At the station, my mother, who always came to meet me, was instantly intrigued and not a little put-out that I should have been shopping (as she supposed) without seeking her approval.

'Now what on earth is that?' she demanded. 'You haven't been squandering your money again?'

'Oh,' I said quickly, 'just a print. For my room.'

'I thought you were saving?'

'It was in a sale.'

The minute we were home, whilst Mother vanished into the kitchen to check the dinner, I rushed up to my room and tore off the wrapping.

I'd been right, it was a painting – though not, as I'd surmised, a print. It was an original oil of a bluebell wood, the background a dark, seductive swathe of blue, the foreground a hot patch of sunlight, in which, laughing and with her arms thrown wide to the spring, lay a girl. Not just any girl, though. The girl spread out in the foreground of this painting was me. She wore the dress I wore to college, her hair was done like mine, even the books that lay, forgotten, on the grass by her side were mine: *Shorthand made Easy, Office Skills for the Fifties.*

At dinner that evening my mother, her face still pinched with disapproval, said: 'And have you decided where you're going to hang the print?'

'Actually,' I said, 'I'm going to take it back. It doesn't go in my room.'

'What's this?' The forced jocularity of my father's tone couldn't mask his irritation at not being party to the topic of conversation. 'Can't the man of the house be let into the secret?'

'Lucy's been extravagant again.'

Which it appeared I had. Without my knowing it, I had squandered something of myself on a total stranger, and he had taken it and turned it into a painting: a good painting, too, for all its student crudities; deft, sure and alluring. But not a painting I could share with my parents, or anyone else for that matter. A painting that had to be kept secret, tucked away at the back of my cupboard and only taken out at night, after my parents had gone to bed and the house had settled into silence. A painting that appropriated me, prising me free of my moorings and casting me adrift into waters that didn't seem dangerous then, simply enticing.

'I wonder when you'll learn that money doesn't grow on trees,' sighed my father, missing the point entirely because, like my mother, he'd been duped into thinking we were discussing my purchase of a print rather than the painting's purchase of me.

The next day he wasn't at Waterloo, nor the one after, and I was just beginning to wonder whether I'd ever see him again, when, on the third day, he was in his usual place under the clock, a bunch of flowers in his arms. This time, when he saw me, he started forward – and, my heart in my mouth, I stopped and waited for him.

'So,' he said. 'Do you like it?'

'It's beautiful.'

'Well, so are you.' He laughed. 'Though not that easy to capture.'

'You seem to have managed.'

'I did my best.' He handed me the flowers. 'Here, these are for you.'

Then, as if there were nothing more to say, he made his funny little bow and vanished.

'And what's this?' queried my mother as I got into the car at Haslemere. 'A new admirer? I thought you had an understanding with Gerald?'

'No,' I said, dropping the flowers in her lap. 'For you. And no, I don't have any understanding with Gerald.'

'He's a good boy,' continued my mother, not pausing to thank me for the flowers. 'Your father and I both think so. Dependable.'

To be depended on for what, though? To provide a living, certainly, and to admire me in a clumsy way. But was that what I wanted? A man who'd been taught to open doors but not his heart? Who coughed and stepped sideways if I returned his affection too forcefully? Who bought me pot plants rather than flowers because they lasted longer? Who worried that my course was in London – where, he said, anything could happen to a girl? Imagining snares more sordid but far less perilous than the one I was walking into. No, I thought, retrieving the flowers so my mother could manoeuvre the car out of the station car-park, Gerald isn't what I want. Not now I have my stranger.

The next day he came with lupins and this time, once he had thrust them into my hands, he took my arm and steered me through the teeming concourse to the sanctuary of the station bar, where we could talk. The day after that it was daisies, then carnations, gladioli, pinks – and each time we spent a little longer at the corner table in the bar, so that I had to arrive earlier and earlier at the station in order not to miss my train.

I discovered that his name was Charles Hamilton, that he was about to graduate from St Martin's, that he came from Hull, where he lived with an uncle who had cared for him ever since his parents had been killed in a car crash when he was five, that all he cared about was painting and that with his inheritance (a few thousand pounds held in trust by his uncle) he intended, after graduation, to rent a cottage in Cornwall and paint.

I also discovered I was beautiful. This may sound strange. Didn't I always know? But you don't. I knew I was attractive, of course, easy on the eye, but the idea I could cause heads to turn, hearts to race, this had never occurred to me until I saw it in Charles' eyes; there and in his painting. And at the risk of sounding smug, I have to say this revelation delighted me. I felt special, set-apart, chosen – in a word, powerful. Though where did I go for confirmation of my power? Not to the mirror, which would have been safe. Not to myself, which would have been usual. I looked instead to Charles, his eyes and the way they followed my every movement, his painting and the way it offered me up for universal admiration. That was where my narcissism delivered me: into the hands of my future keeper.

In the tenth week of my course, on the Monday, Charles announced that if I wasn't doing anything on the Thursday, someone from St Martin's was throwing a party in Fulham.

'He knows the most amazing people. All sorts. You'll love it. I know you will.'

'But . . .'

'His last party lasted a week.'

'But . . .'

He put a finger to my lips. 'It would mean a lot to me.'

'But what about Mummy and Daddy? They'd never let me go to a party like that. Art students and all. And in London too. I've told you what they're like.'

'Lie to them.'

'How?'

'By not telling the truth, stupid!'

So I fabricated a friend on the secretarial course who'd offered me a ticket for the opera, and with whose parents I could spend the night – and because my parents, despite their disdain for the people who created it, were nevertheless in awe of what they termed culture, I was given permission to go.

'It'll be an education for her,' said my mother. 'Covent Garden! Imagine! What will you wear?'

'My blue dress.'

My mother frowned. 'Is that suitable?'

I had to stifle a smile. 'It's all I've got.'

My mother shrugged. 'Well, if you're sure.'

And on the Thursday, trembling with excitement, I effected my transformation from secretarial student into Charles' consort for the evening in the basement loo of the Institute and set out, breathless, to meet my Prince Charming by the ticket booth at Fulham Broadway.

'You didn't need to dress,' he said.

I nearly burst into tears. 'Don't you like it?'

'Silly. Of course I like it. You just didn't need to go to any trouble, that's all.'

'But I wanted to.'

'Why?'

'For you.'

'For me?'

I nodded, nodded and blushed, whereupon he lifted my face very gently to his and for the first time ever, by the ticket booth at Fulham Broadway, he kissed me, the softness of his lips a subtle prelude to the deftness of his tongue, the taste of him so clean and sweet I wanted to swallow him into me.

'Come,' he said, taking my arm. 'We're being stared at.'

The party was an assault on the senses. It took place in a scruffy basement flat off the Fulham Road. There was a minimum of furniture, enormous op-art paintings on all the walls, a table laden with paper cups and a gargantuan bowl of punch in the kitchen, a gramophone player and a pile of records in the front room, and at least two hundred over-excited people – all of whom, it seemed, had dressed to match the paintings. I felt very out of place in my stiff blue party frock and matching shoes, and I kept very close to Charles all evening, hugging his side and eavesdropping on his conversations.

I drank too much too, and drew dutifully on the joints that were being passed through the crowd like batons in a race for oblivion, so that by ten o'clock the room had begun to dip and sway, the paintings had assumed an anarchic life of their own, and I have absolutely no recollection of how we got from the party to the flat of Charles' friend where I was to spend the night.

I woke, though, in the middle of the night, miraculously alert, to find an equally alert Charles in bed alongside me.

'Shh!' he said as my eyes opened in surprise and alarm – and laying a silencing finger on my lips, he began, with the fingers of his other hand, to trace the outline of my face.

'There, there!' He spoke as if to a baby, with exaggerated gentleness. 'There, there!'

Then he brought his face close and kissed me, and when I didn't resist, threw back the covers and began, very lightly and with both hands, to outline the contours of my entire body.

At first I was too shy and frightened to move, but gradually, as I got used to the tickling touch of his fingers, the susurration of his tongue in my ear, it began to feel as if he were calling me into being, delineating me out of thin air, and he created within the confines of my body areas of such exquisite, hidden pleasure that their sweetness was almost painful. He teased into being a creature that opened up to greet him, to swallow him up, subsume him into the wanton ecstasy he was creating. And when – in a sharp flash of pain – he broke into me, fusing his body with mine, so that at last we were one, I bit his neck so that his body, too, would be marked by the occasion as vividly as mine.

We married six months later, much to my parents' horror; so much so, in fact, that to this day my mother maintains it was my marriage to Charles that killed my father.

'He was never the same,' she once told me, 'after you abandoned your course and went to live in Cornwall.'

To the usual list of things (solace, peace, contentment) of which she saw me cheating her, she now added another: her husband.

But was she right? Is it possible that the cancer which

mushroomed in my father's lungs had its origins in the
Chelsea Registry Office, in his disappointment and rage that
I'd broken ranks and refused to settle for Gerald? Or was he
already ill when I took Charles home to meet them, was that
why he behaved as he did, going on at length about Van
Gogh, of all people, implying that it was a prerequisite of
artistic endeavour to be mad or poor or both, and when
Charles politely intervened to mention an artist who was
neither unstable nor poverty stricken, telling him in no
uncertain terms that he was far too young to know what he
was talking about? A neat irony, if so, for it was later that
afternoon that Charles and I first touched, albeit obliquely,
on the subject of marriage.

'God, he's a bigot!'

We were in the garden, dutifully inspecting my mother's
hollyhocks whilst she did the washing-up.

'A naval officer,' I said mildly. 'He's been in the forces all
his life. Most civilians he views with suspicion.'

'Excepting this paragon called Gerald.' He kicked at a
stone. 'Would I approve, do you think?'

'Of Gerald? I don't imagine so.'

He took my hand. 'And how obedient are you, as a
daughter?'

'In what way?'

'I suppose what I'm asking,' he said quietly, 'is who decides
your life? The admiral or you?'

'He's not an admiral.' I withdrew my hand lest mother look
up from the sink. 'Just a man who's lived a very circumscribed
life. Who feels more comfortable with what he knows.'

'That's not life,' said Charles, giving his stone a savage kick.
'That's living death.'

'And anyway,' I countered, turning back towards the
house. 'In answer to your question, I'm the one who
decides.'

His face broke into a sudden, boyish grin. 'That's what I
hoped you'd say.'

Nothing more was said, but it was that conversation, that
moment on the garden path, that led with a subtle and
wonderful inevitability to my saying yes when, after his

graduation, Charles announced he was moving to Cornwall, and capped the announcement with: 'So don't you think we should get married? Then you can come with me. And to hell with the admiralty.'

Up to that point it had truly been, as Andre said, a fairy tale; but what followed next from my bid for freedom and my switch of loyalty from Midhurst to the wild young man who, although so sure of himself, had, I knew, been rattled by my father, what followed next wasn't the expected burgeoning of life but two-fold death: the death for which my mother so liked to berate me and another she knew nothing about – the unplanned baby for which Charles was not yet ready.

When I fell pregnant – in the third month of our marriage and coinciding with the news of my father's cancer – I expected Charles to be delighted. Although we hadn't planned a child, he talked about children often and would shake his head pityingly over our gay friends because, he said, they would never know what it was to be part of the chain of creation. It came as a complete surprise, then, the horror with which he greeted my news. He wanted children, he said, and always had. It was, after all, part and parcel of being married. But now was the wrong point in his career. He was just getting started. How would we pay for it? And what about us? We were still getting to know each other. A baby might upset the apple cart.

I wish I could remember more clearly what, by contrast, I felt, but – not for the first time – my reaction was upstaged by Charles', that and the news from Midhurst that my father had been rushed into hospital. Every day I had my mother on the phone, and between the accusatory force of her grief and Charles' insistence that it was the wrong moment to be having a child, my own feelings simply didn't come into it. I had been, by the time Charles had spoken to a doctor friend and arranged the abortion, quite literally numbed into submission.

It was the end of a chapter. I travelled to London for the abortion and stayed on to see my father die. From there I went to Midhurst to help my mother move into a flat, and in the process of packing up the house, packed up my old room, and with it my childhood.

A sobering process, you might think, especially in the circumstances, but I seized the opportunity to put away not only childish things, but also the guilt and loss I felt about my father and the abortion, so that by the time I returned to Cornwall, which was where I now felt my place to be, I was able to slip with almost indecent ease into the uncomplicated role awaiting me: female half of a model couple.

Some people, I know, thought our lives had to be both lonely and difficult, what with the lack of money and being constantly on the move in our never-ending search for cottages we could afford. But the very reverse was true: we were punch-drunk with youth and promise and each other. Besides which, drawn by our obvious happiness, people came often from London to visit us, and in many of the villages through which we moved, there were small artistic communities (other painters, the odd novelist, film-makers even) over whom, within weeks of our arrival, Charles would always establish precedence. With his talent, his looks and charm, his wit, his warmth, there was never any circle from which he was excluded, at the vivid centre of which he didn't stand.

And for me, as the female half of this model couple, retiring yin to Charles' dynamic yang, it was fulfilment enough, in those early days, to stay in the shadow. I was perfectly content to concentrate on the house and garden, or, in certain villages, to take a job in the local shop, or with the Women's Institute, or involve myself in a round of classes: pottery, tap, brass rubbing, french polishing, weaving. I didn't want a career, and because, of course, I knew in my heart of hearts I was fooling myself to presume my guilt and loss over the abortion as neatly buried with my father as I hoped, it was altogether more comfortable to make myself over to my husband.

For the other thing I did, you see, was model for Charles. Never whilst he painted – he never let anyone into his studio – but almost every evening after dinner, in the garden if it was summer, in front of the fire in winter. It was a ritual, a rite, part and parcel of our relationship, the way he would prepare his things and fill his wine glass whilst I did the dishes; then, his pencils sharpened and the washing-up put away, how he would ease me into the required pose, and reaching for a pencil from the jugful at his side, make two, three, maybe as many as ten quick, darting sketches, each on a separate page of his pad. Sometimes it was just my feet he wanted, or my face, and on these occasions I was allowed to read or sew; but mostly it was my whole body he was after, and then I would have to stretch out painfully on the grass for him, or crouch uncomfortably on the carpet, twist round to look over my shoulder, or hold my hands in front of my face.

He never spoke while he sketched, never let slip the way in which he intended to use the pose, but a month, two months later, he would emerge smiling from the studio with a canvas under his arm, and after he'd set it on the mantelpiece or the kitchen table, invite me to a private view.

And there, in some part of Charles' wood, the wood from his childhood and the day of the picnic, I would always find some part, some echo of myself – either lying luxurious on a carpet of bluebells, or crouching cat-like in a glade, or running scared through a dark, forbidding wall of trees, my hands before my face.

Strange that with a whole world to choose from, there were only these two points of reference: his wood, and me in it. Unsettling that our whole lives can be governed by one or two insights, all that we are and do, that rich profusion of days, the unravelling of maybe a single instant when the carapace that protects us from intrusion is momentarily pierced and we feel the full force of the outside world.

Not that I thought like this then, when I was young and we were a model couple in Cornwall, posing for our happiness. Then, when I looked at the paintings, I would grow big inside to think it was only me he painted, I'd turn to kiss and hug him and tell him how much I liked the painting and he would gather me up in his arms and carry me, Scarlett-like, up the stairs to drop me on the bed, and slipping out of his clothes fit his eager body to mine and probe so deeply into me that my coming was a kind of pain.

So why did it change? How did it change? And when? It was me first, waking up to the fact, after the first dozen years, that it wasn't quite enough, the classes, the modelling for Charles, the house and garden. I wanted something else, something more truly my own. And because I had no special skills – abandoning my secretarial course had seen to that – because my only talent was the talent every woman had, what I wanted was a baby.

This time, thankfully, Charles concurred. Money was still tight, of course, our existence still as marginal as ever, but now, he said, he was ready to share me with a family. Indeed, he'd come to regret his earlier decision. He'd been too hasty, too cautious, too overbearing. I'd make a marvellous mother, and children were, after all, what he'd always dreamed of: the only real claim, he let slip revealingly, on immortality.

So with his blessing I stopped taking the pill, and there crept into our lovemaking another dimension, a striving not merely for pleasure, but for our future, for someone as yet unborn, unnamed. Someone who, with a wave of his or her tiny hand, would dispel the fear from which both Charles and I, in our different ways, now seemed to be suffering: that life might be passing us by.

Except that nothing happened. Try as we might, and over the years we tried everything, from positions to phases of the moon, my stomach stayed obstinately flat, my periods as regular as clockwork, marking off the months that led, inexorably, to a time when I'd no longer be able to give us what we now both wanted more than anything else in the world.

It began to affect our marriage. We made love less and less often, and when we did it was with increasing desperation. We began to snap at each other and, whenever possible, to spend our days apart. It even affected the paintings. Suddenly Charles stopped sketching me. The poses he now used, and with increasing irregularity, so that I featured in fewer and fewer of his canvases, were from memory. That and another more ominous development. He began to put other figures into the wood: strange, shadowy men, who lurked behind trees or drifted in the background, sinister men who didn't have faces, just a masculine shape, and who, if I were present in the painting, dogged me wherever I went. Though how the hell I was supposed to see where I was going was a mystery, for I, too, had lost my face. Where before there had been features: eyes, nose, a mouth, expressions too – happiness, sorrow, alarm – now there was nothing, just an oval void of flesh, an unwritten page, a blank.

For a while it gave his career quite a boost, this intimation of the macabre in his work. Sales hit an all time high, and he was even honoured by a profile in the *Guardian*. Yet the benefits to be derived from this development turned out to be pitifully short-lived. The public soon flitted to the next sensation, and gradually it became more and more of a struggle for the gallery to sell Charles' work, the money I brought in from my part-time jobs now went on groceries rather than luxuries, and Charles turned, for consolation, to the bottle and the artful maintenance of the moody silence.

The fairy tale was turning sour, and in lieu of a rescue attempt by the prince, the princess clearly had to rescue herself. I looked out my old diary and located the number of Charles' doctor friend. He'd moved since our last appointment, but eventually I tracked him down and made a new appointment. I didn't say anything to Charles. I didn't dare. Most obviously because I didn't know what I might discover when I saw the doctor, but also because the mere fact of unearthing my old diary had disinterred those feelings of guilt and loss I'd thought so safely buried with my father. I'd had the abortion acting, as it were, under orders, but all the same, looking back at myself across the years, I couldn't side-step the realisation that I had been culpable too: party, in those early months of my marriage, to too many deaths.

The doctor, unlike Charles and myself, had grown prosperous in the intervening years; prosperous and indecently adept at handling awkward situations.

'I'm so awfully sorry, my dear,' he said at our final consultation, his voice as silky as any lover's, 'but these things sometimes happen. There's nothing I can do. Nor should you blame yourself. You weren't to know.'

What he was telling me, in those practised tones of his, was that because of my abortion, because of the decision Charles and I had taken all those years before, I would never now have children. I might still seem to the naked eye like a whole woman, but examine me closely, X-ray me and probe my internal passages, and there was nothing there. I was, as I'd been sensing subliminally for some time, less than I seemed to be.

Charles was in the kitchen making tea when I got back to the cottage. He saw at once, from the expression on my face – no dissembling now – that something terrible had happened, though it wasn't until he'd put his arms around me and rocked me into a semblance of calm that I was able to tell him what it was. And the funny thing is that it was precisely because we were so at one in that moment, so utterly linked, that I knew we were at one also in what we were thinking: that the person to blame for what had happened was me.

It was essentially then – though it didn't actually happen until a month or so later – that I decided to allow Bobby Alton a taste of summer pudding, then that I set in motion the chain of events which, underscored by Andre's question ('Have you always been so vulnerable to men?') would eventuate in my nemesis, my Benedict.

Veduta

To get to Benedict, I have to fast forward through our first five years on the island to the beginning of summer and the third weekend in April when Charles' maternal uncle and guardian, Ralph, made his statutory annual visit.

Ralph had always been close to his sister, Elsa, particularly since the death of their father, who lost his life in the General Strike of 1926, hapless victim of a bus being less than skilfully reversed out of the depot by a short-sighted scab. He'd given her away when she married her childhood sweetheart, George Hamilton, and eight months later was in church again, this time to say his vows as godfather to the squalling Charles. Thereafter he was very much in evidence in the Hamilton household, popping in on his way home from school with some little treat for his godson, giving him his tea every Wednesday and Saturday whilst Elsa and George went to the pictures, even accompanying the family on their annual holiday to Blackpool.

It was inevitable, therefore, that when Elsa and George were claimed by the car crash, dependable Ralph should assume responsibility for defenceless Charles. Though whether he did this out of duty or love, it was hard to say because love, as typified by Ralph, was indistinguishable from anxiety. Are you sure you're not sitting in a draught? he'd fuss. Or: You ought to eat more fruit, you know. Or: Are you getting enough sleep? Expressions of worry rather than affection that drove Charles up the wall.

He was a strange man, Ralph: mild-mannered and sweet, but not approachable; a man who practised kindness rather than evidenced it, who even while going through the motions of love, forbade any real intimacy. Charles said it was because of a Miss Hornwell, to whom he had been engaged

43

in his youth, but who, like a character from a period play, had abandoned her safe but unexciting teacher fiancé for a travelling salesman with a line in shoes and dirty jokes. Which may have been true, though I had the feeling, I don't know why, that it went deeper than this, that more disturbing forces were at work behind Ralph's mild façade and the rigid ordering of his life (his dedication to his pupils, the weekend he took every Easter with us, his summer walking holiday in the Lake District, the autumn break in the Pennines, his obsessive reading and rereading of the novels of Thackeray and Dickens, all of which he knew almost by heart).

It has to be said, of course, that I'm not the most reliable of witnesses where Ralph is concerned, and I may only be saying this in retaliation against the fact, or the suspected fact, that he didn't much like me. I say suspected because Ralph, gentleman that he was, never actually gave vent to any dislike. He showed an entirely suitable interest in all I did, laughed at my jokes, clucked over my illnesses – but all the same, and for all his politenesses, I couldn't escape the feeling that in his heart he hated me for stealing his beloved nephew and godson away from him.

The net result of which was that I didn't exactly welcome Ralph's annual visits. In fact, each year I prayed that next year the tides would be against it. The visit always fell on the last weekend of Ralph's Easter holidays and some years, thankfully, the tides were awkward. Charles had to go off early on the Friday in order to meet Ralph's two o'clock train and could only return late at night, thus shortening the weekend by a good eight hours. But this year the tides were not in my favour. The causeway opened at twelve, meaning that Charles was able to leave at one, do some shopping, pick up his uncle, and come straight home again with over an hour to spare before the tide cut us off again at four.

It was a lovely afternoon, I remember, spring-warm and suddenly sunny, as if the weather, like the tides, were out to mock my unease. Charles and I had had a sandwich before he set off, and though normally after lunch I read (in the orchard, if the weather was good enough, or else in my bedroom) – with Ralph about to arrive I couldn't settle, so after I'd done the washing-up, laid out some cups for tea and plumped the cushions in the living-room, I decided on a walk along West Beach.

I'd only intended going as far as the first headland, but once there the weather tricked me into continuing, tricked me out of myself too, making me forget my unease and turn my face to the sun, so that I was almost content by the time I reached the causeway and saw Charles and Ralph inching home from the station. Because the causeway is full of potholes and the salt water can, within months, reduce the underside of a car to nothing but rust, we drove very slowly across it, steering with particular care around the potholes, one foot on the clutch, the other on the brake. Knowing it would take at least five minutes for the car to gain the island, I sank onto one of the boulders by the side of the road, and giving myself over to the sun, watched lazily as our battered old Ford laboured beetle-like across the mud-flats. Then, as the car crept the last twenty yards onto the island, I stood up and prepared my face for the moment of welcome.

'Lucy, my dear. How well you look! And isn't it the most perfect afternoon?'

As if he feared to say what he really meant, Ralph made the kind of conversation to which there was never any reply: precisely worded statements of the obvious.

And normally I replied in kind, returning his serve with some banality of my own. But this year his appearance shocked me into brushing his pleasantry aside.

'Ralph, you don't look at all well! Are you all right?'

The face that presented itself to me through the half-wound down window was horribly gaunt, deathly pale too, as if someone had been having difficulty drawing it and had covered the original with a wash of white before embarking with a vengeance on a new set of more sharply defined lines.

Charles leant across his uncle and snapped: 'For God's sake, Lucy, of course he's not well, any fool can see that. Now do stop wittering and hop in unless you want to walk back to the house.'

'I'm afraid I've had pneumonia,' said Ralph. 'But I'm on the mend.'

'Well, do you want a lift or don't you?' demanded Charles.

'No,' I said. 'It's such a lovely day, I think I'll walk.'

'Wise girl,' said Ralph.

'I've put out the tea things, so . . .'

But Charles didn't wait for me to finish. Thrusting the car into gear, he roared off down the road, throwing up a cloud of dust behind him.

I knew then that something was amiss. Usually, during Ralph's visits, Charles was reasonably polite to me, and I to him; we colluded with one another to give Ralph the impression that we were happy, Charles so that Ralph wouldn't be tempted to try and talk him into returning to Hull, me so as to lessen the impact of Ralph's suspected disapproval. Yet here was Charles snapping at me as if we were alone. There was clearly more to Ralph's pneumonia than met the eye.

More resistant than ever to the prospect of the weekend ahead, I started slowly after the car – thinking that to delay my return home, I might stop off in the village and see if Norman, the farm manager, was in the farmhouse – though in the event it was our resident journalist and would-be photographer, the ubiquitous Jorgen, who provided me with my excuse at dalliance. Sprawled shirtless on his lawn, his hairless chest as white and startling as one of his own flashes, and with a dog-eared paperback curling like a stale sandwich on the grass at his side, he sat up and waved at my approach.

'Not in your darkroom, Jorgen?' I called. 'You surprise me.'

'Lucy!' His guttural voice elongated my name, endowing it with a spurious exoticism. 'Fantastic weather, eh?'

'You ought to be careful,' I said, coming to lean on the fence. 'Otherwise you'll burn.'

His eyes dropped to his torso and he frowned.

'I suppose.'

'It's deceptive, this sun.'

He shrugged. 'But fantastic, no? Like making love.' He ran

a suggestive finger down his chest.

'Jorgen!'

He grinned. 'You know we Danes. Too much in the sun.'

I looked at him blankly.

'*Hamlet.*'

'Oh,' I said. 'I see.'

'And you don't let me touch you, so what else do I have, but the sun?'

'Now, now!'

'Love makes fools of us all.'

'Shakespeare again?' I said it as tartly as I could, but it only caused his grin to widen.

'Actually, I can't remember. But one of your writers, yes.'

'You shouldn't keep raking up the past,' I said. 'It isn't healthy.'

Shortly after Charles and I had arrived on the island, in the first or second week, Charles had been summoned to London by Andre to discuss his exhibition. The island happened to be between managers – the last one had had some disagreement with Andre, Norman had yet to arrive – and the only other person in residence was Jorgen. Charles could see I didn't relish the prospect of being left alone in our unfamiliar house, especially without a phone, so he'd stopped at the Lilacs on his way off and asked Jorgen if he'd keep an eye on me. Which was what this relative stranger, the next in line, had come that evening to do – presenting himself, suitor-like, at the kitchen door, face scrubbed, ginger hair slicked back, a spray of wild flowers in one hand, a bottle of whisky in the other: preparations that betokened yet another offer of kindness.

'I'm Jorgen,' he announced. 'From the Lilacs. Come to keep you company.'

We talked first, and awkwardly, about the island, its peculiarities, its history; then, more easily, about islands in general, and why it was that people liked them; and then, as the level in the whisky bottle sank, we shifted imperceptibly to Jorgen's own story. How, in Copenhagen at the age of twenty, he'd married his childhood sweetheart, how she used to nag him to get ahead in journalism and give up photography, which she said would never support them, and how, after their most violent argument over his future, or lack of it, she'd broken into his darkroom and destroyed all his photos, ripped his undeveloped film from its spools and poured his chemicals down the sink, and how, two weeks later, that had propelled him into cutting loose and fleeing to Meldwich on an assignment from a Danish tabloid to cover a local murder. He told his story well, with a mixture of wry amusement, anger and bewilderment, and because of this, because he so obviously still loved the woman who couldn't stand the only other thing he loved, and because I heard in his story a myriad echoes of my own, of Charles and me, Charles and his work, me and the baby I'd never have, and because – in the light of Bobby Alton – I was resentful and suspicious that Charles should have engineered for Jorgen to visit me, I came within a hair's breadth of allowing him, as he so clearly wished, to make love to me. But I was stronger, then, in the wake of our arrival on the island and my conversation with Andre, still resolutely determined to honour my pledge that never again would I look to a man – any man – for a solution to my problems. So, after a couple of fumbled kisses and a drunken paean to my beauty, I sent my tempter, with what little was left of the whisky, back to the Lilacs.

We never repeated the experience. We knew it could only lead to awkwardness. But it bonded us somehow, it meant we shared a secret, made me feel sorry for him, put me subtly in his power – to the extent that even though, even then, I was beginning to find the way he thought his camera gave him a God-given right to record anything and everything around him both intrusive and distasteful, when he asked if he could photograph me, I agreed. Despite my distaste for his methods, it seemed the least I could do, after that night, to help him with what, in punning deference to the group of photographers whose work he most admired, he called 'my magnum opus': a photographic record of island life, an account on film of the seasons, the tides, the fields, the houses, the people, as we all – in our different ways – ebbed and flowed with the year.

Charles, of course, was magnificently contemptuous of the whole idea.

'Fucking upstart!' he'd sneer, fitting his little finger into his ear, then flicking whatever it was he'd found there to the ground. 'Who does he think he's kidding? Magnum opus indeed! Photography isn't art. It's just another form of journalism.'

And he took endless delight (was expert at it, too) in mocking Jorgen's accent, in finding silly alternatives for the titles Jorgen gave his photographs, in aping the earnestness with which Jorgen discussed his 'art'.

I sometimes wondered if Charles had guessed about Jorgen and me, but I knew that wasn't likely. It was just that Jorgen was weak, and therefore easy game; or else that for all his bluster, Charles wasn't so certain of the inferiority of photography and saw Jorgen's work as a threat; or simply that territorially he resented the fact that Jorgen was documenting the island and in the process making it more his than ours. It certainly wasn't that he shared my own misgivings about the intrusiveness of Jorgen's methods: after all, as an artist himself, he too laid unthinking claim to the lives of the people around him.

'So what about the Landies, then?' said Jorgen, his features sharpening into another grin.

'What about them?'

'You mean Norman hasn't told you?'

I shook my head.

'Well, last weekend they came down with that wretched daughter of theirs. To give her fresh air. Get some colour in her cheeks. You know their thing. And she was furious. There was some party in London, apparently, some band was playing. Probably a boyfriend, too. She spent the whole weekend locked in her room. Didn't come out at all, except to go to the bathroom. So Geoff and Caroline got Norman to bring his ladder, and Geoff was climbing up to the window when Harriet opened it and pushed the ladder over.'

'No!'

Jorgen nodded delightedly.

'Was he hurt?'

'Just shaken up.'

I looked across to the Chase and saw that indeed the hydrangea under the window looked rather the worse for wear.

'How is Norman?' I asked. 'I haven't seen him all week.'

Jorgen smiled ruefully. 'So he has a new woman.'

'Another one? What's she like? Have you met her?'

'For a moment yesterday, when I went to use the phone. She works in Meldwich. In the estate agency.'

'And?'

He shrugged. 'Seems nice enough.'

'That's four this year.'

'It is?'

I ran through their names in my mind. 'One a month.'

'How does he do it?'

I glanced over my shoulder to where the old farmhouse, uncompromising and Gothic, formed the focus of the village. 'He bludgeons them into submission. Like a caveman.'

Jorgen shook his head wonderingly. 'Strange what women want. Never what you think.'

'You should go to the pub more.'

'The Jolly Sailor?'

'Yes.'

'Can't stand the place.'

'It's how to score.'

The Jolly Sailor, the pub next to the caravan park, the one Norman always used, catered to the weekenders from the caravans: vulgar men with gold chains round their necks and heavy rings on their little fingers, and prim, censorious wives, who pretended not to notice when their husbands ogled the passing girls in their stretch jeans and high-heeled shoes, and who paid no attention themselves to the masculine bait, the boys with sun-bleached hair and gold rings in their ears, who looked, from a distance, rock-star glamorous, but whose faces, close up, were invariably coarse and dull, uninterested in anything but themselves, and therefore uninteresting.

'No, no,' said Jorgen. 'Better I stick to my work. Work is better.' His eyes lit up. 'Which reminds me. I've got a new batch of photos. From last month. I'd like to show you. And Charles, of course.'

'Well,' I said, 'this weekend's awkward. Ralph's here. You know, Charles' uncle.'

'The old man?'

I nodded.

'I saw the car.'

'But one evening next week, maybe?'

Except I knew we wouldn't. Charles would dream up some excuse, would say he was working, or had his tax to do – anything to avoid looking at Jorgen's photographs.

'Fantastic,' said Jorgen. 'I'm around all week.'

'Us too.' I pushed myself away from the fence. 'Well, I'd better be off.'

He put his hand to his mop of ginger hair in a sort of salute. 'See you then.'

'See you.'

I started off down the road, but had only gone as far as the Institute when he called out: 'Lucy!'

I turned to find he had his camera on me.

'Perfect!' He clicked the shutter. 'Summer suits you.'

I took the short cut back to the house, cutting across the little field where once, in a short-lived agricultural experiment, Norman had kept three rather disdainful Jacob sheep, and, clambering over the section of crumbling wall at the end of the orchard, arrived by the back door to find Ralph and Charles having tea at the kitchen table.

'Ah!' said Charles as I appeared in the doorway. 'The prodigal wife!'

I bent over to kiss Ralph's cheek.

'I'm sorry I couldn't say hello properly on the causeway.'

He smelt funny: a talcum powdery sort of smell, sweet and cloying.

'Now what's this about pneumonia?'

'Don't harass the man,' said Charles.

'Are you all right, though?'

Ralph smiled brightly. 'On the mend.'

But there was something about his eyes, a sort of wariness, which – coupled with the amount of weight he'd lost – belied the fact.

'Who's been looking after you?'

'Oh,' he said, 'I was in hospital.'

'Hospital?'

'But I'm on the mend. Really.'

'I said we'd feed him up,' said Charles. 'Pamper him a little.'

'You always do that,' said Ralph.

'So what can we give him for supper?'

'Goodness,' I said. 'I hadn't given it much thought. Would cottage pie be all right?'

'Your cottage pie,' said Ralph. 'Of course.'

Charles had poured me a cup of tea, and coming round the table with it, he took my face in his hands and gave me a sudden kiss.

'You're looking very beautiful today. Isn't she Ralph?'

I felt myself start to blush.

'I told him,' said Ralph, 'when we saw you on the causeway, I said: Lucy's looking more beautiful than ever.'

Charles put an arm round my shoulder so we stood side by side, as if for a picture.

'Of course she's beautiful,' he said. 'Otherwise I wouldn't have married her. I'm not a total fool, you know.'

It was Charles' habit, when we put on our annual show of marital happiness for Ralph, to embellish his performance with little flourishes of machismo, trying for the sort of masculinity he remembered from his childhood and the environs of Hull. He doubtless thought it gave the performance the stamp of authenticity; and I have to say that usually it worked, eliciting a half-embarrassed, half-delighted murmur from a Ralph both shocked and reassured by his nephew's behaviour. But that afternoon, as he tilted his face upwards to bestow a smile on our antics, there was still that wariness in Ralph's eyes, a kind of pained scepticism.

I disengaged myself from Charles. 'That's enough,' I said, and pulling out a chair next to Ralph's, sat down and reached for my tea. 'So what about school? Are they giving you enough time off?'

Ralph shifted uneasily on his seat. 'I'm afraid I've had to retire.'

'Retire? Why didn't you tell me?' Charles was as shocked as I.

Ralph smiled apologetically. 'I'm telling you now.'

'But how awful!' I said. 'Surely you're not ready to retire? Not for years yet?'

'Well,' he said, 'the thing is this. I knew it was going to take me a while to get better, and I can't expect my pupils to put their education on hold while I recuperate. That wouldn't be fair.'

'So you're no longer teaching?' I could hardly believe it. Teaching had never been just a job for Ralph. It had been his life.

He grimaced. 'Not, mind you, that you'd notice. They still come to me with their problems, and for help with their work. They came to see me in hospital even. Well, some of them did. And when I got back home. A few of them. One of them, little Johnny Huggert, even baked me a cake.' He smiled. 'Not a very successful cake, I have to say, it was burnt on the outside and soggy in the middle – but it's the thought that counts.'

He looked very forlorn as he said this, and I had a sudden vision of him, sitting in an armchair in his neat front parlour in Hull, his precious hoard of ornaments (photos of Charles as a boy, little trinkets Charles had bought him on childhood holidays) arranged with customary precision on the mantelpiece, his leather-bound sets of Dickens and Thackeray immaculate in the glass-fronted bookcase in the corner, waiting patiently for a visit from one of his pupils.

A sudden wave of pity for him swept over me, and without thinking, I put out a hand and patted his knee. He flinched as I touched him, a spasm either of pain or dislike, I couldn't tell which, momentarily distorting his face. I withdrew my hand quickly, and as quickly he turned his attention to Charles.

'But enough about me,' he said. 'What about you? How's the work?'

'So-so.' Charles sounded evasive.

There was a pause.

'Well,' said Ralph eventually. 'Do I get to see it?'

'Maybe,' said Charles. 'After supper. If you can manage the stairs.'

'Of course I can manage the stairs. How do you think . . .' He broke off in mid-sentence, a worried frown flickering across his face: 'Or is it that you don't want me to?' He turned to me. 'He didn't last year, remember?'

'For God's sake,' snapped Charles, 'stop fussing! The work is going fine and I have lots of things to show you – which, if you're good, you can see after supper.'

'Well, that's all right, then,' said Ralph. 'That's all I need to hear.' Then, pushing back his teacup, he grasped the edge of the table and pulled himself to his feet. 'Now how about the daffodils?'

'They're over,' said Charles. 'And shouldn't you be resting?'

'I'll be fine. You can take my arm.'

On his first ever visit to the island, Ralph had brought us a cluster of bulbs which I'd planted along the wall at the far end of the orchard. They'd yielded about twenty blooms in their first year, since when they'd multiplied magnificently, creating, with each passing spring, an ever widening band of buttery yellow beyond the apple trees.

'It's a pity Easter's so late,' I said. 'They were stupendous this year, weren't they Charles?'

'Why don't we go along the beach?' said Charles.

'I'm not sure I can manage the beach,' said Ralph. 'Rather the daffodils.' He began shuffling towards the door.

'I feel like some wine,' said Charles. 'Anyone else?'

Ralph paused in his progress towards the door. 'Do you think you should? It's a bit early, no?'

'Bugger that,' said Charles. 'Now who'll join me?'

'Not me,' said Ralph.

I also shook my head.

Charles shrugged. 'Suit yourselves.'

I got to my feet, and whilst Charles poured himself a glass of wine, began clearing away the tea things. Ralph stood by the door and watched us.

'You have a lovely home,' he said suddenly. 'I hope you realise that.'

I looked at him in surprise.

'Of course we do,' said Charles. 'We're constantly going down on our knees, aren't we love, and thanking our lucky stars?'

'The person to thank,' I said, 'is Andre.'

'Dear Andre,' said Charles. 'Our nefarious benefactor. But enough of this idle chat. See you later!' And skipping over to Ralph, he darted his free hand under his uncle's arm and guided him through the door.

'See you later,' I called.

It was an integral part of Ralph's annual visit, the inspection of the daffodils, usually followed by a walk along the beach. It gave Charles and Ralph the chance to be together, to catch up on news, to air any worries. They were usually gone at least an hour; and though this year it looked as if the shortening of their itinerary would result in an earlier return, I knew I still had ample time in which to rustle up supper.

Humming to myself under my breath, I laid out the various ingredients, got out the requisite pots and pans, and changing my mind suddenly about the wine, helped myself to a glass. Then, alternating between sips of wine and my own, somewhat haphazard rendition of 'Anything Goes', I set about making the pie, and when I'd finished it and slipped it into the oven, prepared a salad and laid the table. I looked at my watch. To my surprise, it had just gone six. Ralph and Charles had been gone an hour and a half.

I went to the door to see if they were still by the daffodils. The orchard was empty. Despite his protestations of infirmity, Ralph had obviously allowed Charles to persuade him onto the beach. What, I wondered, did they have to discuss that could be taking so long?

I gave the oven a final check, ran my eye over the table, then decided I had both the time and inclination to change for supper. I went briskly into the hall and nearly fell over Ralph's scuffed and label-encrusted suitcase, which Charles had just dumped on the carpet. I picked it up. Ralph would never manage it himself, and if left for Charles to take upstairs it would still be a hazard in the hallway when we went to bed.

In the normal course of events I very seldom visited the West Wing where, in the bay above the billiard-room, Charles had his bedroom, and where, tucked away next to the bathroom at the far end of the corridor, was the smaller, meaner room we gave Ralph. But now, as I went down the corridor for the fourth or fifth time in two days (yesterday I'd been up and down it like a yo-yo preparing Ralph's room), it felt almost familiar. Gone was the usual sensation of stepping, Alice-like, through a mirror into a dark and disquieting reflection of my side of the house, a negative that echoed my positive. I put the case on the bed, wondering whether in the light of Ralph's recent illness I should unpack for him, then decided this would be an unwelcome intrusion on his privacy. Instead, I contented myself with turning down the bedspread and drawing the curtains before retracing my footsteps to the East Wing, where, at the far end of that corridor, was Andre's room, and, in the bay over the living-room, I had my bedroom.

Because of their situation in the bays at opposite ends of the house, both master bedrooms commanded views the entire length of West Beach, and now, as I crossed to the window to draw the curtains, I saw that Charles and Ralph were deep in conversation by the pier. Ralph, every inch the schoolmaster, was sitting on a rock whilst Charles, looking in his baggy corduroys and paint-stained shirt like a raffish scarecrow, was leaning over him, talking excitedly and gesticulating as he talked, his empty wine glass catching the dying rays of the sun and flashing a morse-coded message of light, long-short, long-short.

As I stood and watched them, my hand resting on the

curtain, it struck me how strange it was that although my mother and Ralph were so similar in certain respects – both mistrusted their offspring's spouse, both liked nothing better than to run a metaphorical finger over the surface of our lives and tut-tut at the dirt, both were snobbish geographically; Ralph holding a candle for the north, my mother for the south ('Such a vulgar city, Hull,' she'd once said to me) – yet what a very different picture Ralph and Charles made, talking together by the pier, to the image I carried of my mother and myself, circling each other wary as cats.

Perhaps, I thought, it's because Ralph is a parent by proxy only – or else it's down to Charles and the fact that Ralph is his only conduit to Elsa and George, that in order not to feel cut off from the memory of his parents, Charles has a need for Ralph that overrides any antipathy. Yes, I thought, that was it; and that was why, for all the irritation he could engender in Charles, Ralph was allowed and welcomed into our house, whilst my mother I saw only when I made the quarterly effort to visit her. Visits I dreaded even more than Ralph's to us.

'And Charles?' she would query, spitting out his name as if, from the mere mention of it, she risked contamination. 'How is Charles?' Not waiting for a reply, not wanting to hear that he was well or happy; dreading good news of him, in fact, and shivering slightly if I insisted on giving it.

She was scared of him, of course, scared of his power over me and fearful, should she evidence an interest in him, that she would then fall prey to that power herself. My father had been the same. For all his naval bluster and tight, aggressive masculinity, Charles had frightened the pants off him. He was like those tribesmen who believe the camera can steal your soul. He viewed artists, and Charles in particular, as thieves of contentment.

I remembered how, after I'd told my parents that Charles and I were getting married, and as the best reply I could muster to their horrified questions ('But why him? How can he hope to support you?'), I'd fetched his painting of me from its hiding place in my cupboard and stood it on the sofa.

They'd stared at the painting in absolute silence, then my mother had turned and run crying from the room and my father had said, his voice taut with horror: 'You mean to tell me you're going to marry the man who painted you like that?'

I'd seen the fear and hatred in his eyes, the baffled, bull-like fury that another man could snatch from him what he'd thought his for ever: control of his daughter. And because he was my father, because I dreaded more than anything the continuance of that control, I hadn't heeded the warning in his words, had been unable to detect, beneath his fury, an element, however stifled, of love and concern. It was only much later – with Andre, in fact, as we paused by the tank behind the manor house – that I'd been even vaguely ready to take on board any warnings about the kindness of strangers. Though even then – given that everyone, Andre as much as my father, had their own agenda – how could I be certain I was being warned? Who was to say Andre hadn't simply been assessing me for purposes of his own, feeling out my weaknesses the better to exploit them?

I drew my curtains, and going to the gargantuan mahogany wardrobe in the corner got out my one and only Laura Ashley, bought in a burst of extravagance for Charles' first exhibition at the Charn Gallery. It was four years old now and the pattern of cornflowers had faded a little, but it was still my smartest frock – and therefore my best disguise.

Charles was at the dresser, pouring himself another glass of wine, when I made my entrance into the kitchen. Ralph was at the table and, as I'd known he would, he clapped his hands and said: 'Lucy ! You've dressed. How wonderful!'

I dropped a quick curtsy.

'We won't do at all,' he continued, looking from his own rather crumpled linen suit to Charles' paint-spattered shirt and baggy corduroys. 'We'd better change.'

'You'll do no such thing!' Charles' words came out in a burst, like gunfire. 'You'll stay exactly where you are.'

Ralph had placed his hands on the table to lever himself up. Now he retracted them quickly.

'Is anything wrong?' I asked.

Ralph shrugged apologetically. 'We overdid the walking, that's all. I'm a little bushed.'

But he looked more than just bushed. His face was white and drawn, there was a film of sweat on his forehead.

'Why don't you have a lie down?'

Charles turned from the dresser, a glass of wine in each hand. 'For God's sake, leave the man alone.' He thrust one of the glasses in my direction. 'What we need is food. Is it ready yet?'

I met his gaze and held it a moment before replying.

'Yes,' I said eventually. 'It's ready.'

'Well, let's eat then.' He crossed to the table and pulled out a chair. Stifling my impulse to take my glass of wine and throw it at his head, I slipped on my oven gloves and bent to open the oven.

'Right,' I said. 'You dress the salad, then.'

Anyone looking in at the window at that moment would have been hard put to imagine discord in the picture we presented. The light fell warm and soft on the ochre floor, the Aga gleamed invitingly in the hearth, the Welsh dresser was gay with patterned plates, the large pine table a still life of culinary abundance brought to life by an old man holding out a plate, a middle-aged man sprinkling oil and vinegar on the salad, and a woman in a dress scattered with cornflowers distributing cottage pie: as skilful an imitation of domestic bliss as one could possibly hope to find.

But discord there was, sharp and unmistakable, uneasiness too and, following my request to Charles to dress the salad, the kind of silence which, like snow, settles stealthily but insidiously over everything, blanketing the possibility of speech. I darted a look from Ralph, picking at his food with all the precision of a finicky bird, to Charles, who was attacking his with gusto, and realised that unless I said something soon, the silence would become unbreakable.

'You'll never guess what Jorgen told me.'

'Jorgen?' Ralph frowned enquiringly.

'You know. The Danish journalist.'

'Ah, yes. Of course.'

'Well, last weekend . . .' – and I told them the story of Geoff Landie and the ladder.

'I feel sorry for her,' I said. 'Harriet, I mean. The way Geoff and Caroline try and force her to like what they like. It's pathetic.'

'But they're her parents,' said Ralph. 'What alternative do they have?'

'They could leave her in London.'

'To run wild?' ventured Charles.

'How do we know she'd run wild?'

'By looking at her,' he said. 'That Harriet's a right little goer. And you know it.' He reached for the wine. 'Though why the hell we're discussing the Landies I can't imagine. Boring!'

'They happen to be our neighbours.'

'That doesn't make them any less boring.' He held up his plate. 'Is there any more pie?'

'What about you, Ralph?' I asked.

He shook his head. 'I'm afraid I've rather lost my appetite. It was delicious, though, really it was.'

'Some fruit, then?'

Again he shook his head. 'No, I'm for bed.' He looked at Charles. 'After the pictures, of course.'

'Why don't we leave the pictures till morning?' suggested Charles.

'Oh, no! I'd rather see them now. And I can manage. Honestly.'

'Well,' said Charles, 'just let me get a little more of this pie inside me.'

'Talking of pictures,' I said, ladling the last of the pie onto Charles' plate, 'Jorgen's got a new batch of photos he'd like to show us.'

'Oh no!' Charles groaned. 'Talentless, pretentious git. Why doesn't he stick to journalism?'

'My, my!' I said. 'Do you feel anything for the people around you?'

He grinned, and fixing me with a playful, almost defiant look, said: 'Not a lot, no. Why, should I?'

I held his look, reading it for every nuance, then handed him his plate. 'It would make tomorrow easier.'

'Tomorrow? What's happening tomorrow?'

'I've asked Jorgen to tea. To show us his photos.'

'You've done what?' Charles' voice rose in disbelief.

'You heard,' I said levelly.

His eyes didn't leave my face. 'Is this to punish me for something?'

'I happen to like his work.'

'You haven't answered my question.'

'It doesn't merit an answer.' I stood up and switched my attention to Ralph. 'Now are you sure you've had enough?'

'Lucy . . .' said Charles.

'Look,' I said, 'I like his work and I feel sorry for him. That's all.'

I began clearing the table. There was another band of silence, not as long as the last one, but just as oppressive. It was broken by Charles who, as he shovelled the last of the pie into his mouth, said: 'Chuck me an apple, will you?'

I took one from the bowl on the dresser and tossed it to him. He caught it deftly and stood up. 'So,' he said, 'time for the paintings.' He refilled his wine glass. 'You wait here, Ralph, while I set them out. I won't be a minute.'

He made for the door.

'Do you want coffee?' I asked.

He shook his head. 'No, thanks.' Then he was gone.

I took the plates into the pantry, and when I returned, found that Ralph was staring at me, an odd, assessive and almost fearful expression on his face.

'What is it?'

He gave a crooked smile. 'I know that in many ways, after all I've . . .' He paused. 'Well, let's just say after all I've thought and not said over the years, that I don't have the right, but may I say something?'

I tried to keep the surprise out of my voice.

'Of course.'

He paused again – searching, presumably, for the appropriate words for what he was about to say – and over and above my surprise at this sudden acknowledgement of his suspected antagonism towards me, I found myself smiling inwardly that a teacher of English should believe so utterly and completely in accuracy, should confuse it, as Ralph did, with honesty, as if morals were a matter of arithmetic and description rather than choice.

'The thing about looking after someone,' he said eventually, 'is that you can never stop. Even though you might want to.'

'What do you mean?'

'I mean you and Charles. He needs you more than you imagine.'

'You shouldn't worry about Charles,' I said. 'He's well able to look after himself. Thanks to you.'

'He's more vulnerable than you think.'

'You could have fooled me.'

'That's precisely it,' he said. 'I think he has.'

I looked at him.

'Why are you telling me this?'

'You live with him, you know him better than I do, I don't deny that. But I knew him as a child. I know things about him that he hides even from himself.'

'What sort of things?'

He held up a hand. 'That's for him to say. Not me. I'm only trying to tell you what I see. That you and Charles need to be more gentle with each other. Forgive me if I'm speaking out of turn.' A sudden and unexpected grin slithered across his face. 'But it's the prerogative of age, no, saying what you like?'

'Look!' I sat down next to him. 'If something's happened, I really think . . .'

I was interrupted by Charles putting his head round the door.

'Ready, Ralph?'

Ralph pushed back his chair.

'Aye, aye cap'n!' He stood up. 'Forgive me. Duty calls.'

'Of course.' I stood up too. 'I've put your case in your room. And there's a towel in the bathroom.'

'Thank you.' He shot me an apologetic smile, and he looked so contrite suddenly at having started something he couldn't finish, that another surge of pity for him swept over me. I reached for his hand and gave it a squeeze.

'See you in the morning,' I said.

'Indeed.'

Charles let out an impatient cough.

'Coming!'

Ralph returned the pressure of my hand, then slipped his fingers from mine and made for the door.

'I may go for a walk,' I said.

'You should,' said Charles. 'There's going to be a moon.'

'I know. That's what gave me the idea.'

Ralph had reached the door, and he turned to give me one last apologetic smile before Charles had him by the elbow and was propelling him into the hall.

I went through to the living-room, where I saw that as predicted, a fat, yellow moon hung heavy over the estuary. Opening the french windows, I stepped onto the lawn, drew in a lungful of the crisp night air, then, wanting to put some distance between myself and the house, ran down to the complicated craziness of the collapsing pier, a silhouette of chaotic black against the glimmering water. The moon was directly behind it, and as I watched, it edged a little higher into the sky, shedding some of its yellowness. Soon it would be icy white. I looked back at the house. It was in virtual darkness, except for Charles' studio, from which a brilliant bolt of light sliced into the sky like a searchlight. At its base, flickering on the studio ceiling, I caught a suggestion of shadow: Charles and Ralph inspecting the canvases. I shivered, and turning my back on the house struck off along the beach, following the route I'd taken that afternoon.

It was very still out, as if a hand had been laid across the estuary to hold it in check. Apart from the water lapping gently at the beach, licking it as a cat licks its young, nothing moved except the ever-whitening moon. The entire world hung suspended between the end of one day and the start of the next, awaiting developments.

I hadn't gone far when I heard a rustling noise in the copse at the end of the first field. I paused, and as I did so a small, woolly shape came barrelling out of the night and flung itself yelping against my legs. It was Norman's mongrel Bettina, haphazard muddle of parentage, excitable affections and halitosis. I bent down to pat and soothe the animal, but it was useless: my appearance had temporarily deranged her. Laughing, I gave up the struggle, and with Bettina darting in dizzying circles about my feet, clambered the sea wall, peered into the darkness of the copse and called: 'Norman?'

He appeared almost instantly, a gun under his arm, his teeth gleaming sepulchrally in the moonlight.

'A spot of shooting?' I gestured at the gun.

His grin widened. 'No. Just setting a trap for the fox.'

'In the copse?'

'Come!' He took my arm and led me into the darkness. We came to a clearing, in the middle of which stood a large wire cage. The door to the cage was held open by a piece of string that ran, through a series of pulleys, from the door to the dangling corpse of a headless chicken. Bettina threw herself in a frenzy against the cage, yelping furiously. Norman kicked her away.

'Very impressive,' I said eventually. 'Did you design it?'

He nodded. 'Designed and built by Norman Anderson.' He produced a packet of cigarettes and offered me one. I shook my head. The match briefly illuminated his features: his dark brown eyes, his sharply protruding ears, his acned cheeks.

He blew out the match. 'He's getting too big for his boots, our Mister Fox. Two ducks he had last week. And last night a chicken.'

'Will he want another so soon?'

'He's a crafty old bugger, I admit, but I'll get him in the end.' He took a long, hard pull on his cigarette. 'Superior technology. That's what it's all about. That and patience.'

'Well,' I said, 'I wish you luck.'

'Thanks.'

'Though I'm surprised you're not off. Jorgen said you had a new girlfriend.'

He snorted. 'Don't speak to me about women!'

'Trouble?'

He took another draw on his cigarette. 'Tell me something. What is it you women want? Really want, I mean.'

I remembered what Jorgen had said: 'Strange what women want. Never what you think.' Were we really that puzzling to these men who seemed, with their guns and their cameras, to carry everything so effortlessly before them? I shrugged. 'Love, tenderness, to be properly valued. The usual things.'

Norman shook his head. 'Well,' he said, 'funny ways you have of showing it.' He kicked at a stone. 'Too clever, that's the trouble. You're all too clever for your own good.'

Which made me laugh. 'All of us?'

'Oh,' he said, 'you don't fool me, not for a minute. Batting your eyelids, telling us how much you need us, acting dumb. A bloke needs to keep his wits about him, let me tell you, if he's to come out alive.'

Again I laughed, but with less certainty this time. 'Not me, Norman, surely?'

He took a last draw on his cigarette, then flicked it in a glowing arc at the cage. 'That I wouldn't know. That I wouldn't know.' He shouldered his gun. 'Well, I'm for my bachelor bed. See you tomorrow. Bettina!' And slapping his leg to call the dog to heel, he vanished into the bushes.

Unsettled by the uncharacteristic bitterness of his observations and by his dig at me, I stared thoughtfully after him into the darkness. Love, I'd told him, and tenderness. To be properly valued. But was this what I wanted? These things had, after all, been on offer from Jorgen, and Jorgen I'd sidestepped. And in the five slow years since then I'd more or less put my emotions on hold, not sorrowed too actively over the distance that existed between Charles and me, encouraged it even, and welcomed the protection it provided from delving too deeply into what had gone wrong. But now, suddenly, in the wake of Norman's dig, I was made to wonder just how asleep I'd really been, and whether – princess that I was – I hadn't simply been waiting for some skilful prince to kiss me awake. Love and tenderness. They were indeed what I wanted. Always had, and always would.

My gaze fell on the headless chicken in its cage, and despite myself, I took a step closer, intrigue at such an intricate use of one death to effect another causing my thoughts to change direction. It was a subliminal realisation only – gone before I'd properly grasped it, and secondary to the nausea I felt rising in my throat as I came within smelling distance of the decomposing bird – but the chicken in its trap put me in mind of the baby I'd allowed to be taken from me, the embryo I'd never seen, but which hung there all the same, in the undergrowth of my marriage, bait for the future. Then, chickening out, as it were, and tearing myself away from the trap, I ran from the clearing and beat a hasty retreat to the beach.

As I came up the lawn to the house, there was a movement by the french windows and a ghost-like Charles, his face and shirt blanched by the moonlight, stepped into my path.

'Nice walk?'

I managed what I hoped was a suitably non-commital nod.

His eyes shifted to the river. 'It's very still tonight. Almost Chekhovian.'

'Chekhovian?'

'One expects a string to snap.' Then, returning his attention to me: 'What about a nightcap?'

'I'm afraid I'm rather tired . . .'

He cut me short.

'Please.'

Something in his tone brought me up short, so nodding assent, I followed him into the kitchen, where he went straight to the table and picked up the wine bottle.

'Almost finished. Shall I open another or would you prefer a whisky?'

'A whisky would be nicer.'

I sat at the table and watched in silence while he fetched the glasses and ice and played at being barman. He handed me my glass.

'Cheers!'

I knew enough to play my part as well, so raising my glass to his, I returned his salute.

'Cheers.'

He cleared his throat, took a mouthful of whisky; then, his eyes fixed on the liquid in his glass, said quietly: 'Ralph's dying.'

'What do you mean, dying?'

'It isn't pneumonia at all. Or rather, that isn't all it is. It's cancer. Of the stomach. The doctors have told him he can fight it, they're making all the usual, optimistic noises, but he knows they're lying. He gives himself six months.'

I put down my glass. No question now of what part to play. Charles' pain, whether I liked it or not, was my pain too.

'I don't believe it!'

'You saw how he looked.'

'But why didn't he write? Or ring? Why has he kept this to himself?'

'He didn't want to worry us.'

'Didn't want to worry us?'

'You know how he is.'

'So what are we to do? What happens now?'

Charles sat down next to me, the expression on his face not so much sombre as blankly despairing. 'He insists on going back to Hull. He has a nurse who visits, apparently, and there's a bed in the hospital for when it gets worse.'

'But he's all on his own.'

'He insists.'

'You mustn't let him.'

'What choice do I have?'

'He must stay with us.'

I was remembering my father, how he too had kept his death private, and how I had let him.

Charles shook his head. 'He's adamant.'

I extended my hand, and very gently, touched him on the arm.

'Is it me?'

'What do you mean, you?'

'Well you know how wary he is of me.' I stood up. 'God knows why, after all these years. It really is silly. But there you are.'

'You mustn't forget where he comes from.'

'But it's so irrelevant. The disadvantaged north, the affluent south.'

'Not the way he sees it.'

'I don't think he's a lesser person because he comes from Hull.'

'You might not. But lots of people do.'

'Or Mother,' I said. 'Midhurst doesn't make her special.'

'Of course it doesn't. But she thinks it does. That's the point.' He threw back the remains of his whisky. 'Fancy a refill?'

'I'll get it.' I took his glass and went to the dresser.

'Anyway,' I said, 'whatever the reason, do you think it's because of me that he won't stay?'

A look of impatience flitted across his face. 'Hull's his home,' he said. 'That's where he feels secure.'

'But you're his family! Surely that counts for more?'

'Apparently not.'

I handed him his refill.

'So he goes back to Hull,' I said. 'What then?'

'We keep in touch. Monitor the situation. Make sure he has everything he needs. Hire another nurse, maybe.'

'And then?'

'We wait,' he said. 'We wait for him to die.'

'Just like that?'

'What else can we do?'

It sounded as if he was about to cry. The trap had been sprung, and, as I'd known I would – what option was there, after all? – I went to stand behind him and began, very gently, to massage his neck.

'There, there!'

I worked with my fingers to soften the adamantine ridge of his shoulder muscle. Neither of us spoke for a while. Then, his voice under control again, Charles said: 'You know what? I keep seeing him as he was on the day of the picnic. Mother and Father spread out on that tatty old blanket, Mother with her head in Father's lap, and Ralph all prim and proper in his folding chair so he wouldn't muss his clothes. So careful always and so correct. But happy.'

'And you,' I whispered. 'You happy too.'

'Yes,' he echoed. 'Me happy too.'

'Poor Charles. I am sorry.'

Although he didn't talk about them often, I knew how important the memory of his parents was to Charles; how, in a world made up of compromise, imperfection and disappointment, he was nourished and sustained by the knowledge that fixed in the past, where it couldn't be tampered with, was the fact that once upon a time in Hull a man called George and a woman called Elsa had been everything to each other: perfectly, totally, wholly happy.

I remembered a night shortly after we'd married. Recently arrived in Cornwall, we were living in the first of our many homes, a rose-encircled cottage on a hill with a garden shed for a studio. I'd woken to discover Charles' half of the bed empty, and creeping downstairs had found him in the shed, putting the finishing touches to a painting of a peacock and myself in the clearing of his wood. I lay, as was usual at that time in his paintings, supine on the grass, whilst the peacock, its tail extended, towered over me, one claw on my breast, its blank and pitiless eyes defying the viewer to challenge its supremacy.

He heard me open the door to the shed, and without turning put out an arm and pulled me to him. I stood, silent and obedient, in the curve of his arm and watched as he applied the last dabs of brilliance to the peacock's tail.

'What do you think?' he asked.

I shivered. 'It's scary.'

'Oh,' he said, his arm tightening around my shoulder, 'the peacock isn't there to hurt you. He's there to protect you.'

'But he looks so menacing.'

'Otherwise how could he protect you?'

He let go of me and began cleaning his brushes.

'Why do you always paint the same wood?' I asked. 'What's so important about it?'

He didn't reply immediately, and when he did it was in a low, soft voice, almost as if he were talking to himself: 'We went there for a picnic once, the weekend before my parents were killed. Ralph, Mother, Father and me. It was the middle of summer: hot, still, perfect. We took over this clearing and made it ours, we ate and joked, I watched Father fish in a nearby stream, Mother made me wear a hat, Ralph told me a long, involved story about a little boy who ran away from home and found a casket of gold under a paving stone in York. It's the only day I remember us all being together like that.' He paused. 'It was the happiest day of my life.' His mouth twitched as if in a smile. 'And however weird this sounds, the fact that two days later they were dead means no one can ever take that day away from me, no one can change it. It's fully realised, that day, entire, complete. You and me, we change all the time, I can make us change, even, by the way in which I paint you. But that day I can't. That day is undamageable.'

'But surely it hurts? To go on painting it? Reminding yourself of their death?'

'You don't understand. George and Elsa were taken away from me. This way I can keep them with me.'

And now, in Ralph, he was about to lose his only link with that past.

I went on working at his neck with my fingers. 'Tell me,' I said softly, 'did he like the paintings?'

'Ralph, you mean? Who knows?' He shrugged, and in so doing, dislodged my grip on him. 'He always says he does, but I'm never sure.'

'Why would he lie?'

'To please me. Like any' – there was a fractional pause – 'parent.'

Again I was reminded of my father, and how, an hour before he died, he'd looked from my mother to me as we hovered anxiously over his hospital bed and – a smile of bitter satisfaction breaking through the lines of pain on his face – had come out with his final utterance: 'You can't wait, can you? Neither of you can wait for me to be dead.'

'Being their daughter,' I sighed, 'never stopped either of

my parents expressing their disapproval. Of me, I mean. If anything, it encouraged them.'

'Your parents,' said Charles, 'are different. From the snotty south, remember.'

'We won't go into that again.'

'You can't trust parents,' he went on, 'because they'll always love you too much. You can never trust people who love you too much.'

'Oh come now . . .'

He stood up. 'You think I'm being cynical?'

'A little.'

He crossed to the dresser and picked up the whisky bottle. 'Your problem,' he said, splashing more whisky into his glass, 'is that you're too sentimental. Too many fairy stories from Mummy as a child.'

Suddenly I was angry. 'Why are you so scared of emotion? What is it about love, about people caring for each other . . .'

'Not hate?' His tone was quizzical.

'Oh, no,' I said, 'never hate. Hate you've mastered. In all its forms and all its intricacies. You're an expert at hate. But love, simple love, affection, two people putting their arms around each other and comforting each other, that frightens you.'

'Of course.'

'Why?'

'Because love isn't simple. Not real love. It can't be.' He took a swig of his whisky. 'You know that as well as I.'

Then, putting his glass on the dresser, he crossed the space between us and opened his arms.

'Anyway,' he said, 'it isn't true that putting my arms around you frightens me.'

I didn't step into his proffered embrace.

'Why don't you do it more often, then?'

I was remembering the last time we'd made love – here, as it happened, in the kitchen, on the table. It was our second or third day in the house, we'd been moving furniture upstairs, into his room and mine, and we'd broken for lunch. The activity of making the house ours, of overcoming its size, its unfamiliarity, its emptiness, had brought us together, and that, combined with the wine we'd drunk at lunch, meant it didn't come as a total surprise, even though it had been more than a year since we'd made love, when he reached across the table and kissed me, and then, with that mixture of gentleness and ruthlessness that was his and his alone, swept aside the remains of our lunch, nudged me onto the table, and laying me out on the wood, began to pay a far from painterly attention to the still life he'd created. I'd surprised both myself and him, I remember, by pulling at his jersey as hungrily as he was fumbling with my dress, and then digging my nails into his back to force him more deeply into me. My urgency made him rise up over me like a storm cloud, blocking out my light, and for a moment I was able to forget myself, my every particularity, and forget him too, all the damage we'd inflicted on each other. I became part of some other, parallel universe, submerged and liberated at one and the same time, stretching and reaching like him for some point of release that lay outside and beyond the two of us, and which, as we reached it, expunged the tension from our bodies, causing us to fall back slack on the table, our arms dangling over the edges, our heads lolling against the wood.

'If I were to put my arms around you more often,' he said softly, 'I don't think you'd believe me. Not any more.'

'Yes I would.' Suddenly my restlessness, my not wanting him to touch me, my desire to disassociate from him, evaporated. I wanted nothing more than to be in the circle of his arms, enwrapped in the masculine, reassuring smell of him. I wanted to touch his time-battered face, run my hands through his untidy hair, feel the quick, nervous energy of his body, relax against the deftness of his smile, the fullness of his laugh. I stepped forward and let him hold me.

'The first time we made love,' he said, 'you cried out in pain, and I was glad, you know, that I had the power to hurt you.'

'I remember.'

'You were glad too, then, weren't you?'

I didn't answer.

'Weren't you?'

I nodded. He sighed. 'Now we're too familiar with each other. There are a million ways we can cause each other pain.'

'When I was young,' I said, 'I used to believe that if I closed my eyes very tight, really squeezed them shut I mean, then, when I opened them again, everything would be different.'

'Ah,' he said. 'More fairy tales.'

'No,' I said, pushing him away, 'just optimism.'

He relinquished me as easily as he'd taken me to him, and returned to the dresser, where he reclaimed his whisky.

'Well,' he said. 'See you in the morning, I suppose.'

'Yes,' I said. 'See you in the morning.'

Though heaven knows, I wondered to myself as I reached the sanctuary of my bedroom, what the morning would bring. Ralph's visit was proving altogether more than I'd bargained for, dredging up in its wake a wash of emotions and memories which, cut off as I was on my island, I'd imagined past: memories of my father's death, of the abortion, of how once upon a time Charles and I had, like Elsa and George, been everything to each other.

I climbed into bed, and putting an arm round my pillow, squeezed my eyes so tightly shut that they hurt.

Objet Trouvé

The next morning I woke earlier than usual, even though there was only a modicum of light filtering into my bedroom – the result, I discovered when I got up and went to the window, of a thick mist which clung, lover-like, to the estuary, obscuring the mainland. I dressed quickly, then let myself noiselessly out of my room, hopeful that in view of his illness, Ralph wouldn't, as was his custom, have taken possession of the kitchen before me.

As I reached the head of the stairs, however, I heard a noise from downstairs which seemed to indicate that he had. I was on the point of returning to my room to read for a while, when the noise was repeated, and I realised that whoever had made it, it couldn't have been Ralph. The noises Ralph made were invariably as discreet and tentative as he was. This noise was loud and careless. Intrigued, and somewhat alarmed, I hurried downstairs, where my attention was diverted by another noise, quieter, stealthier, emanating from the living-room. Turning, I saw, framed in the living-room doorway, a young man, tall, thin and willowy, his sandy hair thick, plentiful and bright in the light like a halo, his eyes, by contrast, dark and mournful, hinting at sadness.

As I was presented with this unexpected picture, young man in a doorway, and as our eyes met, his so dark and mute, mine so startled, I had the sense that something profound occurred, that we'd made contact more deeply and tellingly than the moment could allow. Is that possible? Can a look between strangers be quite so freighted with meaning? I'll never be certain, but this much I do know, from my meeting with Charles: a total stranger can, in the way he looks at you, appropriate your entire life before you have the chance to raise your defences against him. Love at first sight, they call it. *Coup de foudre.*

But I'm making clumsy, with all these words, something that happened with the speed and clarity of light, literally in an instant, before I was jerked back to reality by Andre appearing from the kitchen and saying: 'Lucy! We've frightened you. I'm sorry. We came on late last night. Benedict and I. This is Benedict.'

'Hello,' I managed, nodding at the young man. He returned my nod with a solemn, graceful dipping of his head.

'I was going to ring Norman and ask him to let you know,' continued Andre, 'but he'd have had to have woken you. We only decided at the very last minute. I hope it isn't inconvenient?'

'Of course not,' I said. 'Just unexpected.'

'I've made some coffee,' he said. 'Want some?'

I followed him into the kitchen, intensely aware, out of the corner of my eye, of the young man stepping, as if from another world, out of his frame to join us.

Andre crossed briskly to the sideboard and fetched an extra cup. Two cups and a jug of coffee already stood on the table. Watching him, I marvelled anew at the speed and purpose with which he moved, cutting through life with an assurance far beyond his years. There was nothing indeterminate about Andre – except, I could hear Charles quip, his sexuality. My eyes darted to Benedict, leaning languidly against the dresser. He wasn't in the least like Andre's usual pick-ups. He wasn't squeezed into denim for a start, neither was he posing against the dresser in order to show himself off. Andre's boys usually wore their masculinity like a suit of clothes, as something with which to embellish themselves, playing at being men, and doing it just that fraction too carefully to convince. Benedict, by contrast, made no effort at all to assert his manliness. In fact, it was almost effeminate, the way he lolled against the dresser. But then, as he straightened himself at Andre's bidding to come and fetch his coffee, his body uncoiled like a spring, and I had a sudden sense that there was something steel-like behind his willowy façade, something tough and flinty and durable. I smiled at the neatness of the thought that had come to me: where Andre's affairs were normally hard on the outside and soft on the inside, Benedict seemed the exact reverse: soft without, hard within.

I noticed something else as Benedict collected his coffee. Andre wasn't behaving towards him with quite the intimate offhandedness that generally characterised his treatment of his boys. His movements were as quick and sure as ever, but they were jumpy, too, and wary – as if too much contact with Benedict could prove dangerous.

'Well,' I said, lifting my cup to my lips, 'it appears we've beaten Ralph to it.'

'Ralph?' Andre shot me a sharp, enquiring look.

'Charles' uncle,' I explained. 'From Hull. You know. He's down for the weekend.'

'Oh, God, of course! I'd completely forgotten.'

'He's usually the first up.' I wondered whether there was any point in telling Andre about Ralph's illness.

'How long is he staying?'

'He goes tomorrow. On the afternoon tide.'

'Lucy, listen!' Andre leant across the table. 'I can't explain now, but I don't want anyone to know we're here: Benedict and I, I mean. I've got to get back this afternoon. Benedict might stay a day or two. If he does, do you think you can keep him away from Charles' uncle?'

'Goodness,' I said. 'What's the problem?'

Andre laid a hand across mine and squeezed it. 'He can stay in his room and feed himself when you've gone to bed.'

'Of course,' I said. 'If that's what you want. No problem. It's just . . .'

'You're an angel!' Andre got to his feet and turned to Benedict. 'Didn't I tell you she was special?'

I ventured a further appraisal of Benedict. He was staring at me thoughtfully and his gaze didn't waver as my eyes met his. I held his look for as long as I dared, then, aware suddenly of starting to blush, turned my attention to Andre. He too had been doing some appraising, I could see it in his eyes, in the way they probed my face, reading it for clues. I felt I had given too much of myself away and looked quickly down at the table.

'I'll explain this afternoon,' I heard Andre say. 'It's a little complicated to go into right at the moment.' I kept my eyes on my cup and saucer, heard rather than saw Andre move to the door. 'Now come on, Benedict, and I'll show you the island.'

I risked looking up again, to where Benedict stood by the dresser, and found that he was still staring at me. He put down his cup, and without removing his eyes from mine, said: 'A tour of the island. Right.'

'You'd better be careful,' I said, keeping my voice as even as I was able. 'Jorgen's about. And Norman, of course.'

'Don't worry,' said Andre. 'We'll be careful.'

Something in his tone forced me to look at him. I saw that like Benedict, he still had his eyes on me, and that like Benedict's, his gaze was uncomfortably assessive and in a strange way challenging. I know, he seemed to be saying, what you are thinking, I can read you like a book, but don't for a moment imagine that anything that might happen won't be without my planning it. I shifted my gaze to Benedict, and throwing down a challenge of my own said: 'So. See you later.'

'Yes,' he said. 'Later.'

Out of the corner of my eye I was aware of Andre turning.

'Come on!' he said. 'Or we'll be discovered.'

They went out through the pantry; and almost immediately, before I'd had a chance to speculate on the mystery surrounding their arrival, or to dwell on the manner in which both Andre and his enigmatic guest had stared at me, I heard a noise on the stairs. Realising with a start that it had to be Ralph, I leapt to my feet and took their cups into the pantry. As I returned to the kitchen, Ralph was coming through the door from the hall. He was dressed in the linen suit he'd been wearing yesterday, and which – perhaps since he hadn't bothered to hang it up overnight – looked more crumpled than ever. There was an apologetic smile on his ashen face.

'I seem to have overslept,' he said.

'Ralph!' I was shocked by the way he looked. He seemed to have grown gaunter in the night. 'Are you all right?'

He lowered himself gingerly onto the chair Andre had been using.

'I didn't sleep too well. It was a bit optimistic of me, I suppose, to think I could make the journey so soon after coming out of hospital.' He looked at me piteously. 'Do you think Charles would mind awfully if I went back today? I feel safer at home.'

I didn't know what to say. I pulled out a chair and sat down next to him.

'Ralph . . .' I began.

He held up a hand. 'Don't misunderstand. I don't mean to be unfriendly. Or ungrateful. But . . .' He paused, and moved his hand to his forehead. 'I'm sorry. I have a headache. Do you have any aspirin?'

I stood up.

'Of course. Upstairs. Let me put the kettle on, then I'll get them.'

The aspirin were on my dressing-table. I caught sight of myself in the glass as I reached for the bottle: untidy hair that cried out for a hairdresser, a neck that was starting to look scrawny, a scourge of lines around my mouth and eyes. It wasn't fair, I thought, that whereas dark people seemed to come into sharper focus as they aged, blond people seemed to fade, their looks to evaporate. I sat down and quickly applied some make-up: lipstick, mascara, eye shadow, a dusting of powder. Then, evaporation resisted, and satisfied that I no longer looked quite so emphatically in my mid-forties, I stood up, and, squaring my shoulders, returned downstairs.

Ralph had his head in his hands. I filled a glass with water and handed him the aspirin.

'Here,' I said. 'Take three.' He did as he was told. 'Right!' I continued brightly. 'Breakfast!'

He shook his head. 'Just some tea and toast.'

'You sure?'

He smiled bleakly. 'Really.'

'Well, if you're sure.'

'Absolutely.'

'So,' I said, sitting down opposite him once I'd made the tea and toast. 'Did you like the paintings?'

He didn't answer immediately, and when he did it was with caution. 'They've changed,' he said. 'They're different.'

'In what way?'

'You haven't seen them?'

I shook my head.

'Then it's not for me to say.'

'Did you like them, though?'

He considered this a moment, then nodded. 'But will the gallery? That's the question.' He toyed with his teaspoon. 'Tell me something. This gallery. This Andre figure. I don't understand. Charles isn't prolific, he hardly painted anything last year, yet the money keeps coming in. How is that possible?'

I couldn't prevent myself smiling. 'What's worrying you now?'

'Well, what's to stop it drying up? What's to stop this Andre character from cutting Charles off?'

I shrugged. 'Nothing, really. Except he hasn't so far. He believes in Charles.'

'Oh, I believe in him too,' said Ralph. 'Don't get me wrong. But – well I find it strange, that's all. Fishy. Wouldn't you say?'

He was interrupted by a noise in the hall, and Charles, looking not so much as if he'd emerged from sleep as than he'd had to fight his way out of it, appeared, ruffled and blinking, in the doorway. Like Ralph, he too hadn't changed his clothes from yesterday: the same loose, paint-spattered shirt, the same baggy corduroys.

'Well, well,' I said. 'The artist awakes.'

Charles smiled wryly, and shambling into the room pecked me on the cheek.

'You look very – in place,' he said.

'I've been up for hours, that's why.'

He went to the table and felt the coffee jug. 'Cold,' he said. 'Like your welcome.'

'I'll make some more.'

I took the jug from him and went into the pantry to empty it. When I returned, he was sitting at the table, munching a slice of dry toast and saying: 'So, what shall we do today?'

'Well actually . . .' Ralph had barely begun speaking when

he stopped again, as if uncertain of how to continue.

'Ralph isn't feeling so hot,' I supplied. 'In fact, he wants to go home.'

'Today?' Charles stared at his uncle in disbelief.

'I'm overdoing it,' said Ralph. 'I'll be better at home.'

'But you can't go today!' said Charles. 'You've only just got here.'

There was such pain and bewilderment in his voice that both Ralph and I were brought up short. There was a silence, then Ralph said, 'No, of course. You're right. But I must take it easy.'

'Of course we'll take it easy,' said Charles. 'I was never suggesting otherwise.' He stood up and crossed to the tide timetable tacked to the back of the door. 'Let's see. The causeway opens at one thirty-eight. We can mooch around here all morning, go off for lunch at the pub, then back in time for tea. Yes?'

'Right,' said Ralph. 'Yes. That would be perfect. Yes.'

'And,' I said quickly, 'we need some things from the shop. You could get them afterwards.'

Charles raised an eyebrow. 'Aren't you coming?'

I shook my head. 'I've got things to do.'

'Like?'

I shrugged. 'Things.' I turned to Ralph. 'Like making a batch of brownies for tea. You like my brownies?'

Ralph nodded. 'And of course there's your guest.'

'My guest? How the hell did you know about him?' It was out before I could stop myself.

Ralph looked surprised. 'You told us last night.'

'Last night?' Then, thankfully, it dawned on me who he meant. 'Oh,' I said, 'Jorgen! You mean Jorgen.'

'Of course,' said Ralph. 'Who else?'

'Anyone would be preferable to Jorgen,' grunted Charles.

I turned on him. 'Well, he's coming,' I snapped, 'and that's that!'

'So,' said Charles, 'that's the programme. Lunch at the Jolly Sailor, followed by shopping, followed by Jorgen. Bloody fucking marvellous!'

He began to clear the table.

'No, no!' I said hastily. 'I can manage. Really. You two start mooching.'

And before he could argue, I snatched up the plates and darted into the pantry to wash up the evidence of Andre and Benedict's arrival.

When, about an hour later, having made the brownies and written out a shopping list, I put my head round the living-room door, Ralph was settled in the chair by the french windows, reading.

'Need anything?' I asked.

He looked up and shook his head.

'Where's Charles?'

'In the studio.'

It was so like it should have been, each of us going quietly about our business, placid and undisturbed, that it was all I could do not to break out in nervous laughter.

'Well,' I said, 'I'm going upstairs. There's a list of things we need from the shop on the kitchen table.'

'Right,' said Ralph. 'I'll tell Charles.'

On entering my room, I went straight to the window. A sullen sun was struggling to make itself felt through the thinning mist, but without any real success. The day was grey, drab, utilitarian; also without the slightest sign of human life. Frustrated, and with an abundance of time to kill before Charles and Ralph left for the pub, I crossed to my dressing-table, removed my make-up and began, in careful stages, to reapply it. That done, I threw myself onto the bed, took up my book and tried to read.

At half past one I heard the car start, and returning to the window, saw it accelerate in a swirl of dust up the path leading to the village. I had until half past three, I reckoned, before they returned. I snatched up a cardigan and ran downstairs.

On the lawn, I hesitated a moment, deciding which way to go. Then, because it was the most deserted part of the island, and therefore the best for lying low, I turned left along the beach, heading towards the bunker.

Where yesterday had been summery, all sunlight and sparkle, full of promise, today everything was a negation of that promise: on hold and in abeyance. Yesterday the weather had differentiated between the elements: the sea had sparkled, the sky had been an improbable blue, the land green with encroaching spring. Now everything was shrouded in grey, as if the world had been put away again, cloaked in dust sheets, to await another, less transitory taste of the summer to come.

I reached the bunker without seeing a sign of life, and paused a moment to gather breath. At this, its easternmost point, the island protruded into the estuary like the prow of a ship, set in endless sail towards the squat twin cylinders of distant Broadwake. I knew very little about the power station, except that it was one of the oldest in the country and under constant threat of closure. Although it dominated the skyline at the river's mouth, it felt very remote to me – part of another, parallel world. Even when the earnest women in their hand-knitted jumpers and open sandals who were always protesting about nuclear power in Meldwich High Street buttonholed me with their pamphlets and petitions, I never signed. Not because, like Charles, I found their dress sense laughable, simply because I didn't feel touched, on the island, by the menace which Broadwake symbolised; preferred to ignore its solid, stolid ugliness and concentrate, instead, on the gracefulness of the passing yachts, the wheeling dance of the gulls.

I frowned, remembering what my history teacher, irritated by my constant giggling at the back of her class, had once said: 'You're a silly girl, Lucy Boyd. Not stupid, just silly.' She'd been right, I supposed. I was silly – silly and selfish. I should, after all, have gone with Ralph and Charles to the pub. Ralph was dying, Charles was my husband, they were more important than being out here by the bunker with the gulls, looking for a man who – who what? I shook my head. I didn't want to think about it.

I turned my back on Broadwake and continued along the sea wall, past East Meadow, past the old sewage farm and its cluster of apple trees, to the creek, where, as in my dream, I saw Benedict leaning against Norman's *Sprite*.

I came quickly down off the sea wall, and as I did so, he detached himself from the boat and took a step forward. We came to within a couple of feet of each other. I stopped, suddenly shy. He smiled. I returned his smile. There was an uneasiness between us, like undischarged electricity.

'So!' I said. 'This is where you are.'

'We've been on Andre's yacht.' He gestured to where the yacht lay tilted on the mud floor of the creek.

'You can't have been sailing, surely? There's no water.'

He shook his head. 'Just inspecting it.' He continued to stare at the yacht. 'She's very beautiful. Sleek. Wouldn't you say?' His praise, even as he uttered it, sounded uncertain, resentful almost.

'They've gone off,' I said. 'My husband and his uncle. To the pub. They'll be gone another hour at least.'

'I know,' he said. 'We saw them go.'

I looked about me. 'Where's Andre?'

'Gone to fetch the car.'

'He's leaving?'

'He has to.'

There was another silence, under which, as a sort of ironic, percussive accompaniment, I was aware of the rigging on Norman's boat tapping rhythmically against the mast.

'It's a pity you weren't here yesterday,' I said eventually. 'We had sun.'

'It must look different in the sunlight.'

'It does.'

'Have you lived here long?'

'Five years.'

'You're very lucky.'

I shrugged. 'I suppose. It can get lonely, though.'

'But you can be on your own. Properly on your own.'

I smiled. 'Sometimes that can be rather intimidating.'

He looked out over the creek towards the skyline. 'I long to be on my own,' he said. 'Really alone.' The grey of the backdrop threw his pale, sharp profile into stark relief.

'Is that why you're here?' I ventured. 'To get away from someone?'

His face darkened. 'In a way.'

'And how long, exactly, will you be staying? Andre said a few days.'

He shot me a look. 'Would you mind if it was longer?'

'Gracious, no! That would be lovely. As I said, it gets rather lonely on the island. Just Charles and I. Rattling around in that house. Company's always welcome.'

He made a little bow. 'The kindness of strangers.'

It was then, as he uttered those words, that it crystallised, the thought that had been with me ever since I'd seen him in the doorway: that here, perhaps, was the prince I'd been awaiting. And so what if his author were Andre? His mumbled reference to the kindness of strangers suggested that like me, he too knew all about dependency on others.

Though all I said, and glancingly, was: 'Tennessee Williams.'

'You know the play?'

I shook my head. 'No, no. It's just . . .' And then I stopped. I realised I didn't want to explain, it would involve telling him too much about myself. And I wasn't ready yet for that. Nor did I want him to tell me about himself, or who he was escaping. Our mutual dependence on Andre was bond enough.

'Have you known him long? Andre, I mean?'

'God, no!' His reply was almost too quick. 'Just a couple of weeks.'

'A lot can happen in a couple of weeks.'

'It isn't that. Not what you think.' Again the words came tumbling out of him. 'Not what you think at all.'

'I'm not sure I think anything,' I said quickly. 'Not yet, at least.'

He was in danger of overstepping the mark. Although what he'd indicated was, of course, exactly what I wanted to hear, I didn't want the details. Details were finite. They reduced one's options.

'Something has hurt you, though,' I continued. 'I can see it in your eyes. But you mustn't be frightened. Not here. Not of me.'

'I mustn't?'

I answered his question with one of my own.

'Has anyone ever told you how beautiful you are?'

Just as earlier, in the kitchen, he'd held my gaze longer

than propriety allowed, so now he did the same again; only this time there was a gratifying flicker of alarm and pleasure in his eyes, a tempting, teasing vulnerability.

'Yes,' he said finally. 'On occasion.'

'But you don't like it?'

'Do you?'

It was another bond between us, another shared affliction. Stifling an impulse to throw my arms about him in relief and joy, I looked quickly away. 'The tide is turning,' I said. 'Soon the creek will be full.'

There was a shout behind us, and turning, I saw the compact figure of Andre waving from the sea wall.

Benedict snapped to attention, and breaking into a run, made for the sea wall. I followed more slowly.

'Poor Lucy,' said Andre the moment I came within earshot. 'You must forgive me. All this coming and going, this secrecy.'

I looked at him expectantly.

'Benedict got into a spot of bother in London, nothing serious, but it seemed advisable to stow him away for a bit. A couple of weeks at the most.'

I looked enquiringly at Benedict. He was staring at the ground and a lock of hair had fallen across his eyes, concealing their expression.

'I can't say more now,' said Andre, 'but I'm sure you understand. And I hope it won't be a problem, keeping him from prying eyes?'

'No, no!' I said. 'As long as he doesn't mind staying in his room and feeding himself when we've gone to bed.'

Andre clapped me on the shoulder. 'You're fucking remarkable, you know that? Charlie's a lucky man.'

Now it was my turn to say: 'Thank you.'

'Tell me something, though,' he continued. 'Does he always keep his studio locked?'

I nodded. 'Why?'

'Well, when I was up at the house dropping off Benedict's things, I thought I'd have a look at how the painting was going. Just keeping an eye on my investment, you know. But the door was locked.'

'He doesn't let anyone in. Not even me.'

Andre shrugged. 'It'll have to wait till next time.'

'But it's going well, I think. Or so he says.'

'Good, good.'

There was a pause.

'So,' I said, 'you'll be down again soon?'

'Within the fortnight.' He turned to Benedict. 'Your things are in the room, and Lucy can always ring me from Norman's if you need to make contact.'

'Right,' mumbled Benedict, his eyes still on the ground.

'So!' Andre leant forward and did something he'd never done before: planted a kiss on my cheek. 'You're a woman in a million. I won't forget this.'

He touched Benedict lightly on the shoulder, then sprinted down the side of the sea wall to his car, leapt in, gave us a final wave, and sped off in a cloud of dust.

'Well,' I said, embarrassed in the wake of Andre's departure to be alone with Benedict again; wanting and yet not wanting to pick up where we'd left off. 'We'd better be getting back.'

'Can we see him go off?' asked Benedict, 'From here?'

'If you want to.' I pointed towards the mainland. 'You can't see the lowest part of the causeway from here, but over there on the mud-flats by the farthest bank, there's a telegraph pole. See it?'

He nodded.

'That's where the causeway reaches the mainland. In ten minutes or so we should be able to see the car.'

'Do you mind waiting?'

'Not at all.'

We stood in silence after that, our eyes fixed on the far bank – until, eventually, there was a glint of colour on the mud-flats.

'That's him!'

'Where?'

'Just below the telegraph pole.'

Except that as I spoke, the car breasted the sea wall on the opposite bank and sank from view on the other side.

'Too late,' I said. 'Gone.'

'How long till we're surrounded by water?'

'A couple of hours.' I looked at him. 'Why, will you feel safer then?'

He shook his head. 'Just curious.'

I wanted our eyes to meet again, to rediscover that strength of contact which Andre had interrupted – but he avoided looking at me.

'Right,' I said. 'Well, I have to go back through the village. There's someone I need to see. Do you . . .'

He cut me short. 'I'll go back the way we came.'

'Along the sea wall?'

He nodded.

'Well, you'll hear the car when Charles and Ralph return, but until then, please, the house is yours. Help yourself to anything you want. There's bread, cheese.'

'I'll be fine,' he said. 'Don't you worry about me.' And still without meeting my eye, he turned and strode off along the sea wall. Compelled by the willowy and oddly insubstantial figure he cut against the skyline, I watched until he'd reached the apple trees and vanished from sight. Then, turning back to reality with reluctance, I set off myself along the road into the village.

As I approached the Chase, I saw, to my horror, that the Landies' car was parked on the verge. Hard to bear at the best of times, the thought of them now was unbearable. They had a habit of sitting out in the garden, ostensibly to get the best of the sun, but in reality – or so we all suspected – to get the best of us. It was impossible to do anything in the village when the Landies were down without bluff, overbearing Geoff, nervous Caroline twittering away at his side, providing a running commentary on whatever it was one was doing. I prayed that today the weather would be keeping them indoors, but the island gods were not on my side. As I drew abreast of the house, I saw that Geoff and Caroline, in company with another couple – obviously Londoners, from the impeccably rural way in which they were dressed, all oatmeal tweed and wellingtons – were clustered in a circle round the damaged hydrangea, inspecting its injuries.

'Lucy! Good to see you!' Geoff, of course, had heard my

approach, and now he detached himself from the group. 'How are you keeping?'

I was forced to stop, and as I did so, the others transferred their attention from the hydrangea to me.

'Hello Geoff,' I said. 'Caroline.'

Caroline returned my greeting with her habitual worried nod of the head.

'This is Henry and Margaret,' said Geoff, indicating the solid and dependable-looking couple behind him. They smiled at me politely. He lowered his voice. 'Last weekend we had a bit of a run-in with Harriet, and Henry here is a child psychologist, an old friend of Caroline's, he's here to tell us what we should do.'

'Children!' said Caroline theatrically, casting her dark, uncertain eyes heavenwards.

And as if on cue, like a rather disgruntled cuckoo from a clock, Harriet poked her head out of the upstairs window and demanded: 'Is there any toilet paper in this house?'

The four adults in the garden looked up in startled, almost fearful unison.

'Harriet, really!' chided Geoff. 'Where are your manners? Say hello to Lucy.'

Harriet graced me with a perfunctory smile, then returned to the subject at hand: 'Well, is there?'

'In the bathroom cupboard,' said Caroline, 'where it's always kept.'

'No there isn't,' said Harriet. 'I've looked.'

'In the cupboard under the stairs, then,' said Geoff. 'There's a whole box of the goddamned stuff.'

'There's no need to swear,' said Harriet, withdrawing her head and banging the window shut behind her.

'You've no idea,' said Caroline, turning to me, 'how lucky you are not to have children.'

'So it would seem.'

'Lucy, here,' said Geoff, managing to make me sound like a part in one of the burglar alarms he manufactured, 'Lucy here is married to that painter chappie I was telling you about. They live in the manor house, up by the front.'

'Now is that the house?' asked Henry, 'where the industrialist lived? You know, the one you were telling us about, who crashed his plane in the river?'

Geoff nodded. 'And threw all the parties. That's the one.'

'How marvellous!' said Margaret, her matronly features radiating envy. 'It's such a splendid house.'

'Well,' I said, 'a little big for us. Just Charles and I.'

'And how is dear old Charles?' asked Geoff. 'Still beavering away at his canvases?'

'More or less.'

'Artists!' Geoff gestured extravagantly. 'It's a mystery to me where they get it from. Their ideas. Their – what do you call it? – their inspiration.'

'From life, surely?' said Caroline, frowning.

'Or they have a muse,' put in Margaret.

'You do yourself a disservice, Geoff,' said Henry, removing his glasses. 'If you picked up a brush, I bet you'd be surprised at what you could achieve.'

'I certainly should,' said Geoff, winking at me. 'And so would a lot of other people.'

'You should try it some time,' continued Henry, now in the process of polishing his glasses with a handkerchief which, judging from its laundered perfection, he kept solely for that purpose. 'It's wonderful therapy, apart from anything else.'

'The only person who needs therapy in this family,' said Geoff, 'is that brat upstairs.'

'Geoff, really!' Caroline dug her husband in the ribs. 'There's no need to make a meal of it.'

'Well,' I said, 'if you'll excuse me, I must be getting back. We have a guest.'

'Of course,' said Geoff. 'Andre, no? I thought I saw him driving past.'

'He was down, yes, but only for the tide. I meant Charles' uncle. He comes every year about this time.'

'Of course,' Geoff turned to Henry. 'Andre's the other chap I was telling you about. The one with the gallery in town. Where Charles exhibits, in fact.'

'I'm with you.'

'He owns the island, that's how we came to get this house. I did the burglar alarms for the gallery.' Geoff smiled. 'Most crucial, in that line of business, burglar alarms.'

'Especially with the prices paintings fetch these days,' said Caroline. 'I mean, did you see what that Van Gogh went for?'

'More than Charles gets, I'll bet,' I said.

'Ah,' said Geoff, 'but just you wait. When he's dead, he'll be worth a fortune.'

'What a comforting thought.'

'Honestly Geoff!' Once again, Caroline dug him in the ribs; this time, so sharply that he winced.

'I didn't mean it like that!' His normally smug and imperturbable features reddened slightly. 'I only meant . . .'

'I know,' I said. 'Don't worry, I think it too. But I really must be getting back. See you around, no doubt.'

'Sadly,' said Margaret, 'we're only here until tomorrow. Busy workers, and all that. You know.'

'Well,' I said, 'maybe tomorrow then. Bye!'

'Bye!' they choroused, and stayed in a group by the fence, their eyes trained on me as I walked away. I looked back once, as I approached the Lilacs, and they were still watching me. I gave them a final wave, then turned into Jorgen's garden, knocked once, and without waiting for a reply, let myself in.

'Jorgen?' I called. 'Are you in?'

There was silence. I tried again.

'Jorgen?'

This time there was a muffled reply.

'In the living-room.'

I stepped over the muddled heap of wellies that Jorgen kept in the hallway (not, I think, because he ever used them, simply because he regarded them as emblem and totem of English life) and pushed open the living-room door. Jorgen lay spreadeagled across the carpet, his extended frame taking up almost all of the floor space of the small, square room. He grinned up at me sheepishly.

'Ah!' he said. 'You!'

'What the hell are you doing?'

'It's my back. It's been giving me trouble.' He placed his

hands in the small of his back, lifted his legs into the air, and began to open and shut them, like scissors. 'Exercises,' he explained.

'That's good for your back?'

He nodded, made a few more scissor movements, then lowered his legs and levered himself upright.

'Now what can I do for you?'

The size of him in the little room would have been overwhelming, intimidating even, were it not for his boyish smile.

'I was wondering if you felt like coming up to the house this afternoon to show Charles your photographs . . .'

His smile became, briefly, a puzzled frown. 'But you have his uncle with you, no?'

'We do, but it's such a filthy day, and we're not doing anything.'

The smile returned, broader than ever. 'But of course! That would be fantastic. Of course. Fantastic. When?'

'In about an hour?'

'Fantastic, yes!'

'Good,' I said. 'In an hour. Now back to your exercises.'

I retraversed the wellingtons and let myself out. It had started to drizzle, forcing the Landies indoors. The village was deserted and, in the absence of people, rather forlorn-looking. My spirits, however, were anything but forlorn, and it wasn't just the satisfaction of knowing I'd succeeded in engineering Jorgen to tea. Jorgen and the Landies, all the familiar, cramping ties of my island life, had suddenly been loosened by the arrival of my stranger. Ever since my conversation with him at the creek, all through my exchange with the Landies, and afterwards with Jorgen, running under these encounters like a hot and pulsing accompaniment, had been the growing and delicious realisation that I was about to cast caution to the winds and make a play for Benedict.

I remembered how, just the day before, Jorgen had lifted his camera to me and said: 'Summer suits you.' He had been more right than he knew. Summer had always suited me, just as love had, and being loved. I was, after all, as Norman had so timeously reminded me, still a functioning woman.

Nothing more, perhaps, but certainly nothing less.

Pausing in my tracks and closing my eyes, I feasted on the image, electric in my head, of the wraith-like man who, when asked if he minded being beautiful, had replied: 'Do you?'

I was awoken from my reverie by a tapping sound, and, snapping awake, saw the pale moon of Norman's face bobbing at the farmhouse window. He beckoned me over, eased down the window, and grinning at me conspiratorially over the top of the sash, said: 'Andre's told me.'

'Told you? Told you what?'

'About the mystery guest.'

'Really? What did he say?'

'Just that he was staying a week or two. Some trouble in London, right?'

In normal circumstances, I would have liked nothing more than to join Norman in speculating on the facts behind Andre's behaviour; but now, under the spell of my new-found happiness, I didn't want to share the stranger with anyone.

'Something like that.' I said it dismissively, then, forcing the discussion to a close, added quickly: 'But I'll get soaked if I stand here gossiping.'

Norman regarded me quizzically. 'Well, don't let me keep you.' And, with a curt nod of the head, he withdrew into the gloom of his living-room.

The drizzle was worsening, so I took the short cut back to the house, through the orchard and past the old fish-pond, where I paused. The drizzle had wetted the concrete, deepening its colour and releasing a dank, indefinable smell from its cracked and crumbling heart. On impulse, and despite the rain, I knelt, and closing my eyes, did what I most liked doing when I visited the pond, stocked it in my imagination with the sleekest and most wonderful of fish: carp, salmon, trout and bass. I rested my cheek against the chipped rim of the pond, took its smell deep into my lungs, and still with my eyes closed, swam with my imaginary fish through the cool green water, alive in every muscle to the darting, flickering beauty of my silent companions. Then, aware that I was getting drenched, I stood up and hurried for the house.

Entering the kitchen, I found it empty and, superficially at least, exactly as I had left it – except that when I looked again, I noticed that the butter dish was on the table, not the dresser, the fruit bowl was slightly to one side of where it usually stood and two of the brownies, which I'd left on a wire rack to cool, had been taken. The still life that I thought of as me had been subtly rearranged.

I went into the living-room, which was also empty, and then upstairs, where I hesitated at the end of the corridor leading to his room. His door was closed. I wanted to approach it, knock, and ask whether he'd had enough to eat, but the all pervasive silence in the house prevented me, made me turn instead to my room, where I discarded my damp clothes and changed into a warm woollen dress, my blue one, with the high, nun-like collar – a fitting garment, I thought, in which to administer tea. As I struggled to do it up at the back, I heard the car, followed by the sounds of Charles and Ralph in the kitchen. I went downstairs.

Ralph was standing at the window, swaying metronomically, whilst a rather unsteady Charles was struggling to plug in the kettle.

'So,' I said brightly, 'how was the pub?'

'Fucking plug!' muttered Charles, without turning. 'Who invented these things?'

Ralph stopped marking time to whatever song was playing in his head and, turning, said with an apologetic smile: 'The pub was just fine.'

'Don't make coffee.' I relieved Charles of the kettle. 'Jorgen will be here in a minute, then I'll make tea.'

'Jorgen?' Charles stared at me blankly.

'Just how many pints did you have?'

'Jorgen! Ah yes, Jorgen! Of course.' He drew himself up to his full height. 'Well, in that case I shall wait in the living-room.' He gestured to Ralph. 'Come, Uncle, we have a social duty to perform.' And still holding himself majestically erect, he swept unsteadily from the room.

'I'd better keep him company,' said Ralph.

'You better had,' I agreed.

He crossed to the door, then paused.

'About Charles . . .' he began.

'Yes?'

But he only shook his head. 'No,' he said, 'nothing. That's a lovely dress.'

'Thank you.'

He gave me a final apologetic smile, then followed Charles into the living-room.

A moment later Jorgen appeared in the kitchen door, a large cardboard box under his arm.

'Not too early, I hope?' He'd brushed his hair and changed into a pair of crisply ironed jeans. He looked as spruce and nervous as a teenager on his first date: exactly as he had, in fact, on the evening we'd met.

'Just perfect,' I said. 'Here!' I thrust the brownies at him. 'You can take these through to the living-room.'

When, seconds later, I followed him with the tray, he had put the brownies and the cardboard box on the coffee table and was hovering over the figure of Ralph, who sat prim and upright on the window seat, whilst Charles lay sprawled in the armchair.

'That's right,' he was saying, 'the oldest resident. By quite a few years.'

He caught sight of me and stepped forward to help me with the tray. I smiled him away.

'I can manage, thanks, if you just clear a space on the table.'

He moved the brownies to one side, and picked up his box, clutching it to his chest. I put down the tray, arranged myself on the edge of the sofa, and began to dispense tea.

'And you're a photographer,' said Ralph, 'is that right?'

Jorgen nodded.

'And a journalist,' added Charles. 'Don't forget the journalism.'

'For the money,' explained Jorgen. 'I'm a journalist for the money.'

'The *News of the World*,' said Charles.

'Really?' said Ralph.

'No, no!' Jorgen shot Charles an unsettled look. 'I work for a Danish paper.'

'Like the *News of the World*,' replied Charles.

'We deal,' said Jorgen stiffly, 'in human interest stories.'

'Oh, come on!' A note of exasperation had crept into Charles' voice. 'Inhuman interest, more like.' He turned to Ralph. 'Incest. Murder. Child abuse. Buggery. That sort of thing. There's good copy, apparently, along this coast.'

A silence followed this remark, which I broke by handing Jorgen his tea. He managed to take it without relinquishing his cardboard box.

'I can't remember if you have sugar?'

He shook his head. 'No thanks.'

Charles had sat up and was staring at me. 'Just look at her,' he said to Ralph. 'Like a painting, eh? Woman with teapot. The very picture of charm and elegance!'

'Your tea,' I said as severely as I could, holding out his cup. He shambled to his feet, and taking the cup, moved to the centre of the room, where he stood, legs apart, like a headmaster giving an end of term address.

'Jorgen and I have an ongoing debate,' he said to Ralph, 'as to whether or not photography can qualify as art. What do you think?'

'Well,' said Ralph, shifting uncomfortably on the window seat. 'I haven't really . . .'

'Your tea,' I said, getting up and going to his rescue.

'Thank you.' He smiled at me gratefully.

'Will you have a brownie?'

He nodded.

'To my way of thinking,' continued Charles, 'photography is a form of journalism.'

'Ignore him, Jorgen,' I said, 'and show us the photos.'

'Perhaps it's better if I don't,' he said quietly. 'I'd hate to upset Charles.'

'You must ignore Charles.' It was Ralph, his voice surprisingly firm. 'I'd like to see your photographs, even if no one else would.' He got to his feet. 'What are they exactly? Portraits? Landscapes? A mixture?'

Jorgen put down his cup. 'A mixture. What I've been doing, ever since I got to the island, is trying to keep a record of the place. Its different moods and seasons. How they complement or contradict each other. And the people. How they fit into the island. Or don't. Depending.'

He got to his knees, opened the box, and taking out some ten or fifteen photos, laid them out in three rows on the carpet. Ralph went to stand over them.

The first picture was of Norman with his gun, silhouetted like a statue against the sky.

'Mm,' I said, 'I like that.'

'Indeed,' assented Ralph.

'That's Norman, the farm manager,' explained Jorgen. 'He goes everywhere with that gun.'

'Jorgen!' My eyes were drawn to the picture underneath Norman's. 'I don't remember you taking that!'

It was a long distance shot of me picking my way across the causeway, a basket under my arm: an unlikely Little Red Ridinghood in a wolfless environment.

'What's that?' Charles came up behind me. 'Which one? Where?'

'There!' said Ralph. 'Below the one of Norman.'

'When did you take that?' There was a sudden harshness in Charles' tone, a note almost of threat.

'I can't remember,' said Jorgen. 'Last spring, I think.'

'Do you know, Lucy?'

I was intensely aware of him at my back, towering over me. 'No,' I said. 'It must have been summer, because of the dress, but otherwise . . .'

'I think,' said Jorgen, 'it may have been . . .'

He was interrupted by Charles.

'Given your training as a journalist,' he said, his voice now icy, 'I'm sure you find it difficult not to snoop. All the same, I would appreciate it if you didn't spy on my wife.'

'Charles, please!' I twisted round so I could look at him. 'Just what are you playing at?'

He ignored my question, his attention utterly on his sudden adversary.

'And what do you do, then, in your paintings?' demanded Jorgen, getting to his feet. 'You also snoop.'

'Not snoop,' said Charles. 'Never snoop. I remember,

recreate, transform. Never snoop. There's a difference.'

'And you own what you paint?'

'Of course not.'

'Then let me see her too. Lucy's part of the island. I'm
recording the island; you don't control the island.'

'Oh, photograph the trees and fields, by all means,' said
Charles, 'the causeway and the mud-flats. But leave Lucy out
of it.'

'You're jealous!' said Jorgen. 'You're jealous because I see
her differently to you, because I give her another existence.'

'Stop it, both of you!' I raised my voice as shrilly as I could
against their senseless male competitiveness. 'What do you
think this is, some kind of market where you can haggle over
me as if I didn't exist?'

'But my dear!' said Charles, looking down at me for the
first time since the argument had started. 'We all of us only
exist insofar as other people see us. We rely on other people
to bring us into being. Surely you know that?'

'In that case,' I said, rising, 'let me relieve you of a duty. I'll
find someone else to bring me alive.'

And not caring that I was walking across the photographs,
not caring that I might scuff or damage them, I ran from the
room.

It had backfired terribly, my game of inviting Jorgen to tea.
It hadn't put Charles in his place at all. The only people it
had hurt were Jorgen and myself – and doubtless Ralph, who
hated confrontation of any kind. I fought back the tears. Why
did creative people thrive so on manipulation, on setting
people against each other? Was it that the act of creation gave
them a taste for playing God, or was it simply that by pushing
people to extremes, they were better able to observe and
understand the complexities of human behaviour? This was
apostasy, I knew, but I had, in my time, seen more cruelty
perpetrated in the name of art than could ever justify the end
result.

'Lucy, wait! Not so fast!'

I turned to see Jorgen hurrying up the road after me, his
cardboard box tucked tightly under his arm, his pale face
creased with concern.

'That was very wrong of us,' he said, drawing abreast of me. 'You're worth twenty of Charles or me. You're sweet and kind and generous. We're just jealous because we can never make you as perfectly as you've already been made.'

'I think,' I said, 'I'd prefer it if you stopped talking about me like that. And anyway, it isn't true.'

'Oh but it is. You're one of the most beautiful women I've ever known.'

'Even though,' I said, the words escaping me before I could stop them, 'I play such tricks on you?'

'Tricks?' For a moment he looked blank. Then it dawned on him what I meant. 'That's all it was? A trick?'

I put out a hand and touched him on the arm. 'I'm not a lovely person, Jorgen. I'm silly and self-obsessed. I get bored and I get angry with Charles, sometimes I . . .'

He didn't let me finish. 'And of course you hate it that we both find you beautiful.'

His saying that put me in mind of Benedict and our shared affliction.

'Well, wouldn't you?'

But he seemed not to hear me. 'We don't really know you,' was all he said. 'We think we do, but we don't. What do you want, really?'

I shrugged. 'Too much, it would seem. But right now, at this very moment, all I want is to apologise.'

'Apologise?'

'Your photographs,' I continued firmly, 'are very good indeed. Charles snipes at journalism because he's frightened by its simplicity. His own work is so, I don't know, so cluttered with his own emotions, he's lost the ability to see clearly any more.'

Jorgen glanced at the box under his arm. 'Ingrid, my wife, she hated my work also,' he said. 'All the people I value hate it.'

'Except me.'

He smiled at that. 'Of course.'

'What you have to do is arrange an exhibition. Speak to Andre.'

'He only handles painters.'

'He'd know where you should go. Or else there's that gallery in Meldwich. You know, by the market square.'

'No one ever goes there.'

'It's a start.'

'Perhaps you're right.' He frowned. 'Yes, I must stop relying on what Charles thinks of me, just because he's the only artist I know. I must stand on my own two feet.'

'Precisely.'

He looked at his box. 'Good or bad, this is my life. Mine, and no one else's.' He smiled at me oddly. 'So – thank you for the trick.'

'You mean you'll come again?'

'We learn,' he said. 'Learn and get stronger. People who stay at home cannot grow.'

He leant forward suddenly, and clumsily kissed me on the cheek.

'Go carefully,' he said. 'And don't you worry what we think of you. What we think doesn't matter.' Then, shifting his box of photographs from the crook of his left arm to his right, he strode off down the road to the village.

I watched until his gangling frame had dwindled to a speck, then turned and walked down to the beach. Although the rain had stopped, the sea and sky were still variously grey, like a canvas on which, for purposes of comparison, had been mixed every gradation of the colour, as if the weather couldn't decide which shade to use – whilst over Meldwich, for contrast, there was a tear in the sky, through which a shaft of late-afternoon sun promised a different tomorrow.

I closed my eyes, whereupon, to my surprise, the view became another sort of canvas, one of Charles', of me in his wood. No sooner had this image established itself than the figure that was me came urgently to life, and, turning her back on the men who watched her from behind their trees, stepped out of the picture and ran towards that tear in the sky.

'I owe you an apology,' said a voice at my elbow.

I turned to face my husband. My first impulse was to ignore him, to push past him and go back into the house, busy myself with supper, but something in his eyes made me decide to have it out with him.

'Me and Jorgen both.'

'Jorgen can take care of himself.'

'I'm not sure that he can.'

'It's you I feel badly about. I shouldn't have spoken like that.'

'Even though you meant it?'

He raised an eyebrow. 'Did I?'

'I imagine you did.'

'No,' he said. 'It's Ralph. This whole weekend. I'm finding it very difficult.'

'So you lash out at Jorgen and me?'

He hung his head. 'I know I'm a shit.'

'Yes,' I said, 'and so do I.' And now I did make to push past him.

'Hold me,' he said. 'Like you used to. Put your arms around me. Just for a moment. Please.'

I hesitated, but only fractionally, and then, without knowing why, I found myself opening my arms to him. He stepped into them and hugged me with surprising force.

'Without you,' he said quietly, 'my world has no centre. Everything revolves around you. You do know that, don't you?'

'But of course,' I said. 'It all whizzes like mad around me. That's why I'm such a dizzy blonde.'

'Laugh if you like,' he said, 'but it's true.' He took my hand. 'Now, how can we make supper special tonight?'

'For Ralph, you mean?'

'For all of us.'

'Well,' I said hesitantly, 'I could make a starter, I suppose, and . . .'

He interrupted me. 'Yes! And candles and that bottle of Rioja we've been saving. The whole works.' And keeping my hand in his, he pulled me towards the house.

We entered the kitchen to find Ralph putting away the last of the tea things.

'Ralph!' said Charles sternly, causing the old man to start guiltily. 'What do you think you're doing?'

'Just tidying up.'

'Well, you sit down. Lucy and I are going to prepare us a meal to remember.'

'There's really no need . . .'

'Sit!'

Ralph did as he was told.

Charles fetched the Rioja from the wine rack.

'Pass the glasses,' he said. 'I want to propose a toast.'

I handed him the glasses, he opened the bottle with a flourish, then suddenly he stiffened.

'What?' I said. 'What is it?'

'A noise,' he said. 'Upstairs.'

I felt my blood run cold. 'What sort of noise?'

He held up a hand. 'Listen!'

We listened in silence, but thankfully, whatever noise it was that Benedict had made, it wasn't repeated.

'Probably the pipes,' I said hastily, 'or a window banging.'

But Charles had moved on already and was handing out the wine. He lifted his glass ceremoniously. Ralph and I followed suit.

'To us,' he said solemnly. 'To family.'

'To family,' echoed Ralph dutifully.

I was still listening fearfully lest Benedict make another noise, and Charles had to clink his glass against mine to bring me back to the event at hand.

'To family,' I repeated guiltily.

The meal that followed was, against all the odds, surprisingly festive. From somewhere deep inside himself, Charles dredged up a host of anecdotes that had Ralph and me in stitches. By the time I put the cheese on the table, and Charles had located a cobwebbed bottle of port, all three of us were weak with laughter.

'Now,' I said, crossing to the dresser for some biscuits to go with the cheese, 'anything else?'

'I'm dying,' said Ralph.

I froze, then turned to look at Charles, who was staring at his uncle, horror-struck.

'I'm dying,' repeated Ralph, 'for a cup of coffee.'

And as quickly as the horror had engulfed us, it receded, leaving an unsettled silence in its wake.

'Right,' I managed, 'coffee. For you too, Charles?'

He nodded.

'Coffee coming up.'

After coffee, and after we had finished the last of the port, I got rather unsteadily to my feet. 'We'll leave the washing-up till the morning, agreed?'

Charles, I realised, was grinning at me – rather too fixedly. 'Poor Lucy,' he said. 'She's had one over the eight.'

'Eight what?'

Charles shrugged. 'God knows. It's a silly expression I always thought.'

'Well,' I said, 'whatever they are, they've got the better of me and I'm going to bed.'

'You're giggling,' said Charles. 'You haven't giggled like that since . . . since . . .'

'Since when?'

'I forget.' A sudden shaft of sadness dimmed the mischief in his eye. 'A long time anyway.'

'Thank you,' said Ralph, 'for a most delicious meal.'

'Yes,' said Charles, 'thank you.'

'Don't mention it,' I said, 'and don't stay up too late, you two, or you'll regret it in the morning.'

The darkness on the stairs did nothing to disturb the warm cocoon of laughter in which the evening had wrapped me, but as I turned down the corridor to my room, my eyes were drawn with eerie inevitability along its length to the dark rectangle that was Benedict's door – and, a painter suddenly, I found myself filling it, lineament by delicious lineament with Benedict's subtle and collusive image.

Anti-Cerne

That Sunday the causeway opened at two thirty-nine, which meant we had the entire morning to get through before Charles drove Ralph to the three o'clock train. The first person up was Benedict, though the only one to know this, of course, was me, and then only because I was the next up, and when I set about the washing-up from the night before, I found a wet plate and mug on the draining board. I'd only just finished the washing-up when Ralph appeared, his tentative smile more grimace than grin, a response less to the outside world than to his internal cycle of pain. I made us both coffee, whereupon a rather withdrawn and thoughtful Charles put in his appearance. We had breakfast, then Charles excused himself to go to his studio and Ralph, moving to the window, said: 'It's cleared up. I think I'll take my book into the orchard.'

I fetched a couple of deckchairs from the shed and put them by the pond; and after a bath, went to join him. Limp-limbed and slack-jawed, his book unopened on his lap, he was dozing. I thought of slipping away for a walk, but I'd already been round the island once that weekend, and living on an island one learns not to over-use its possibilities. So, like Ralph, I settled into my deckchair and gave myself over to the distant strains of the music to which Charles invariably worked: a selection of operatic arias and choruses. Ralph woke in concert with the slave's chorus from *Nabucco*, whereupon I brought us out tea and what was left of the brownies and tried to cut short the silences that kept opening up between us by gossiping about Jorgen, Norman and the Landies.

Charles emerged from the studio at one, and after a lunch of bread and cheese in the kitchen, followed by coffee in the living-room, we all trooped out to the car.

The relief Ralph felt to be going home was written all over his face.

'Now promise you'll ring Norman,' I said, 'the minute you get in, and if you get ill again, if you need anything at all . . .'

'I'll be fine. Really!' He darted forward to kiss me on the cheek.

I caught hold of him and hugged him. 'Look after yourself,' I commanded.

'Of course,' he said, wriggling free. 'Why on earth wouldn't I?'

'Come on!' snapped Charles, who was in the car already. 'We don't want to miss the train.'

I held open the door for Ralph, then closed it, thinking: 'I may not see you again.'

'Do we need anything from the shops?' asked Charles.

I shook my head and stood back as they pulled off down the driveway, my hand lifted in a dutiful wave. Ralph's hand, raised in an answering wave, was still extended through the window when the car vanished round the corner leading up to the village.

I went inside to seek out Benedict.

When Charles got back at four, he found me in the kitchen, making tea.

'So,' he said, rubbing his hands together. 'Alone at last!'

'That's what you think.'

'What do you mean?'

'Andre came on whilst you were taking Ralph to the station. He brought a friend. A boy called Benedict. He wants him to stay for a couple of weeks.'

'A couple of weeks?' Charles looked dismayed. 'Why?'

'He's been ill and needs a holiday.'

'Another of Andre's pick-ups?'

'Actually, no.' My denial was a shade too quick, a touch too certain. 'A business acquaintance, I think.'

Charles shot me a speculative look. 'Well,' he said, 'how nice for you. To have company.'

'I'm sorry,' I said. 'I didn't plan this.'

Charles patted me on the shoulder. 'No, no,' he said, 'of course.'

I handed him his tea.

'How was Ralph when you put him on the train?'

'Tomorrow I'll ring the hospital, speak to his doctor.'

'And then?'

He shrugged. 'Who knows? Wait, I suppose. Just wait.'

'I'll go up with you if you want. To Hull.'

'I'm not going to Hull.' He turned for the door. 'Now please, don't call me till dinner's ready.'

'About eight,' I said, 'if that's okay.'

He reached the door, then paused. 'Not a nice weekend,' he said. Where yesterday the untidiness of his attire had seemed cheerfully Bohemian, today he looked merely dishevelled.

'No,' I echoed. 'Not a nice weekend.'

It was eight thirty and almost dark by the time dinner was ready. I'd been alone downstairs ever since Charles' return and it was silent and dark in the hallway when I emerged from the kitchen to summon Charles and Benedict to table. I turned on the light, then stood at the bottom of the stairs and called up into the gloom: 'Charles! Benedict! Dinner!'

Benedict appeared first. He had bathed and changed and his hair was still damp. He looked so young and clean it was almost painful to look at him. I found myself imagining what might happen were I to put out a hand when he reached the hall and touch the albescent beauty of his hair. Such was its brilliance, I was sure I would burn myself.

He was half-way down the stairs when an untidy and distracted Charles appeared on the landing above him. Benedict turned, and Charles, despite his tiredness, came suddenly alert, and in a single glance took in everything about this new arrival before bounding down the stairs and saying: 'So! You must be Benedict! Welcome!'

Then, side by side, Charles with a fatherly arm around Benedict's shoulder, the two of them descended the last of the stairs.

'I'm ravenous,' said Charles, 'and I'll bet our guest is too.' He looked at Benedict. 'Eh?'

Benedict nodded. He didn't meet my eye. I turned and led the way into the kitchen.

The meal that followed was not in any way unusual. I played hostess, Charles was liberal with the wine, and

Benedict listened in attentive silence while Charles gave him the low-down on the island and its inhabitants, running wittily through Norman and his gun, Jorgen and his photographs, the Landies and their guests.

'They take the cake,' said Charles. 'Chewing on the cud of rural England and wittering on about the magic of the causeway.'

'Well,' I said, 'you must admit, it is pretty magical.'

'When we came on,' said Benedict, uttering what I think was his first complete sentence of the evening, 'it was like . . . I don't know . . . crossing over.'

'The problem with the Landies,' said Charles, 'is that they never do cross over. Not properly. They just cross back and forth. They're the sort of people who think they're growing just because they're on the move.'

'Enough of the Landies,' I said. 'Or we'll talk them out of existence.'

'Would that we could,' chuckled Charles.

After dinner, he stood up and said: 'Well, I'd better pop over to Norman's and phone.'

'Give him my love,' I said.

'Who? Norman?'

'No, stupid, Ralph.'

'I wouldn't mind some coffee when I get back.'

'It shall be done.'

I filled the kettle, then turned to Benedict.

'I told him what we agreed,' I said. 'That you've been sick. That you work with Andre.'

I expected him to greet my remark with another nod of his head, so silent had he been throughout the meal, but looking up from the mound of orange pips he'd collected on one side of his plate, he said in a tone of almost aggrieved surprise: 'He doesn't seem very interested.'

'No, no,' I said, 'don't get him wrong. It's just that he likes to take his time.'

'Before what?'

I had to think a moment before finding the appropriate word: 'Engaging.'

Then, because I didn't want to talk about Charles, and

because all through supper it had been as much as I could do
to keep my eyes off the haunting delicacy of Benedict's face,
the way he handled his knife and fork, his lips as they parted
to take in his food, I used the excuse of going round the table
to fetch some cups from the dresser to rest my hand, ever so
lightly, on his shoulder. 'Could you get the tray?' I'd been
going to ask, but he withdrew so sharply from my touch, as
if I'd electrocuted him, that instead I found myself saying:
'What is it? What's hurt you?'

He didn't reply, but just as at the creek I'd seen it in his
eyes, so now I could read it in the set of his shoulders, that
something awful, something deeply wounding, had happened to him. I managed not to make the mistake of
touching him again, but as I fetched down the cups and laid
the tray, I did add quietly: 'You're quite safe here, you know.
And if you need to talk, then I'm ready to listen.'

Still he didn't reply, and though again it was as much as I
could do not to take him in my arms, to hug away his pain,
whatever that pain might be, I forced myself to finish
preparing the coffee as if nothing untoward had passed
between us. Then, taking up the tray, I said: 'Let's go through
to the living-room.'

We hadn't been settled long, Benedict on the window seat,
myself in the armchair, when we were joined by Charles, a
sketch-pad under his arm.

'So?' I queried, handing him his coffee.

'Got in safely and about to go to bed.'

'And tomorrow you'll ring the hospital?'

'Tomorrow I'll ring the hospital.' He turned to Benedict.
'And you, young man – you've also been sick, or so Lucy tells
me.'

As if he were seeking confirmation that this was what I'd
meant about Charles taking his time to engage, Benedict
shot me a look of mild enquiry; then, without waiting for my
confirmation, he turned to Charles and nodded.

'Nothing serious, I hope?'

He shook his head.

'My uncle,' said Charles, 'is dying.'

'Charles! Please! Do you have to?'

'Yes,' he said, subsiding onto the sofa. 'You've no idea what a relief it is, just to say it. My uncle is dying.'

'I'm sorry,' said Benedict. 'That must be awful for you.'

But Charles seemed not to hear him. He'd opened his pad and was looking at me. 'Now, Lucy: would you mind sitting for me?'

'I don't believe it!'

'I know it sounds callous, but what do you expect me to say? I just pray that it's quick.'

But it wasn't Ralph I'd meant. The last time I'd sat for Charles had been in Cornwall, more than ten years ago. In those days, when he deployed me in his paintings, I'd still had a face, features, my own reality.

'And to what do I owe the honour?'

He didn't choose, however, to answer my question.

'Stay where you are, but put your legs over the arm of the chair.' And when I didn't move: 'Please, Lucy. It won't take long.'

I rearranged myself as directed.

'Perfect!' He sat forward and pulled a pencil from his pocket.

I darted a look at Benedict. He'd turned his back on the room and was looking out of the window at the night. There was nothing to be gleaned from the line of his shoulders except, perhaps, a desire to be alone.

Charles lifted his pencil at arm's length and squinted to measure my proportions.

'Well,' I said. 'This takes me back.'

'To where?' His concentration didn't waver as his pencil went from arm's length to pad and back again whilst he blocked my vital measurements.

'Cornwall, of course.'

'But I draw you all the time.'

'Do you?'

In your head, I was thinking, and your memory, yes, you make free with me there; but not in the flesh, not as I am, not in reality.

'You're in everything I do,' he said. 'Absolutely everything.'

'Bits of me,' I said. 'Bits and pieces.'

'I like to tantalise.'

He was frowning as he worked. I twisted round in the chair to steal another look at Benedict.

'Keep still,' muttered Charles.

'Sorry. I was just wondering . . .' I raised my voice a notch. 'Are you all right over there, Benedict?'

There was a momentary pause: then, his voice low and clear, he said: 'Yes, thanks. Fine.'

We sat in silence after that until, with a flourish, Charles put down his pencil and held his pad at arm's length to scrutinise it. 'There! That'll do for now.' He dropped the pad onto the coffee table.

I got out of the chair and stretched. 'Let me see.'

He had drawn me like a cat, coiled supine and voluptuous over the armchair.

'Goodness!' I said.

'Yes?'

I shrugged. 'You make me look a lot more comfortable than I felt. Almost – I don't know . . .'

'Sexual?' It was the most oblique of queries, as sly as his drawing.

I met the challenge head-on. 'All right,' I said. 'Sexual. If that's how you see it.'

Benedict had got up from the window seat and come to stand at my elbow.

'Nice,' he said. 'You've captured her perfectly.'

I could feel the warmth of his breath on my neck, and as he spoke his hand brushed my upper arm, just as my hand, earlier, had brushed against his shoulder. I wanted to lean back and have him enfold me in his arms, but when I did take a tentative step backwards, he moved sharply to the side.

'Tomorrow,' said Charles, 'I may draw the two of you. You make a pretty picture, the two of you.'

'Absolutely not!' A flicker of alarm disturbed the depths of Benedict's eyes.

'But why?'

'If someone paints you . . .'

'They steal a piece of your soul?' Charles let out an

explosive laugh. 'No, no! That's photography. It's the camera that steals your soul. And anyway, it's a primitive belief.'

'Beliefs have to be primitive,' said Benedict. 'Otherwise they become ideas.'

'How interesting!' Charles got to his feet. 'So you think . . .?'

But Benedict raised a hand. 'I'm sorry. I can't really talk about it. And anyway, I'm rather tired.'

'Of course,' said Charles, 'you've been ill. Tomorrow, perhaps?'

Benedict shook his head. 'I'm not a good talker.'

'Honestly, Charles! Leave the poor man alone.' I risked placing a careless hand on Benedict's arm, and this time he didn't withdraw. So, turning quickly to face him, I followed up my advantage with: 'Now. Have you got everything you need?'

Having submitted himself to my touch, though, he now made a point of avoiding my eye. 'Absolutely. So if you'll excuse me . . .'

I tightened my grip on his arm. 'Sleep well,' I said. 'And sweet dreams.'

He bobbed his head in acquiescence, then – disengaging himself from my grasp – slipped, wraith-like, from the room.

'Well, well!' said Charles as the door closed behind him. 'What a strange young man. Interesting, though. And quite unlike the usual pick-up.'

'He's not a pick-up,' I said crossly, 'as I keep telling you.'

'No,' said Charles, 'obviously. Mm, I wonder . . . Most interesting.'

'What?'

He raised an eyebrow. 'You tell me.'

'I think we're all tired,' I said. 'It's been one hell of a weekend.'

The expression on my face must have been fiercer than I'd intended because, dropping this line of enquiry as abruptly as he'd started it, he turned to the window.

'Do be careful, though,' he muttered. 'I have a feeling it's a race, this, and you know what races are.'

'I do?'

'Only one person wins.'

'I haven't a clue what you're talking about.'

'You haven't? Well, that's all right, then. I'll say good-night. And, of course, sweet dreams.'

Perhaps I should have confronted him then and there, told him there was nothing (as yet) to worry about. But because, at heart, I wanted him to worry, and because I hoped there was something there, I merely returned his last, ironic serve with a 'sweet dreams' of my own before following Benedict out of the room.

Upstairs, seated at my dressing-table, I stared disapprovingly at my face in the glass, ran a reproachful hand slowly through my untidy, straw-like hair, felt out, as punishment, the lines about my eyes, the rawness of my lips. Then, reaching for my reflection in the glass, and pressing my fingertips to its cold, stark surfaces, I sent up a silent prayer that I would prove equal to the course ahead.

Bozzetto

A race, Charles had said, and the days that followed that first weekend certainly bore out the aptness of his words. The instant Benedict's presence on the island was no longer a secret, everyone, it seemed, was after him.

Norman came more than once to the house to gossip about the new arrival, to guess at what he might have done, to wonder at how Andre fitted into the picture and to grumble at the fact that I didn't seem to share his curiosity. And on the Wednesday, bumping into Benedict on his way out, he invited him to go shooting: an invitation which, to my surprise, Benedict accepted and apparently so enjoyed that the next two evenings, too, he vanished into the fields with Norman, gun at the ready.

It took Jorgen longer to find out about Benedict's existence, but once he had, he dropped by as often as Norman to ferret for information. And Charles, caught up though he was in his worries over Ralph and whatever it was he was painting, who spent his days locked in his studio, only emerging after six to join me in the kitchen for a glass of wine, would, instead of staying to talk with me, go into the living-room to await Benedict's return from his shooting expeditions, and then, putting a paternal arm round his shoulder, force him into a lengthy walk along the beach. Even Geoff Landie – who, on the Tuesday, caused a minor stir by arriving, alone and hang-dog, in the wake of some row with Caroline – even Geoff, despite his depression, showed a surprising level of interest in the fact that we'd netted a new arrival.

Or do I exaggerate? Do I make too much of unremarkable things? It's possible. We were a small community on an isolated island, any newcomer was bound to engage us. Perhaps I was only so horribly aware of the interest of the others because I wanted our guest for myself, resented having to compete for his time of which, in any case, he was extremely jealous. I hardly saw him at all on the Monday, Tuesday or Wednesday, and though the Thursday was a slight improvement, in general he kept very much to himself – either in his room or out on Andre's yacht, which every day, and for as long as the tides would allow, he took into the estuary. By the Friday all I'd been able to discover about him was that he came from a village in Cornwall, that he played the drums in a band called The Unknowns, that he'd been unemployed for almost a year, that he had a room in Kentish Town, but that he didn't much like London, it was only the band that kept him there.

It wasn't until the Saturday evening that I was able to be properly alone with him – and then only for the briefest of moments. Although overcast, the afternoon had been warm, and I had spent it in the orchard, reading. At six I closed my book and walked round the house to the lawn, where I stood, listening to the faint lilt of Charles' background music, waiting for Norman to appear, a gun under each arm, to collect Benedict for the day's shooting. Then I remembered that Norman had been invited to a party in Meldwich and was going off to hunt a different prey: a new woman. There would be no shooting tonight.

I walked up to the living-room, and putting my head through the french windows, called: 'Benedict? Benedict?' There was no reply. So, depositing my book on the window seat, I set off along the beach to see if I could find him.

I don't know what it was that made me pause at the copse, but something, some sixth sense, made me relinquish the beach at this point and approach the trees – and there, on the far side of the clearing, as wraith-like as ever, stood Benedict. He had his back to the trap and was peering intently into the undergrowth. He didn't hear me until I was almost in the clearing; then, in instantaneous reaction to my tentative 'Benedict?' he swung round sharply: 'Lucy! Shit you startled me!'

All I could do by way of reply was wrinkle my nose, for no sooner was I inside the clearing, than I was overpowered by the smell of the decomposing chicken.

'Ugh!' I said. 'That smell!'

His eyes went to the trap.

'Horrible,' he agreed.

'How can you stand it?'

'You get used to it.'

I fumbled in my pocket for my handkerchief and put it to my nose. He smiled, almost apologetically.

'But then I'm being silly,' he said.

'Silly? How?'

'I was watching for the fox.'

'Watching for the fox?'

He nodded.

'But surely he won't come when someone's here?'

'That's what's so silly.'

'And anyway, you don't have a gun.'

'No, no!' he said quickly. 'Not to shoot him. Just to warn him.'

'Warn him?'

He gestured to the trap. 'Make him wary.'

Something about the expression in his eyes, a certain sad determination, made me realise that this was no idle pastime.

'So you feel sorry for the fox,' I said softly.

'Of course.' He sounded surprised. 'Don't you?'

'I hadn't thought about it.'

'All day and all night, that chicken hangs there. Like all of us, the fox gets hungry. One day he'll fall for it.'

'I don't understand,' I said. 'You go shooting with Norman. Why go shooting if you're on the side of the fox?'

'That's different,' he said. 'Learning to use a gun.'

'How? You're out hunting.'

'Norman is. Not me.'

'What are you doing then?'

'Just learning to use a gun.'

'But why, if you don't intend to use it?'

'It's a useful skill.'

'If you want to kill.'

'Or if you need to protect yourself.'

There was a pause.

'And do you?'

'Don't we all?'

It wasn't as if he'd said a great deal – he'd been right in telling Charles he wasn't a good talker – but even so, his words confirmed me yet again in my suspicions. Here was a man who'd been wounded by life. And because I saw myself as wounded too, especially in that clearing, and because, looking at him over the trap, I saw not just a young man, but a hint of the child who might have been, an alternative, sunnier future – and because that brought to mind, and painfully too, an image of Charles with his arm around Benedict's shoulder, I let out a little cry.

'Are you all right?' Although we were separated by the trap, and the light in the clearing diffuse, there was no mistaking the concern in his eyes.

'I'm fine,' I stammered. 'Just fine.'

He skirted the trap and came to where I was standing.

'What?' he demanded. 'What is it?'

I shook my head. 'You wouldn't understand.'

'Try me.'

Whereupon, taking him at his word, I reached out with both hands and ran them through his hair. He stiffened, but at least he didn't pull away.

'What brought you here?' I whispered.

He ducked the question with a quick, ironic smile. 'Andre, of course.'

'But is it what you want? Is it what you need?'

He shrugged, and reaching up to lift my hands from his hair, fastened them in his.

'Do any of us have what we want? Do you?'

'You haven't answered my question.'

'Nor you mine.'

I managed a smile. 'Sometimes. Almost.' And leaning forward, I brushed my lips ever so lightly against his.

Again he didn't pull away – nor even, this time, stiffen. He just stood there, rooted to the spot, as if awaiting some command. I was suddenly very embarrassed. Freeing my hands, I hid my face in my handkerchief and blew my nose.

'You must be careful of Andre. He's very powerful.'

'I know that.'

'It doesn't do to be too passive.'

'I know that too.'

And as if to underline his words, he felt for my hands again and lifted them to his lips and kissed them.

I stared as hard as I dared into his sad, brown eyes.,

'Who are you?' I asked. 'Really?' And when he didn't reply: 'What exactly happened in London?'

He shrugged. 'I got involved in something that didn't work out.'

'A relationship?'

He grimaced.

'A woman?'

'In part.'

'And Andre?'

Now he smiled. 'Andre rescued me. Brought me here. Told me you'd look after me.'

'Just me?'

'Just you.'

'And am I?'

But once again he avoided my question.

'You tell me.'

'Well,' I said slowly, 'I'd certainly like to. If you'll let me.' And moving carefully, so as not to startle him, I made to touch his face.

He caught my hand before it could get to him, and very serious suddenly, as if he were the one who had to do the comforting, he said: 'Andre told me how lonely you were.'

'He did?' I wasn't sure I liked hearing that. What Benedict and I discovered together, I wanted us to discover alone, not in response to Andre.

'And now I see why.'

'The island, you mean?'

'In part. But only in part.'

'What else?'

I was expecting him to make some reference to Charles, but instead he threw me completely by saying: 'It isn't easy being beautiful.' And then, before I could muster a reply, or indeed a response of any sort, he took a step towards me. For one glorious, heady moment, I thought he was going to take me in his arms, but he simply brushed past me.

'Now come,' he said, 'we'd better get out of here if you don't like the smell.'

And ducking quickly out of the clearing, he left me no alternative but to pocket my handkerchief and follow him onto the beach.

'There,' he said. 'Better out here. No?'

I couldn't agree. Its smell apart, at least we'd been alone in the clearing, intimate, close. Here on the beach we were dwarfed by the sea and the sky, made minuscule. But this was not something I knew how to say, so I merely nodded, and together we began to walk back towards the house.

'I shall miss it,' he said after a moment, his eyes fixed on the horizon, his soft lips puckering. 'This estuary.'

'But you've only just arrived! It's not even been a week. Andre said a couple.'

He heard, of course, the dismay in my voice, and it made him smile. 'Oh, I'm not going yet. But when I do, then I shall miss it.'

'I hope you stay all summer.' I tried to eradicate all urgency from my tone. 'You really are most awfully easy as a guest, no trouble at all. As I said when you arrived, it's nice having company.'

He looked from the horizon to my anxious eyes.

'You're very sweet,' he said – then, suddenly, he tensed, and without any warning, turned, took me in his arms and hugged me so tightly I could hardly breathe.

'Benedict!'

'Ssh!' he replied. 'Don't say anything. Ssh!'

He kept me in his vice-like embrace, and because, of course, it was what I'd wanted him to do since that first morning, that first sight of him in the doorway, I closed my eyes and gave myself over to the insistence of his arms, the softer, subtler pleading of his body, his stomach, groin and legs. But even as I did this, even as I relaxed into him, fitting my body to the curve of his, he let go of me and took a quick step backwards. I opened my eyes, and on the sea wall looking down at us I caught the flash of Jorgen's startled, white face and round his neck the ubiquitous camera.

'I'm sorry,' said Benedict. 'I shouldn't have done that. I don't know what came over me.'

'Please!' I cried. 'Don't apologise. It's perfectly all right, really it is, you mustn't think . . .'

He cut me short. 'Don't let's talk about it. We'll only complicate things.' And turning sharply, he strode so quickly towards the house that I almost had to run to keep up with him.

As we came up the lawn, he said: 'I need to freshen up. I'll be down later.' And with a curt, embarrassed nod of the head, he vanished into the house.

I wanted to call him back, shout out that he was welcome, at any time, to take me in his arms – but he'd obviously meant it when he said he didn't want to talk about it. And anyway, there was a chance that up in his studio, Charles could be watching. A lilting waltz (*La Traviata*? *Rigoletto*?) was pouring in a liquid wave of sound from the studio window – and suddenly, despite my abandonment by Benedict, it lifted me, this waltz, into a mad, reeling dance. A wave of irrepressible joy rose up in me, and as it broke I closed my eyes, threw my arms wide and careered round the lawn until, out of breath and with my head spinning, I collapsed onto the grass and lay staring at the ceaseless shifting of the clouds.

Benedict had taken me in his arms! Benedict had hugged me so tight it had hurt, had nuzzled his face into the hollow of my neck! What did it matter that Jorgen had seen us, or that Charles, if he was looking, would be wondering at my dance, my sudden happiness? I felt, at that moment, as blessed as the island itself, caught between the security of land and the freedom of the open sea, whilst all around me, the world was opening out not just into summer, but into a fuller, heightened version of itself.

That evening, appropriately, we changed the clocks and went onto summer time. And oh, if only it could have continued like that, as sure and certain as the seasons. But, setting aside my awesome ability to delude myself, there were other even more irrepressible forces at work, other less predictable runners in the race. As, indeed, I was to discover the following Thursday.

On the Thursday, just as soon as he'd finished his breakfast, Benedict went out for a walk. I was about to tackle the washing-up when there was a tap at the window and Norman, his nicotine-stained teeth bared in a jaunty grin, appeared in the doorway.

'Morning, Luce! Any chance of some coffee?'

I gestured to the jug on the table.

'And to what do I owe the honour of such an early visit?'

'Our lord and master.' He settled himself at the table and reached for the jug.

'Which one? I have so many.'

'Andre. He's just rung to say he's coming down for a day or two.'

'Today?'

Norman nodded.

I crossed to the tide chart. The causeway closed at one thirty-eight and opened again just before ten.

'This morning?' I asked. 'Or after ten?'

'He didn't say. Just that he was coming down. Something about some archaeologists.'

'Archaeologists?'

'I think that was the word.' He shrugged apologetically. 'You know me. Only the one O level. Not in English.'

'Archaeologists!' I repeated. 'Whatever next?'

'And he wants to check on Benedict, of course.'

I stiffened despite myself. 'Of course.'

Norman twirled his spoon in his cup. 'I know you think because Andre wants to keep the whole thing quiet we shouldn't talk about it, but do you think he's – Benedict, I mean – do you think he's one of Andre's, you know, blokes?'

'Why should you think that?' I asked sharply.

Norman chuckled. 'No, that's the point. Usually I can tell a poofta when I see one. But this time I'm not so sure.'

'Good!' I said decisively. 'Because, since you ask: no, I don't think he is. In fact, I'm sure he isn't.'

'Ah, ha!' He tugged at his ear, a characteristic gesture and the reason, I always thought, why his ears stuck out from his head as they did. 'Been giving you the eye, has he?'

'Certainly not! It's . . .'

'Go on,' said Norman. 'I'm listening.'

All I could say, though, was: 'Just a feeling I have.'

'Female intuition, eh?'

'If you like.'

I didn't care for the way in which he was staring at me.

'What?' I demanded. 'Why are you looking at me like that?'

'You're a dark horse,' he said, 'and no mistake. One would almost think . . .'

'Yes? What would one think?'

But he merely shrugged. 'That you were in on the conspiracy.'

Well, I thought, better you think that than anything else, so I didn't protest, and after a moment he pushed back his chair.

'But I must be getting on. Thanks for the coffee.'

'Don't mention it. And thanks for the message.'

Nothing further happened until the afternoon, even though I'd been expecting, come lunch-time, that Andre would have appeared, Andre and Benedict both. Benedict couldn't have gone sailing, I knew, because there wouldn't be water yet in the creek. Neither of them did appear, however, so at two thirty, knowing that now Andre couldn't come on till the evening, I set off on a walk to see if I could locate our antisocial lodger.

Ever since Ralph's departure, the weather had been indecisive, warm one day, chilly the next. The only certain proof of impending summer was the cow-parsley gathered like lace round the edge of the fields, a smattering of old-fashioned dog roses in the hedgerows, and the sleek, self-satisfied clusters of lilac along the road to the village. That Thursday was no exception. There were spring flowers everywhere, whilst the sun – such as it was – vacillated behind banks of baleful cloud.

I went first through the village – which, thankfully, was deserted – then stopped at the creek. That, too, was deserted. Even though the causeway would be closed by now and the tide was rising fast, the incoming water had not yet lifted Andre's yacht from where she lay on the mud. I could, and perhaps should, have pushed on along the sea wall, but instead I decided to return to the house, and if Benedict still wasn't there, then to follow the sea wall to the bunker, and from the bunker back to the creek.

This time the village was not deserted. Geoff Landie was on his knees in a corner of his garden, weeding the edge of his recently mown lawn. It was an island joke, the obsessive regularity with which Geoff mowed his lawn. Most weekends he was at it, and if he stayed on the island for as long as a week, then it was every third or fourth day. The rest of us let our grass grow until it was almost jungle-high; the Landie's lawn was never less than impeccably suburban.

'Geoff!' I said. 'Still here?'

He looked up.

'Will Caroline not have you back?'

He smiled broadly. 'No, no. We've sorted that out, thank God. On Henry's advice – you remember Henry, the friend of Caroline's? Child psychologist?'

I nodded.

'Well, he suggested Harriet spend a couple of days with Caroline's mother and Caroline's coming down tomorrow so we can have a weekend on our own. *Sans* the monster.'

'But you usually do.'

'Not without worrying. This weekend we'll know where she is. You haven't met Caroline's mother?'

I shook my head.

'Formidable lady. Quite terrifying. As Henry says, more than enough to make Harriet appreciate her poor parents.' He let out a sorrowful laugh. 'Caroline's right. You don't know how lucky you are not to have children.'

'Perhaps.'

'Nothing but trouble.'

'Perhaps.'

'Now!' He became suddenly conspiratorial. 'You'll know the answer to this. I've bought two salmon steaks from that fishmonger in Meldwich as a little treat for Caroline, but I haven't a clue how to cook them.'

'Geoff, really!' I couldn't disguise my astonishment. 'You mean you can't cook fish?'

'I don't have much call to go in the kitchen,' he said stiffly.

'Well, you put a dab of butter on the steaks, some dill and black pepper, then you simply grill them, three minutes a side.'

He looked at me in disbelief. 'Is that all?'

'Fish is easy.'

'That's really it?'

'That's really it.'

He rolled his eyes in amazement. 'God, if I'd known, 1 would have done this years ago.'

'What you also need,' I said, 'is flowers and a good wine and baby potatoes.'

'Got all of those.'

'Then it's a second honeymoon.'

He grinned like the little boy he was. 'I've also been hoovering,' he said. 'All morning. Good, eh?'

'Good?' I said. 'You're a positive saint.'

And I left him to it, kneeling over his lawn as if in penance or prayer, religiously removing all traces of weed from its emerald perfection. I took the short cut round the side of the Institute back to the house, and as I reached the orchard was distracted by a metallic glint in the grass by the grain shed. Going down the track to investigate, I saw to my surprise that Andre's BMW was parked in the long grass by the side of the shed.

So he had arrived after all! But why should he park his car here instead of going straight to the house? There was nothing in the shed except grain, and Andre was not noted for the interest he took in the life of the farm. Overwhelmed by curiosity, I approached the car and peered through the windscreen. A copy of that day's paper and a shoebox tied with string lay on the passenger seat. More curious than ever, I was wondering if I dared slip my arm through the open window and lift out the box when I was startled by a noise to my left. I swung round to find Jorgen, camera in hand, striding towards me through the grass.

'Lucy!' he said loudly. 'What are you doing here?'

It took me a moment to regain my composure. When I had, I hissed an angry 'I might ask you the same' in reply.

'And why are you whispering?' He made no attempt to

lower his voice. 'Are we out of bounds?'

'Of course not,' I snapped. 'I . . . I . . .' I paused. Much as I would have liked to have berated Jorgen for his intrusiveness, now didn't seem the moment. 'I was just wondering what Andre's car was doing here, that's all.'

'Oh,' he said, looking at the car as if he'd just noticed it. 'Of course, that's Andre's, isn't it?'

'Have you seen him?'

'Afraid not. But then I was busy with this.' He indicated his hateful camera, then slipped it round his neck. 'And now I'm off home for some tea. Want some?'

I shook my head. 'I was going for a walk.'

'It's Earl Grey. Your favourite.'

'No really, I'd rather finish my walk. Try Geoff instead. He needs refreshment.'

'Really? Why?'

'He's been mowing again.'

Jorgen shuddered. 'The man's mad. It's a – how do you say it? – personality misorder.'

'Disorder.'

'Exactly.' He sighed resignedly. 'Well, see you around.'

He strode off through the grass, his camera bouncing against his chest. I let him reach the path, then, not bothering to tiptoe any more, I abandoned the car and rounded the corner of the shed. The main door was open. It took me a moment to get accustomed to the gloom, but once I had, it appeared that apart from its mountain of grain, the shed was empty. Then, as my eyes accustomed themselves more precisely to the gloom, I thought I could make out a shape on the far side of the grain, the shape of a man: the shape, more particularly, of Benedict.

'Benedict?' I ventured, my voice echoing eerily in the cavernous depths of the shed.

There was no reply.

'Benedict?' I tried again. But still there was no reply, nor did the shape so much as waver. I closed my eyes, waited a moment, then opened them again. The shape hadn't moved. Only now I wasn't so sure it was Benedict. It could have been a shadow, some trick of the light.

And suddenly I felt somewhat silly, standing at the entrance to the shed peering into the gloom, silly and also, it has to be said, rather frightened. So, turning tail, I scampered down the path after Jorgen calling: 'Wait! I've changed my mind! Wait!'

I got back to the house at four to find Charles prowling tensely round the kitchen, drumming the fingers of his right hand against the palm of his left.

'You didn't tell me Andre was coming down,' he began the minute I was through the door.

'Why? Is anything wrong?'

'Of course not! I just like to know, that's all. Especially when I'm working. You know that.'

I pushed past him to the Aga. 'Well, as it happens, I only found out myself this morning. And as for telling you . . .' I turned to face him. 'You don't like me disturbing you whilst you work.'

'Not when it's something trivial.'

'Andre's that important?'

'I like to know what's going on in my own house, that's all.'

I reached for my apron. 'Very well. Next time I'll come up and disturb you.'

'Please do.'

'But don't you dare yell at me to bugger off like you usually do. Now! What do you fancy for supper? Would pasta be all right?'

But he'd turned his back on me and was staring out of the window, his shoulders bunched, one hand fiddling distractedly with his greying curls.

'What is it?' I asked eventually. 'What's bothering you?'

He didn't reply.

'Is it the work? Don't you want him to see it yet?'

He turned. 'I just want us to be on our own. That's all. Just you and me. On our own.'

'Really, now! He won't be down long. He never is. And anyway, you and I, cooped up here on our own, we drive each other mad, you know we do.'

'You don't understand.'

'Understand what?'

Again he didn't reply.

'Understand what?'

But he merely shrugged, and coming away from the window, threw himself into a chair.

'Forget it,' he said. 'It's nothing. I'm just a bit jumpy, that's all.'

The light from the window fell at an angle across his face, highlighting its crags and crannies.

'The work?'

He smiled. 'All right. If you like. The work.'

'I know it's early,' I said brightly, 'but why don't you open a bottle of wine?'

He looked at me in surprise. 'No tea?'

'I've just had gallons with Jorgen.'

'Dear Jorgen!' He got up to fetch the wine. 'Still snapping away?'

'All the time.' I was tempted to pass some more damning comment, but that would only have set Charles off, and for all the annoyance I felt at Jorgen's persistent snooping I wasn't in the mood, at that precise moment, for one of Charles' tirades against his artistic rival.

'And is it full house in the village still?'

'It will be tomorrow. Caroline's coming down to make it up with Geoff. This psychologist friend of theirs has bundled Harriet off to Caroline's mother.'

Charles laughed. 'Whose side is he on, the psychologist?'

'According to Geoff she's a harridan. Well able to cope.'

'Here!' Charles handed me my glass of wine.

'Thank you,' I said, and then – because our little skirmish seemed to be over: 'So tell me. Where is he, then? Andre?'

Charles sat down heavily at the head of the table before replying.

'Out sailing, I think.'

'Out sailing?'

I wasn't able to keep the surprise out of my voice. Charles shot me a puzzled look.

'What's so odd about that?'

'Oh,' I said quickly, 'nothing. Is he on his own?'

'No, no. He went with Benedict.'

'With Benedict?'

'Is that so unusual?'

'And did he say when they'd be back?'

Charles threw up his hands in mock surrender. 'Sorry! I didn't speak to him. I just heard his car, then saw the two of them walking up towards the village in their life-jackets.'

'In their life-jackets? But they keep those on the boat!'

Charles shrugged. 'Well, they had them on. Rather odd, they looked. Like inflatable men.'

I wanted to pursue the conversation, but that would only have aroused Charles' suspicions; and anyway, it was obvious that I wasn't going to learn anything of any real use until Andre and Benedict returned and could explain their movements themselves. So, reaching for a lettuce, I thrust it at my unhelpful husband.

'Instead of just sitting there,' I said, 'why don't you make the salad?'

'All right. Pass me the board.'

I handed him the board, some tomatoes and a knife.

'Imagine this!' I continued brightly. 'Geoff Landie doesn't know how to cook fish.'

'Doesn't surprise me in the least,' said Charles. 'The man probably has to follow a manual in order to fuck. More wine?'

We were well on the way to finishing the bottle when Andre and Benedict, looking cold and windswept, burst into the kitchen and made a bee-line for the Aga.

'Shit, it's cold!' Despite his thickly quilted jacket, Andre was shivering. 'Like winter almost!' He held his hands over the stove to warm them. 'Sorry to break in like this, but we were freezing out there, weren't we Benedict?'

Benedict, who had joined Andre at the stove, nodded in silent assent.

'Have some wine,' said Charles. 'That'll warm you.'

I fetched two glasses, and once Charles had filled them, handed them to Andre and Benedict. The cold seemed to have altered the features of both, tightening Andre's and throwing his uneven nose and belligerent chin into sharper relief, while on Benedict it had had an opposite effect, causing his face to close in on itself, to become even less decipherable.

'So,' I said. 'Welcome!'

'You got the message?' As he asked the question, Andre took a sip of his wine, but without losing eye contact.

'Norman popped in this morning.'

'It's not inconvenient?'

It may have been my imagination, but Andre's eyes seemed to be boring into me as if in search of something he suspected was hidden behind my polite demeanour.

'Not at all,' said Charles. 'Not in the least.'

'Good!' Andre maintained his inquisitional stare a fraction longer, then looked towards the Aga and wrinkled his nose appreciatively. 'Just as long as there's enough of whatever it is you're cooking to include me?'

'Of course,' I said briskly. 'Sit and we can eat.'

Andre crossed to the table. Benedict turned to follow suit, and as he did so, caught my eye. I tried, by raising an eyebrow, to ask a question of my own, but it was impossible to gauge anything from the blankness of his expression; his gaze was as unfathomable as the darkness in the shed.

'So!' said Andre, a touch jocular suddenly, as if – having started his silent inquisition into the state of my mind – he now wished the incident closed. 'What island news?'

'You mean Benedict hasn't brought you up to date?'

Andre laughed. 'Not satisfactorily.'

So, while Charles dished up the food and Benedict passed the plates, I dished up the latest gossip about Geoff and Caroline and Harriet.

'God!' said Andre. 'Am I glad I don't have children. Aren't you?'

There was a pause.

'Actually,' said Charles quietly, 'it's something we both regret, isn't it Lucy? Not having children.'

I didn't attempt a reply.

'But your work!' Andre's disbelief was evident in his tone of voice. 'Just think if you'd had to worry about children, feed them, spend time with them, how your work would have suffered.'

'Everyone,' said Charles, 'seems to think my work is everything.'

'And isn't it?' Andre sounded surprised.

'No,' said Charles, 'not by a long chalk.'

There was another pause.

'But you're someone who wants to leave a mark,' said Andre eventually. 'Isn't that why you paint?'

'In order to leave one's mark,' said Charles, staring levelly at Andre, 'one doesn't have to paint. There are other options.' He turned his stare on me. 'One could, for example . . .'

'And what about Benedict?' I interrupted quickly. 'What do you want to leave behind?'

At first he didn't answer. Then, looking up sharply and rescuing me from the continued intensity of Charles' unsettling stare, he said: 'Me? Nothing.'

'Not anything?'

'Why should I?'

'Well,' I said, 'on this island it's impossible not to leave a mark. Not with Jorgen around.'

Was it my imagination, or did he flinch?

'His photos, you mean?' Spectator-like, Andre's eyes were flickering from Benedict to me and back again, assessing the state of play.

I bowed out of the game by dropping my head and nodding, whereupon, taking his cue from me, Andre leant back in his chair and wiped his mouth. 'Lucy, that was fantastic!'

I stood up. 'Well,' I said, 'that's a relief, at any rate. Now, if you'll pass me your plates, there's some fruit on the dresser.'

In the relative safety of the pantry, I paused a moment to regain my composure, then turned on the tap and began methodically to rinse the plates. Almost immediately, I heard a noise behind me. Swinging round, I found Andre in the doorway, the salad bowl in his hands.

'Where shall I put this?' he asked.

I nodded towards the draining board.

He put the bowl next to the pile of plates, and, running a finger along its rim, said: 'Everything all right?'

'Meaning?'

'Benedict. Charles. You know.'

'Of course,' I said. 'Why shouldn't it be?'

'An interesting boy,' he continued. 'Our Benedict. Not very articulate, but certainly more than just a pretty face.'

'Indeed,' I said stiffly. 'It's very refreshing having him around.'

'Confused, though,' said Andre. 'Very young and very confused.'

We might have left it there, and maybe we should have, but his last remark goaded me into asking: 'What are you trying to tell me?'

'Oh,' he said, 'I just think people should know what they're dealing with, that's all.'

'In that case,' I said, 'maybe you can tell me why you're here. I have a feeling – am I wrong? – that you and Benedict are up to something.'

'Ah,' he said. 'Me. Well, I'm always up to something. The entrepreneurial spirit, you know. Dies hard.'

'But you're not going to tell me what it is?'

He shrugged, a trifle too elaborately. 'There's nothing to tell. Except, of course, that I'd hate to see you get hurt.'

'And how would that happen?'

'With any luck it won't. Not if you're careful.'

And then, cutting short the conversation as sharply as he'd started it, he flicked a finger against the salad bowl, making it ping, and ducked back into the kitchen. Not knowing what to make of his enigmatic utterances, and remembering too late what Benedict had told me, that Andre had said I was lonely (part of the plot, perhaps?) I abandoned the plates and turned off the tap. Drying my hands on the cloth that hung from a hook on the wall, I went to the outside door, threw it open and drew deeply on the cool evening air. Then, feeling at least revived, if not any the wiser, I returned warily to the kitchen.

'What you have to realise,' Charles was saying, 'is how much we had been affected by the fifties. It was a very flat decade, the fifties. One dimensional. Suburban. Materialistic. The outlook was limited, pinched. People watched their feet, not the horizon.'

Andre snorted. 'So were the sixties that different? The eyes moved up a notch, that's all. From the foot to the navel.'

'Oh, it's easy to laugh at the sixties,' said Charles. 'Too easy now. But people were searching for something.'

'Of course,' said Andre. 'Gratification.'

'No!' said Charles sharply. 'It wasn't that at all.'

Andre leant forward. 'Oh, come on, Charles! People are people. They don't change.'

'But they do change!' said Charles. 'That's exactly it.'

'So what's become of the sixties, then? All that cosmic energy? All that love and peace? Flower power! Where are your hippies now?'

'These things are cyclical,' said Charles. 'Just because . . .'

'I'll tell you what was wrong with the sixties,' said Andre. 'You were soft in the sixties. Money was easy, so was housing, work. You had it all – and you blew it. It was indulgence, not liberation.'

'And you're going to get it right, are you?' countered Charles. 'You're going to last?'

Andre stood up, and, quite unselfconsciously, as if it were the most natural thing in the world, went to stand behind Benedict and rested his hand on the younger man's shoulder. 'You made one great mistake in the sixties,' he said. 'You thought people were basically good. We have our blind spots, I know, but at least we see people for what they are.'

'And what's that?' demanded Charles.

'Greedy, self-obsessed shits.'

'All of us?'

'All of us!' Then, executing a drum roll with his fingers on Benedict's shoulder, Andre threw back his head and let out a single, barking laugh. 'But enough of this philosophical crap. Show me the new paintings.'

'Now?' Charles was clearly caught off guard by the change of subject.

'Why not?'

Charles got reluctantly to his feet. 'All right, if you insist.'

Andre sensed the reluctance in Charles' voice. 'Don't you want to?'

'No, no!' said Charles. 'You have every right. After all, you do own me. Or the parts that work, at any rate.'

And opening the door ceremoniously, he ushered Andre into the hall.

'So!' I said, when the door had closed behind them, and trying, with the brightness of my tone, to eradicate the image of Andre with his hands on Benedict's shoulder. 'What does Benedict think of the sixties then?'

He squirmed in his seat. 'I was a baby. I don't remember.'

'And Andre? Is he right, would you say? About us being self-obsessed?'

'Who knows?'

I got up and filled the kettle. 'I'd rather,' I said – as bright, still, as a button – 'believe Charles. Wouldn't you?' I switched on the kettle. 'I mean, which would you be, ideally? Good or bad?'

He looked puzzled. 'If I had the choice, you mean?'

'But of course you have the choice!'

He shook his head. 'Some people. Some people have choices. Not all of us.'

'Nonsense! We all can choose. We all have to choose, all the time, how to live our lives, how to do things, what things we should do, what things we shouldn't.' I stopped, and my voice, when I continued, was so low I don't suppose he could have heard me. 'Like you and me, like what's happening to us . . .' I faltered, and going, like Andre, to stand behind him; I put my hand where Andre had put his, felt out the muscles along his neck. They were strung like a bow from his frame: taut, expectant, musical.

'Tell me,' I said. 'This afternoon. Where were you?'

He reached up, and taking my hand in his, squeezed it so hard it hurt. Then he stood up and, backing away, said formally: 'Can I help with the coffee? Get the cups, perhaps?'

'Please,' I whispered. 'You mustn't be frightened. There's nothing to be frightened of. I won't hurt you, I only . . .'

But he was at the dresser already, reaching down the cups.

'These blue ones, yes?'

'Please!' I began again. 'I only . . .' And then, realising the futility of trying to pursue the conversation, gave up with a dull: 'That's right. The blue ones.'

I turned back to the kettle.

'Pretty!' I heard him say.

'A wedding present,' I said. 'From a school-friend. In fact my oldest friend. Though I haven't seen her since the wedding. We've lost touch totally.'

All my old friends, I was thinking, I've lost touch with all my old friends. Couldn't even remember what they looked like, some of them.

'Anything else?' he asked.

'Just the sugar and milk,' I said. 'Then we're done.' As stiff still as a butler, he laid the tray, then held open the doors for me as I carried it into the living-room.

'How long before the others come down?' he asked.

I managed a nonchalant shrug. 'It depends how many canvases.'

'You don't know?'

'Charles never lets me into the studio.'

I began to pour the coffee. 'Sugar? Milk?'

He took his cup and crossed to the bookshelves at the far end of the room, where we kept the turntable and tape deck that Andre had given us when we moved into the house.

'May I play something?' he asked.

'Of course.'

He bent over the equipment and switched it on. When he straightened up, it was to the mournful precision of a Latin American tango.

'Nice,' he said. 'No?'

It was as if everything, not just the people, but inanimate objects too, were conspiring against me.

'But that's not ours!'

'Andre brought it down.'

He put down his cup, and closing his eyes began, with slow, meticulous seductiveness, to sway to the music. It was all I could do to prevent myself leaping up and flying into his arms, and it was only Andre's sudden appearance in the doorway that rescued me.

'Ah!' he said. 'Coffee! Great! He came to sit next

to me on the sofa.

With trembling hands, I passed him his cup. 'So, how were the pictures?'

'Different.'

'How different?'

'Good different.' He grinned. 'In fact, very good different.'

'Still the wood?'

'Still the wood.'

'So how are they different?'

'You'll see when he's ready.' He felt in his pocket and drew out a white envelope; then, reaching for one of the copies of *Vogue* I kept in a pile under the coffee table, laid it next to the coffee tray, tapped a little mound of white powder and a razor blade out of the envelope, and began to cut the powder into lines.

'I hope you don't mind,' he said, 'but it's been a heavy week.'

'No,' I said. 'Of course not.'

There was a noise at the door, and Charles appeared. He paused, frowning, to take in the disparate activity in the room – Benedict swaying by himself in the corner, Andre marshalling his powder troops on my old copy of *Vogue*, me pouring the fourth cup of coffee – then came forward smartly to collect his cup. Glancing up, Andre noticed the frown on Charles' face.

'Not your scene?' he queried.

Charles' frown deepened. 'You seem to forget,' he said. 'We're of the sixties. It's pot for us. As in "going to".'

'Oh come now,' said Andre. 'I didn't say that.'

'Didn't you?'

'Andre says he likes the paintings,' I interposed quickly.

'Very much,' said Andre, 'very much indeed.'

'Well, that's a relief,' said Charles.

'But I keep forgetting,' continued Andre, 'the reason for my visit.' He put down his razor blade. 'There's a group of archaeologists from Cambridge who've uncovered evidence of a stone age village on the mud-flats, just to the right of the causeway. I've given them permission to camp in the Institute for the summer. I don't think they'll get in your way, they'll be out digging in the mud all day, but if they do, you must just let me know.'

'Archaeologists!' I said. 'Goodness! When do they arrive?'

'Tomorrow, at the end of the tide.'

'And they stay until?'

'August, September.' He shrugged. 'However long it takes them. Now the problem is this. I have to go off tomorrow when the tide opens.'

'But Norman said you were down for a day or two?'

'That's what I'd hoped. But,' and here he favoured me with a crooked grin, 'something's come up. So, I have a favour to ask. I would ask Norman, but you know what he's like. Can you meet these archaeologists, show them the Institute, make them feel at home?'

'We'll organise a welcoming party,' said Charles. 'Meet them in style.'

Andre took out his wallet, extracted a five-pound note, and began to roll it into a tube. 'Their leader's called Imogen Kalberer.'

'Imogen Kalberer?' Charles let out a laugh. 'God, what a name! I can just see her, a sort of archaeological Valkyrie, driving her troops across the causeway.'

Andre put the rolled-up note to his nose and bent over the cocaine. 'There are still some showers that work in the Institute, and all the loos. Norman knows. I went through it all with him this afternoon.' He sniffed his way expertly along the first of his lines, paused, then sniffed a second line through his other nostril.

'Fine,' I said. 'No problem.'

'Benedict!' Andre held out the rolled-up note. Benedict abandoned his solitary dance and, coming to kneel in front of the table, went through the same procedure. Then he and Andre rubbed what was left of the powder into their gums.

'Lucy!' said Andre. 'What about you?'

'Me?'

'Don't you want some?'

I shook my head.

'Come on!'

'How exactly does it make you feel?'

'Toned up. Sparkier. Good.'

'Go on,' said Benedict. 'Try it.'

I looked at him, and this time his eyes weren't expression-less. Quicksilver as a fish, there was a flicker of recognition in their liquid depths.

'Don't be silly, Lucy,' I heard Charles say, followed by my own: 'All right. I think I will.'

'Good on you!' Andre busied himself with dividing up another two lines.

'Lucy, don't be a fool!'

'I'm not going to become an addict,' I snapped. 'Not if I try it the once.'

'But why?' asked Charles.

I looked up and met the baffled incomprehension of his gaze.

'Because I want to,' I said. 'That's why. Because I bloody well want to.'

Andre handed me the rolled-up note, and following his example I leant forward and sniffed up the two lines he'd laid down for me.

'Okay?' he asked.

I nodded.

'Feel anything?'

I shook my head.

'You will in a minute.'

Out of the corner of my eye I was aware of Charles crossing to the window, but my eyes didn't follow him, they were fixed on Benedict who very slowly, very languorously, got to his feet, and holding out his arms said: 'Come on, you two! Dance!'

And before I knew it, Andre and I were in his arms, matching the music together, our every gesture a homage to its sad, seductive rhythms. Dancing as no doubt they'd danced in Mr Benson's time, with their band on the lawn and fairy lights and waiters all in a row.

I was brought back to reality by a crash, a giggled 'Oops!' from Charles, and Andre breaking free of our circle. I opened my eyes to see Andre on his knees by the coffee table picking shards of china from the pile of sludge to which

Charles had reduced the cocaine by dropping his coffee cup into the midst of it.

'Oh dear,' said Charles. 'How clumsy! I am sorry. I must have drunk more than I realise. I'd better go to bed.' And turning to face Benedict and me, he said: 'Enjoy what's left of the evening, children!' and swiftly left the room.

'Fucking moron!' Andre prodded the cocaine once or twice with his finger; then, with a disgusted snort, got to his feet and stalked away. I went to the table and picked up a sliver of blue china.

'Her name was Matilda,' I said. 'We used to do ballet together and go to the cinema on Saturday afternoons. She was very thin and she had a brace.'

'Your friend.' It was Benedict, who'd come to stand beside me.

'She didn't think I should get married. "Why?" she said. "What do you need a man for? You can't trust them, you know." And yet of all our wedding presents, hers was the prettiest.' I dropped the piece of china into the sludge on the magazine.

Benedict bent down to pick up the magazine, and holding it over the coffee tray, took out his handkerchief and wiped the mess onto the tray.

'You know what I found the other day?' he said. 'A whole lot of magazines with Andre in them.'

'Upstairs, you mean?'

He nodded. '*Vogues, Arenas, Cosmopolitans.*'

'So!' Andre had returned from the far end of the room and thrown himself onto the sofa. 'Been snooping, have we?'

'Who put them there?' asked Benedict.

Andre shrugged. 'They're very old. From another time.' He sat up. 'Much more interesting is Lucy's album.' He turned to me. 'You know. The one you showed me last Christmas.'

'Oh no!' I said quickly. 'Benedict wouldn't like that.'

'What's this?' The speed with which Benedict asked the question was, in the light of his usual reticence, more than a little surprising.

'You see!' said Andre. 'Of course he would.'

'No, really,' I said, suddenly very uncomfortable. 'Not now.'

'Oh, come on!' said Benedict. 'Why not?'

'Because,' I said firmly, 'you'll only laugh at me.'

'Me? Laugh at you? I'd never do that.' And narrowing the gap between us, he brought his face so close to mine that for an instant I thought he might meld with me. Blinking my eyes to bring him back into focus, I became aware of something soft and warm on the bare flesh of my arm. It was his hand.

'Please,' he was saying. 'Please let me see it.'

When, a minute later, I got back to the living-room, the album under my arm, either Benedict or Andre had pushed back the rug, and the two of them were dancing to more of the tango, their bodies so practised together they might have been partners. I should have left then, of course, just slunk away, the album safe still, in the crook of my arm; but the spell they cast with their bodies kept me there mesmerised until Andre looked up and noticing me, reluctant in the doorway, pushed Benedict aside and held out his arms to welcome me back.

'Right!' he said. 'Photo time!'

I positioned myself in the middle of the sofa, and the two of them came to sit on either side of me.

I opened the album and – as always happened when people saw the photographs for the first time – there was a sharp intake of breath from Benedict.

'David Bailey,' said Andre. 'Not bad, huh?'

'Did he pay you?' asked Benedict. 'Or did you know him?'

'Neither. Charles knew him slightly, but how this happened, I was walking down the King's Road one Saturday and this man came up and asked if he could photograph me.'

'They're amazing!' said Benedict. 'Why haven't I seen them before?'

'He used some of them in an exhibition once, and one of them . . .' I turned the page. 'That one there, on the cover of ue. It was the first time they'd used an amateur model. Or hey said. Then . . .' I shrugged. 'I don't know. He went on ther things.'

'Give here!' Benedict took the album from me and continued to page through it.

'You see,' said Andre, shooting me a grin. 'Not a total waste, the sixties, not if they could produce you.'

'You can say that again!' enthused Benedict. 'God, you were beautiful!'

I should have expected it, of course. What am I saying? I had expected it. It was why I'd been loath to fetch the album in the first place. But even so, it still came as a shock, his careless, unthinking use of the past tense. Were. Were beautiful.

I reached across and, releasing the album from Benedict's grasp, dropped it onto the coffee table.

'Enough!' I said. 'Enough of photographs. Don't you think?'

And before he could protest, I got up and crossed to the french windows. If it had been light, I would have been able to see the old pier and the estuary, the opposite bank and the sky beyond. Because it was night though, what confronted me as I reached the window was not the estuary, but what could have been a painting: an out-of-focus woman in the foreground, looking out towards the viewer, and behind her on the sofa, the vivid outlines of two young men sitting side by side, the one as compact as a tightly balled fist, the other as fluid as smoke.

I took a step closer to see if I could bring the woman into focus, but in doing that, I merely caused her to vanish. Whereupon the background of the painting altered too, and Andre came to stand at my shoulder.

'Still very beautiful,' he said, nodding at the window. 'This amateur.'

'But an amateur, all the same,' I said. 'A rank amateur.'

'In some things, maybe. Not all.'

'Tell me something,' I continued. 'Why set someone up if you don't want them to get hurt?'

'What do you mean?'

'I was hoping you'd tell me.'

'All I can tell you,' he said, taking my hand in his and lifting it to the window, where my image had reappeared on the glass, 'is that you should concentrate on this. Nothing else. Just this. The rest is unimportant.'

Then, pulling my body away from the window and towards his, he said: 'Another dance?'

I shook my head.

'No. I'm tired. I'm going to bed.'

'Right,' he said, letting go of me. 'See you in the morning, then.'

I crossed to the door, and as I reached it, but without turning, said: 'Good-night, you two. Sweet dreams.'

'Good-night,' echoed Benedict. 'Sweet dreams.'

Upstairs on the landing, I thought I heard music, soft music, subtle where the tango had been sharp, issuing from Charles' studio. It seemed to be beckoning me, and letting myself be drawn by it, I followed it up the stairs to the second floor, along the length of the dim and dusty corridor to the next set of stairs, and then, very quietly, all the way up to the studio itself. It had, though, been an illusion. There was no music here – even though the strip of light under the door indicated that Charles was working – only silence. In fact, so silent was it on the landing, so utterly devoid of sound, that I knew Charles must have heard me coming up the stairs and was listening, like me, on his side of the door, for evidence of further movement. Daunted suddenly by the sheer intensity of the silence, and by all the things that had happened that day, and which, try as I might, I could neither understand nor welcome, I turned and tiptoed back to the floor below, where I did hear music, the unmistakable rhythms of the tango, and over them, carnival-like, a sudden burst of laughter: Benedict's I thought, though at that distance I couldn't be sure.

The next morning I overslept, and by the time I'd bathed and dressed it was gone eleven. There was a note from Andre on the kitchen table thanking me for supper and for agreeing to meet the archaeologists, to which Charles had appended a scribbled PS: 'Aforementioned due at twelve. Rendezvous in front of house at eleven forty-five.'

I made myself a cup of coffee and took it into the living-room. Someone had tidied up after last night. The tray of coffee things had been returned to the kitchen, the copy of *Vogue* was no longer in evidence, the rug was back where it belonged. The only trace of the evening was my photo album, which lay on the coffee table where I'd left it.

I picked it up and opened it at random. A slim young woman, whose coltish legs were encased in patterned tights and capped by a narrow strip of dress no wider than the belt which pinched her waist, hung at a crazy angle from a lamppost outside a Georgian house. Her hair was prevented from obscuring her face by the sunglasses perched on the top of her head, and she had what looked like a necklace of ceramic onions round her neck. She wasn't smiling, but the fearlessness with which she confronted the camera intimated she was happy.

Or did it? Had she been happy? I tried to remember. She'd giggled a lot, that I knew, and been excited, and when, after the session, Charles had met David and herself for a meal, she'd loved the way everyone's eyes in the restaurant had been on her, David's and Charles' most obviously, but men from the other tables too, even some women. I frowned. Had that been happiness? That slightly breathless, excited state in which this silly woman had passed her twenties? Or had it simply been naivety? Innocence? Worse than innocence. Stupidity? Narcissism? And why, since she looked as foreign to me now as a total stranger, someone from another time, did I still share her foolishness?

Troubled, I put down the album, and crossing to the french windows, sipped thoughtfully at my coffee. It was almost eleven forty-five. Any minute now Charles would appear, also Benedict. Unless, of course, which was more than likely, our recalcitrant guest chose to duck out of welcoming the archaeologists.

My question was answered by Benedict himself, who, as I finished my coffee, appeared on the lawn looking as if, like me, he'd just that minute got out of bed. His body was more gangling than usual, loose-limbed and oddly angled, as if it hadn't had time to marshal itself properly and were still tangled about itself in the bedclothes. His hair too was all awry, standing up in haphazard spikes, and his clothes, which he'd obviously thrown on hastily, hadn't had time to arrange themselves properly to his body. He looked half-finished, like a sketch someone had abandoned half-way, before getting the proportions right. Then, as I watched, he yawned enormously, throwing back his head and stretching as he did so, and suddenly his body settled into itself, was complete again, of a piece. At that moment Charles appeared round the side of the house, rubbing his hands in expectation of the adventure awaiting us. Not at all certain that I was ready for either of them, I put down my cup and stepped reluctantly through the french windows.

'Ah-ha!' said Charles. 'So there you are! I was wondering if you'd make it.'

I didn't give him the satisfaction of rising to his barbed enquiry. 'So!' I demanded of Benedict. 'Did you sleep well?'

He answered my question with one of his own: 'Did you?'

'I think so. I'm not really sure.'

'I wouldn't be surprised,' said Charles, 'if last night was lost in a total blur.'

'Not at all,' I said sharply. 'I remember everything.'

'Everything?' queried Charles.

I met his gaze. 'Everything. Now, shall we go?'

'Indeed!' Charles clapped his hands. 'Let's give our Miss Kalberer a reception that will thaw her archaeological heart.'

The village, as we went through it, was empty. As we passed the Landies' house, I noticed that the upstairs curtains were still drawn. Either Geoff was resting up in preparation for the weekend ahead, or else the second honeymoon was already underway.

We passed the creek.

'Do you think they'll have any luck?' Benedict asked. 'These archaeologists?'

'Who knows?' Charles didn't sound particularly concerned. 'But they'll have a lot of fun, messing around in the mud. People always do.'

We reached the causeway to find a bizarre caravan wending its cautious way towards us. At its head was Norman's battered old van, behind that a capacious mini-bus, and behind that an open truck piled high with what looked like tables and chairs. Bringing up the rear was an ancient Citroën 2CV, from whose open roof protruded a number of brightly coloured poles.

'God!' said Charles. 'What a sight!' Then he frowned. 'What's Norman doing, though? Do you think he went out to meet them?'

I shook my head. 'I should imagine he's just coming back from a night on the town.'

'That makes three of you,' he said, continuing to stare at the approaching procession. 'Though what really puzzles me is why Andre was so keen for them to come. Do you think they're cover?'

I was aware of Benedict stiffening.

'What do you mean?' I asked. 'Cover?'

I must have spoken more sharply than I intended, for he shot me a look, and one at Benedict, before shrugging and returning his attention to the causeway. 'You know. A diversion. To take his mind off things. Stop him getting bored.'

I looked at Benedict. He too had his eyes on the cars, but there was a tight, white line down the side of his jaw.

We stood in silence after that, until Norman's van came bouncing up the last stretch of the causeway.

'So what's with the reception committee then?' he queried, sticking his head out of the window.

'Andre's orders,' said Charles. 'Make them feel welcome.'

'The way you lot look, they'll turn right round and scuttle back to Cambridge.'

'Have you spoken to them yet?' I asked.

He shook his head. 'I only noticed them once we were on the causeway.' He slipped the van back into gear. 'Well, you say hello to them, and when you've finished, tell them I'll meet them at the Institute.'

He hit the accelerator and shot off in a cloud of dust.

By now the mini-bus was almost upon us. Charles stepped forward and motioned it to halt. The woman driver wound down her window.

'Miss Kalberer, I presume?' Charles gave the question a rococo flourish.

The woman was visibly taken aback. Then, as someone no doubt accustomed to the eccentricities of island dwellers, she recovered herself sufficiently to say: 'Mr Charn?'

Charles shook his head sorrowfully. 'Unfortunately not. Hamilton's the name, Charles Hamilton, and this is my wife, Lucy, and Mr Charn's companion, young Mr Benedict.'

Miss Kalberer nodded cautiously at each of us in turn. She had what I call British Council looks: nondescript hair, donnish glasses, quizzical eyes, not a trace of make-up. A professional spinster.

'Andre was called back to London so he asked us to meet you,' continued Charles. 'He hopes your stay on the island will be profitable.'

Miss Kalberer essayed a smile. 'How very kind. I'm sure it will.'

'You'll find us in the manor house, if you need us. Otherwise Norman will see to your needs. He's waiting for you now at the Institute. Just follow the road into the village. You can't miss it. It's the ruin on your left.'

Miss Kalberer blanched at this last piece of information. 'Right,' she said. 'Yes, well, thank you very much. You've been most kind.' Although she looked so utterly English, she enunciated her words with the precision of a foreigner. Swedish, I thought, or German, if her name was anything to go by.

Charles stepped back, and with a deep bow, beckoned the mini-bus forward. It drew off with a jerk (we'd obviously made Miss Kalberer nervous), to be smoothly followed by the truck, which was indeed piled high with tables and chairs, then the Citroën. In each vehicle rows of curious eyes, all framed by spectacles, peered uncertainly at us as they drove past.

'Why the table and chairs, do you think?' I asked.

'I've no idea,' said Charles, who now that the official greeting was over was brushing his hands on his corduroys as if to wipe away the formality. 'Perhaps they plan to throw dinner parties in between exhuming skulls.'

'You are awful,' I said. 'That poor woman didn't know how to take you.'

'Good,' said Charles. 'Then she'll leave us alone.' He threw an arm round my shoulder. 'Shall we go back via the beach?'

'If you want.'

He looked at Benedict. 'Coming?'

Benedict shook his head. 'If you don't mind, I'd like to walk on my own. I'll go the other way.'

'Right,' said Charles. 'See you back at the house.'

'Are you sure?' I tried to keep my voice light and non-committal. 'Wouldn't you rather come with us?'

'No,' he said. 'Really.'

I managed a quick smile. 'See you later, then.'

'Yes,' he said. 'Later.' And without returning my smile, he strode off along the beach.

'Funny lad,' said Charles; then turning to me, grinned broadly, his face suddenly boyish. 'Aren't I the lucky one though? Having Lucy all to myself.'

Pentimento

In the fortnight following the arrival of the archaeologists, summer came properly to the island at last. It was as if a door had been opened somewhere, and we had stepped from a cell without windows into a universe flooded with light. The days blazed with sunshine, the fields and hedge-rows were tumid with growth, boats bobbed and skimmed across the estuary, their sails mirroring the puffs of cloud plumped up on the horizon; cloud which, in the evening, was taken by a valedictory sun from white through vulgar shades of purple and pink to the most subtle and tender of greys.

And at night, when I went to stand at my window and look out across the estuary before getting into bed, the two green lights that shone, the one above the other, at the end of the pier seemed like a roman candle which had been suspended mid-explosion: my own personal firework display, continuously celebrating the promise of tomorrow.

Norman shook his head worriedly and tugged at his ear. 'I don't know,' he muttered. 'It's only the middle of May. I don't like it. I don't like it at all.'

But Norman's pessimism notwithstanding, the weather showed no signs of changing. As the month drew to its close, summer day still followed summer day with total surety, each more saturated by sun than the last. Even in mid-week now, there were yachts in the estuary, and at the weekend the water was stiff with them. And in the sky there appeared from the airfield near Meldwich a plethora of gliders, hang-gliders, microlites and old-fashioned propeller planes, the latter droning their solitary way across the seamless blue like images out of a distant war.

By the beginning of June, the cow-parsley, unequal to the heat, had faded from white to a nondescript green, robbing the fields of their lacy surround. But by now there were other compensations. The horse chestnuts lining the road to the

157

village had thrown up pyramids of blossom that stood proud
of their branches, beacons to the trees' extravagant fertility;
poppies peeped from between the corn; dog roses ran riot in
the hedgerows; and in the orchard behind the manor house,
the more cultured variety laid out by Mr Benson in the
thirties established easy sway over the other flowers, their
blood-red blooms wanton with perfume.

Then, as June melted into July, and as sunny day still
followed sunny day, it was the fields that took precedence.
Literally baked by the heat, the corn began to rise, its
feathery crust to brown; and as it did so, blackbirds would
skim its surface, escaping the pie. Larks flirted with the fields
too, teasing them with song until, stricken by silence, they
would plummet earthwards to make amends. Whilst, higher
overhead, bigger, more serious birds flew longer, more
serious distances, their wings churning the air like machines;
and higher still, the propeller planes criss-crossed the sky at
regular intervals, doggedly travelling back and forth from
that war.

Occasionally, to break the monotony, there would be an
overcast morning, or a storm out to sea. I would stand on the
bunker, and out past Broadwake sea and sky would amalga-
mate into a layer of black. But always, or nearly always, where
I stood the sun would continue to shine, and on the opposite
bank the fields would continue green and brilliant in its
light. Respectful of our privacy, the storms skirted the island,
bypassing our oasis of summer.

With the exception of Charles, who kept to his studio,
these sun-drenched days brought us all out of ourselves, out
of our houses and into closer contact with one another. From
dawn to dusk Norman could be found in the fields, or
around the grain shed, his gun at his side, a cheery grin on
his face. Jorgen, too, stalked the fields and outhouses, the
beach and the Institute, but with a camera as his gun, a look
of abstraction in his eye. The Landies, now reconciled,
introduced a stream of guests to the island, a new pairing
each weekend, some with children, some without, but all in
awe of the island and those of us who lived here permanently.
And on a couple of weekends there were parties at the Chase,

at which we were made to tell these guests our island tales, and on other weekends in the farmhouse, where we met Tracy, Samantha or Denise – whoever it was who was sharing Norman's bed that week.

Up in Hull, where it was also hot, though not as hot as on the island, Ralph complained bitterly of the heat, said it meant he couldn't sleep, and was, for a worrying ten days, readmitted to hospital. Charles was on the verge of travelling up to be with him when he was discharged, though this didn't prevent my mother, when I told her about the incident over the phone, from commenting: 'So this is what I have to look forward to, is it, when I fall ill? Being totally ignored.'

Our other outside force, Andre, remained for the most part in London, busy, he said, with the gallery; though every ten days or so he would visit the island, and once, in the company of two men I'd never seen before, I caught sight of him in Meldwich, going into the estate agents.

Most obvious though, most in evidence, were the archae-ologists. There were fifteen of them excluding Miss Kalberer, and on every tide they would drive their mini-bus to the other side of the causeway, unload their tables and chairs, and having lugged them laboriously across the mud to the site of the village, set them up in a semi-circle, then settle with their heads down like obedient schoolchildren to sift the mud for artifacts until the tide forced them back to the Institute. There they'd gather round the trestle tables they'd erected in the downstairs rooms to clean, label and box their precious fragments of pottery. Plundering their environment for evidence with the same degree of intensity, though in a different way, and with a different goal, as Charles and Jorgen.

All this summer behaviour would have meant nothing, of course, would have been unbearable, if Benedict had, as originally threatened, left after the first two weeks, or if he'd continued to keep so vehemently to himself. But something unexpected, and for me miraculous, happened with the arrival of the archaeologists. Whereas up till then Benedict had made it abundantly clear he didn't want anyone, least of all Lucy, to encroach on his territory, now – for some unknown reason – he seemed to drop his guard. He still took his daily sailing trip, but when not on the yacht was to be found either out in the fields helping Norman, or visiting Jorgen and the Landies, or else just sunning himself in the orchard. And that wasn't all. He condescended to come shopping with me in Meldwich, helped me spring-clean the downstairs rooms, and once the good weather had really taken hold even asked me if I'd like to go sailing with him – and seemed genuinely disappointed when I told him that sailing frightened me.

'My element,' he said. 'The sea. You can be free on the sea.'

I had to smile. 'Sounds like a jingle.'

'I'm not advertising,' he said. 'Just sharing a secret.'

At first I didn't know how to take it, this sudden and unexpected change in our guest. I wasn't sure, even, that I liked it. His initial mysteriousness had been most appealing, besides which – after the oddness of Andre's remarks in the pantry and the sense I'd had then that something was afoot – I'd rather determined to hold myself aloof, to tread warily, keep my wits about me. But with Benedict about me, and so willingly too, I was quite disarmed. It was magical to see him happy, to see him laughing, to sense a lessening of his pain. And though he still didn't tell me that much about himself, and though – for the time being at least – I was careful not to let my feelings show too blatantly – it was happiness enough to giggle with him over island doings, to teach him the names of flowers, and to hear back from him about the band he'd drummed with, the books he'd read or the films he'd seen. The slender threads from which we weave our lives. And as we spun this tapestry of growing, if tenuous intimacy, as time became somehow elastic, minutes with Benedict elongating into hours, hours into days, the interstices between one encounter and the next humming with possibility, so came the realisation that maybe Andre, for all his omniscience, didn't hold the key to everything. That maybe I knew things about the boy that Andre didn't. And thinking back to the evening we'd had the cocaine, remembering them in each other's arms, I would reappraise the

picture, pick out with hindsight how wary Benedict had
seemed in Andre's embrace. Familiar as I was fast becoming
with his various expressions, the ways in which he held his
body, the manner in which he moved, I was able to rearrange
him like a lay figure, find other positions for him, other
avenues of being: avenues that led, as the summer itself
seemed to be leading, and endlessly too, into the heart of a
greater happiness.

Though before I'd had the chance to capitalise on this
new-found power, or to act in any way decisively on what
suddenly seemed not merely possible, but probable, Charles,
the ever vigilant Charles, who must have been observing me
as closely as I'd been observing Benedict, mounted a typically
subtle counter-attack.

It was mid-July and I was sitting by the fish-pond, my cheek
against its sun-warmed rim, my eyes on the roses, when
something came between me and the sun. Looking up, I saw
Charles standing over me. He had come from the direction
of the village.

'If only you could see yourself!'

'What?'

'Abandoned.'

'Abandoned?'

'Day-dreaming.'

'It's the sun,' I said. 'The heat.'

'A mermaid out of water.'

'A thoroughly contented woman.'

He frowned.

'What is it?' I said. 'Is anything wrong?'

'Why?'

'You look serious. Where have you been?'

'Phoning.'

I sat up. 'Ralph?'

'No, he's fine.'

'You talked to him?'

He nodded. 'The doctor was in to see him this morning,
says he's more than holding his own.'

'What is it, then?'

He dropped to his haunches and ran his thumb slowly,

testingly down the side of my face.

'I wish I had my sketch-pad. I'd like to capture you like this. This moment.'

I brushed away his hand.

'What?' I demanded. 'What is it?'

'But you don't want that any more, do you?'

'What the hell are you talking about?'

He turned to stare at the roses. 'You,' he said softly. 'You and me. This summer.'

'Look!' I said. 'If you think . . .'

He held up a hand. 'I've also been talking to Andre.'

'Oh, yes?'

He stood up and thrust his hands into the pockets of his jeans. 'I have a feeling that our young friend may be about to desert us.'

'What do you mean?' This caused me, of course, to sit up even further. 'What did Andre say? What's happening?'

He shrugged. 'Andre said nothing. He never does. It's just a . . . let's say a premonition.'

He hovered over me like a cloud, a barrier between me and the sun.

'Why are you telling me this?' I demanded. 'What are you playing at?'

He smiled. 'The perfect husband,' he said. 'What else?'

Then, turning sharply, he marched off towards the house.

'Charles!' I scrambled to my feet. 'Charles! Wait!'

But it was as if he hadn't heard me; as if, having delivered his line, he couldn't wait to leave the stage. Reaching the house, he ducked in through the kitchen door without once looking back.

I kept very much to myself for the rest of the day, sneaking into the house to make myself a sandwich when I knew the others wouldn't be there, and come seven o'clock pleading a headache so as to miss out on supper too. There had been earlier indications from Charles that he knew how I felt about Benedict, but nothing as definite or as challenging, nothing which – especially in the light of his suggestion that Benedict might be leaving – so forcefully impelled me to act, and act now, before the opportunity to act was taken from me. Did it disturb me that it was primarily my husband's prescience that was making me think like this, that it was his gauntlet I was picking up? A little, perhaps, but only subliminally. I cared less who had flicked the switch than that I'd been given the green light – which was how, as I stood at my window before turning in, I saw the lights at the end of the pier: invitations to a clearer, more decisive tomorrow.

I woke at seven to a flawless day. Scared that I'd miss him if I didn't hurry, I dressed, did my make-up in minutes, and was in the kitchen by twenty past. Just as well too, for he was there before me, in a T-shirt and shorts, crouched over the radio, frowning.

'Morning!' I said. 'Why so solemn?'

'The weather's going to change. There's a low coming in from the west.'

'Today?'

'No, tomorrow maybe, or the day after.'

I waited for him to switch off the radio and straighten up before speaking again.

'I have a favour to ask.'

'A favour?'

'I've changed my mind. About the sailing. I'd love to go with you.'

'Today?'

'Why not?'

He was frowning again. 'Today I was . . .'

I interrupted him. 'Please! I won't be sick or anything. I can pack us a picnic lunch, there's some cold chicken from the other night, and if the weather's going to change, then surely today. . .'

'But why?' His frown was now tinged with suspicion. 'Why this sudden change of heart?'

I couldn't tell him, of course; that would have been to reveal too much, on his side as well as mine, so I tried making light of it.

'Your element,' I said. 'Remember? You said the sea was your element. I'd like to see you in your element.'

Which seemed, as I'd hoped it would, to allay his suspicions. The look of wariness didn't leave his face, but after a

moment, with a shrug that was as reluctant – though I chose
not to notice this – as it was acquiescent, he said: 'All right.
I'll take you sailing. But we leave in an hour.'

'You angel!' It was all I could do to stop myself throwing my
arms round his neck.

'Though what about Charles? Wouldn't he like to come
too?'

'Good heavens, no! He's working.'

He looked at me quizzically. 'Well, if you're sure.'

'Of course I'm sure. And anyway,' I added, suddenly
reckless in the aftermath of this, my first success, 'I want you
all to myself. Just you and me. Alone in your element.'

He didn't acknowledge my double-edged joke.

'You'll have to do exactly as I tell you,' he said seriously.
'You don't play around with the sea.'

'I'm all yours,' I said, still reckless despite his seriousness.
'Entirely and utterly yours.'

And indeed I was. From the moment we stepped into the
dinghy to row out to the yacht, Benedict took command. He
told me exactly where to sit, where to put our provisions, and,
once we were aboard the yacht, how to find my way about the
cabin, where to store the sail covers under the seats in the
cockpit, how to slip us free of the mooring.

'My, my!' I said, marvelling at the deftness with which he
darted from point to point, unfurling the sails, freeing ropes,
passing them through pulleys, testing them. 'You certainly
know what you're up to!'

'I told you,' was his terse reply. 'You don't play around with
the sea.'

Eventually we were ready.

'Now just do as I tell you,' he said, 'and don't be alarmed
when we tilt. She's meant to do that.'

I smiled as brightly as I knew how. 'Aye, aye, cap'n!'

This time he returned my smile. 'Right! Anchors away!'

I released the rope attaching us to the mooring, scrambled
back off the deck into the cockpit, and almost immediately
we were slanting elegantly away from the island.

'So,' I said, 'where to?'

'The river mouth?'

'You mean past Broadwake?'

He nodded. 'The open sea.'

'Isn't it rough out there?'

'Not today.' He pulled at the sail, and the boat tipped further to the side, causing me, despite myself, to tense – though only momentarily and not, I'm happy to say, so blatantly that he would have noticed.

He squinted at his watch. 'We'll have the tide with us all the way down. Then, if we anchor somewhere for lunch, it'll have turned by the time we come back.'

'How obliging.'

'The tides are there to be used.'

We passed a pair of speedboats. Their skiers bobbed hopefully in the water, waiting to be driven off, whilst the boats circled them like sharks.

'God!' I said. 'Those names! *Shi Tot* and *Funk You*! How vulgar can you get?'

He frowned. 'They have a right to the river too.'

'I didn't say they didn't.'

'Sorry. I just hate people being snobby about boats. Right! We're going about.'

He explained what I had to do, and I found to my surprise that I was able to follow his instructions, to duck the boom, pull on the ropes and adjust myself to a different angle with only the tiniest surge of fear. Delighted at how easily I seemed to be falling in with the day, I let out a yelp of triumph.

'I'm beginning to enjoy this.'

He grinned at me. 'Told you so.'

He looked very at home, sitting knees apart in the stern of the yacht, one hand resting lightly on the tiller, the other cradling the ropes. He hadn't been exaggerating when he'd said the sea was his element. He seemed more relaxed out here, more at ease, more truly himself. Though where this led me, of course, as I deflected my eyes from the provocative line of his legs as he braced himself against the side of the cockpit, was to the realisation that I still had no idea what held him so rigidly in check on the island. That and the concomitant thought that if, as seemed evident, he only felt free on the yacht, where he was so clearly in control and on his own, the land behind him, then where did this leave me?

'Look!' he said. 'A race.'

I followed the direction of his arm and saw, in the distance, a collection of brightly coloured sails skimming the water like a scattering of butterflies.

'Where are they racing?'

He shrugged. 'Search me. Round the island. Or up to Broadwake and back. It's a club.'

'Will they overtake us?'

He laughed. 'God, no! We're miles ahead of them.'

All the same, and for all the speed with which we continued to slice through the water, it took us the best part of two hours to reach Broadwake.

Close up, its twin towers looked less impressive than they did from a distance. From the island they dominated the entire horizon; here they were overtaken in immensity by the open sea. Suddenly there was no bank, only water, and on the skyline an enormous tanker, two or three times the size of Broadwake. It's all, I thought, a matter of perspective. No such thing as objective reality. Only what we see, what we choose to see, and the angle from which we view it.

I stood up, and clinging to the side of the cockpit stared about me at this infinity of water.

'Scary, huh?' said Benedict, his sombre eyes fixed on me with unusual intensity.

'I'm not sure I like it.'

He smiled, and gestured with his left hand at the horizon. 'Freedom!'

'It's so vast, though. And empty. It frightens me.'

I sat down.

'Do you want to go back?'

I nodded. 'If you don't mind.'

He swung the tiller, and the boat came round in a long, slow arc. 'Just past the power station,' he said, 'there's an inlet. We can anchor there for lunch.'

'Heavens!' I said. 'Just when you think you're alone!'

He raised an interrogative eyebrow.

'That boat there. Just behind us.'

He spun round, and I thought I heard a muttered 'fuck'.

'What is it?'

For a moment he didn't reply, then – letting out a sudden laugh – he turned back to face me, rearranging his body, as he did so, into its pose of relaxed control.

'Just the coastguard.'

'Is it following us?'

He essayed another laugh. 'Shit, no. It's always out here. Going up and down.'

'Doing what?'

'Keeping an eye on things.'

I twisted round to study the boat more carefully, but it must have changed course: it looked very small suddenly, very far away.

'Gone,' I said. 'Going, going, gone.'

It took us the best part of an hour to sail to the inlet, which was in fact a smaller, subsidiary river that ran into the main estuary about a mile upstream of Broadwake.

'The view could be better,' said Benedict, shading his eyes and grimacing at the twin towers of the power station, which now that we were back in the lee of the land had reasserted their brooding primacy. 'But at least we're sheltered.'

He made me hold the tiller while he scrambled along the deck to drop the anchor and furl the sail.

'Right!' he said. 'Now how about some lunch?'

This was the moment I'd been angling for, the moment when Benedict and I could talk, really talk, though now it was upon me, I wasn't sure I welcomed it. More frightened, suddenly, by our lack of movement than by the sailing itself, I silently busied myself with arranging the food on deck whilst Benedict, as self-absorbed, mercifully, as I, saw to the wine, and, having poured us each a glass, left the bottle in the cabin to keep cool.

'So!' Kicking off his sandals, he lay down lazily alongside the food, his head propped up on his elbow, the negligent youthfulness of his body almost more than I could bear. He lifted his glass in a toast: 'To summer days.'

All I could come up with, in response to this, my first cue, and feebly too, was a quick: 'To your staying.'

'That too.'

'And happiness,' I continued blindly. 'Happiness for all.'

He frowned. 'Don't overdo it.'

'Why? Does it scare you? Happiness?'

'Wanting too much,' he said. 'Being unrealistic. That's what scares me. As it ought you. But we should eat. I'm starving. Aren't you?'

He was, I realised, the captain still, I his crew; and because I didn't know what my next step should be – nor, indeed, whether there was a next step – I followed his command, tucking obediently into the food, and finishing off with the peaches I'd bought in Meldwich that Monday, and which, as we bit into them, cascaded juice down our chins.

'Mm!' he said, flopping onto his back. 'Heaven!'

I leant over the side to wash my hands, then, suddenly exhausted by my panicked passivity in the face of what I'd been pursuing, lay down myself and closed my eyes. Now that we weren't moving, the sun was like an assault, pinning my limbs to the deck, robbing me still further of energy.

'Tell me something,' he said. 'You and Charles. Have you ever . . .?'

Suddenly I was alert.

'What?'

'Do you mind talking about him?'

I managed a laugh. 'Of course not.'

'Why haven't you ever had children?'

It wasn't the question I'd been expecting, and for a moment it rendered me speechless.

'You'd have made rather splendid children, I imagine,' he went on, 'and I hope you don't mind me saying this, but for you on the island, with nothing really to do, surely it would have relieved the boredom?'

'Boredom?'

'Aren't you bored?'

He'd scored not one, but two direct hits, and it was an age before, weakly, I could cobble together a reply.

'So that's what you think. That I'm bored.'

'Am I wrong?'

'No,' I said eventually, 'you're absolutely right. Bored and silly and self-obsessed. That's me. That's Lucy.'

And turning onto my side, so he wouldn't see the tears that had sprung to my eyes, I lay very still, not even stirring when I heard him get to his feet to fetch the bottle of wine.

I heard the clink of the bottle against his glass, then, faint as the breeze that stirred in the rigging, his apologetic: 'I'm sorry if I said the wrong thing. I didn't mean to imply...'

'No, no,' I said quickly. 'You're absolutely right.'

'Would you like some more wine?'

I shook my head, and curling in on myself, snuggled against the deck.

'Sleep then,' he said very gently. 'Sleep.'

'First,' I said, 'you tell me something.'

'What?'

'How long can you stay?'

There was a pause.

'All summer?'

Another pause.

'Would you like that?'

'What do you think?'

'I'm not the solution,' he said.

'Solution? To what?'

'You know.'

'All I asked was if you could stay.'

'I'll stay,' he said, 'as long as I can.'

'That's all I wanted to hear.'

'That's all I can promise.'

After which, mercifully and rather to my surprise, I slipped into a strange, sun-drugged, dream-muddled sleep, in which I floated like a fly in treacle, unable to clamber out. I dreamt I heard voices, and movement in the cabin, then movement all around me – and coming to with a start, sat up to discover we had weighed anchor, slipped out of the inlet and were heading home.

'Goodness!' I said. 'I was out like a light.'

Benedict smiled at me over the tiller. 'An hour and a half.'

I clambered into the cockpit.

'Good sleep?'

I nodded, and turning to lean over the side, breathed deeply on the cool, reviving air. At a distance of some twenty or thirty yards, another yacht was tagging us. The man at its helm looked naggingly familiar.

'I know that man.'

'Which man?'

I pointed, whereupon the man gave me an answering wave.

'You probably know all the faces around here,' said Benedict. 'After five years. Now, we need to go about.'

After the numbing heat of the inlet, it was surprisingly cool on the water, chilly almost, so as soon as we'd gone about, I went into the cabin to fetch my cardigan. As I bent forward to put it on, I caught sight of myself in the little mirror above the sink.

I know I'm vain and never pass up the opportunity of inspecting myself in the glass, but that wasn't why, or how, I looked at myself then. It was with an odd, detached curiosity, as if I were a stranger to myself, that I studied my salt-stiffened, wind-blown hair, my sun-burnt nose and cheeks, my pouting mouth and sky-blue eyes, the tracery of lines that ran from feature to feature, trapping me in its web. Charles has his painting, I thought, and Ralph his teaching, Jorgen his photography. But I have only myself, this tenuous configuration of skin and bone, this trap to which time has begun to take his hammer, chipping away at it here, undermining it there, until – what? I shuddered. A trap, but a trap not simply of self, not merely of time, but of how I saw myself, and therefore allowed myself to be. Pretty as a picture, yes, and powerful with it, for looks are potent, but all the same, less than I truly was. Childless, hopeless, loveless, a disappointment not only to Charles, but to all the people in my life, my mother, father, Bobby Alton, Jorgen, Ralph – and most importantly, me. An image made in other people's eyes, for other people's pleasure and their dismemberment.

'Lucy!'

Benedict's voice released me from one predicament to face another: a predicament which, given his comments about boredom, I now wasn't sure I wanted or needed to face. Pulling my cardigan over my head, I turned my back on my reflection and went above.

'There's something I'd like to tell you,' he said as soon as I'd settled myself opposite him in the cockpit. 'Something you should know.'

There was an odd look in his eyes, at once speculative and serious, uncertain yet determined. I'd not seen this look before.

'Yes?'

'You know Andre said there'd been some trouble in London? To do with me, I mean?'

'Yes?'

'I'd like to tell you what it was.'

I frowned. 'You don't have to. Not if you don't want to.'

He held up a hand. 'No, I'd like to put the record straight. I think I . . .' He paused.

'Yes?'

'Owe it to you.'

'I'm not keeping a record.'

'All the same. I don't want you thinking . . .'

'What?'

'Wrong things. But first we need to go about.'

So once again we went about – and indeed, through all of what followed, at regular intervals through his explanation of himself, we went about. I would release my rope, duck the boom, crawl to the opposite side of the cockpit, whilst Benedict handled the tiller, dealt with the ropes, judged our angle to the wind, before resuming his story.

'I had this friend. His name was Nick.' His voice took on a sing-song quality. 'We grew up together, lived in the same road, went to the same school, were in the same class. We did everything together. Homework, paper rounds, all the crazes: marbles, kites, skate-boarding, girls.'

'I see,' I said. 'Simply a craze, are we?'

'Then we left school, we came to London together, to look for work, we found a flat, well, rooms in a flat, I started drumming with the band, Nick got a job in this gallery, as a sort of messenger boy, general dogsbody, man Friday.'

'This gallery,' I said. 'It wasn't Andre's by any chance?'

He nodded. 'Then,' he said, 'I met this girl. Wendy. Wendy Phillips. It wasn't that serious, but we were – well, a feature.

And the three of us, Nick, Wendy and me, we'd go places together, to the movies, or the pub, she didn't come between us, he seemed to like her, and I know she liked him.'

We went about.

'Then what?'

'Then she vanished. Wendy. She disappeared. Just like that. One day she was there, then she was gone.'

'You mean . . .?'

'I mean she vanished.'

'But where? How? Why?'

He took my questions in turn. 'Back to her parents. By train. Why, I don't know.'

'She didn't explain?'

He shook his head. 'I was pretty cut up about it, I can tell you. I know it hadn't been that serious, Wendy and I, but all the same, no one likes being left, so Nick – my old friend Nick – he suggested we go drinking, which we did, and when he'd got me totally plastered, which he did, he took me home, and when he'd got me home, he put me to bed, and when he'd done that, when he'd undressed me and pulled the sheets over me, he got into bed with me.'

'Without any clothes on?'

'Without any clothes on.'

There was a pause.

'Then he told me he loved me, and that was why Wendy had gone away, because he'd told her how he felt about me, and he hoped I didn't mind, because he'd always loved me, ever since he could remember, it was just he'd been too frightened to say it.'

I pulled my cardigan more tightly round my shoulders.

'And then?'

His voice dipped to a whisper. 'Then he touched me, and I let him touch me, and we fell asleep.'

I found I couldn't bear to look at him any longer, so I looked away, to where the sea met the sky, and after a long time I heard him say: 'The next morning I told him I wasn't like that, that what had happened had happened, but we couldn't do it again. And when he began to argue, because he did, he was an argumentative bugger, I pulled him out of bed and I held him against the wall and I hit him, I hit him as hard as I could, in the face and in the stomach, until he bled.'

At that point I had to look at him, and I saw that the colour had drained from his face and that his knuckles, too, were white from the force with which he was clenching the tiller.

'Later that morning,' he said, 'when I came out of my room, I found he'd also vanished. Just like Wendy. Gone. His room was empty, so was his bit of bookshelf in the living-room, his section of fridge. All empty.'

A silence fell on the boat, broken only by the slap of the water against the hull, the mocking cry of a gull.

'And have you heard from him since?'

Again he looked at me, but craftily this time, as if I might be out to trick him. 'What do you think?'

'Benedict,' I said. 'You have to tell me what happened.'

'Well, through the gallery, through Andre, he met these people, not very nice people, they wanted him to do some job for them, drugs, running drugs, something like that, and because he was desperate, because he had nothing to lose, he agreed.'

'And?'

He shrugged. 'I don't know. No one knows. He's been gone three months now, and nobody knows.'

'That's awful,' I said. 'Quite awful.'

'My only mistake,' he said, 'was letting him touch me. If I hadn't let him touch me, we could have gone on as normal.'

We went about.

'And Andre? How does Andre fit into the picture?'

He smiled, a dreamy, half-unbelieving smile. 'When Nick went missing, Andre came round to the flat, he could see how upset I was, he said I could come down here, be on my own for a bit, until I got over it. Until I was myself again.' He threw back his head and let out a short, explosive laugh. 'We have to be so careful,' he said, 'so careful of who we love.'

Then, before I could frame a reply to a remark which, I knew, had been meant as much for my benefit as his, he nodded over my shoulder. 'But see! We're almost home.'

I turned to look, and indeed, the island had come into

view: a long, low, sullen hump of land spiked at intervals by the jagged outlines of long-dead elms, monuments to the might have been.

'You take the tiller,' he said, 'and just keep her on course.'

I swapped places with him, and while I concentrated on holding the silhouette of the Institute in my sights, he clambered onto the deck, dropped the mainsail, and as we glided up to the mooring, leant overboard, snatched the rope out of the water, and made us fast. I helped him tie up the sails and replace them in their covers, stow away the ropes and remove the ensign; then, the yacht shipshape, I fetched the lunch things from the cabin and let him hand me into the dinghy. We rowed silently ashore.

It had just gone eight, and after the noise and movement of being out on the water, the buffeting activity of the day, evening had brought with it an almost preternatural calm: there was no wind in the creek, no sound except the occasional bird, and the light had lost its attack, was dimming towards dusk.

He helped me ashore, pulled the dinghy clear of the water, and came towards me to relieve me of the basket.

'Let me carry that.'

'Just a minute!' I put the basket on the ground and reached with both hands for his face.

'I know it's over,' I said. 'Over before it began. Goodbye before hello. But it would have been glorious.'

His face went out of focus as I pulled it down to mine. The taste of him, however, was sure and sharp and sweet – the taste of the wind and of the sea and very faintly of peach; and his back, when I ran my hand down it, seemed to go on forever. Ironic confirmation of the palpability of that which couldn't be realised.

Then, without any warning, he'd broken free of me and was sprinting towards the sea wall. I was about to call after him when I saw a movement on the wall, and peering more closely, made out the shape of Jorgen, crouching by a bush with his camera. He sprang to his feet at Benedict's approach, and turned to make his escape, but before he'd got more than a couple of yards, Benedict was upon him and the two of them had merged into a struggling, writhing whole. I heard grunts, then a cry of 'Not my camera, no!', then I saw the camera fly in a graceful arc to land with a squelch in the mud.

'My camera!' Jorgen slithered down the sea wall.

For a moment it looked as if Benedict might follow him, but instead he just shrugged, and tugging his T-shirt back into place, raised a hand to beckon me.

'Come!' he called. 'Let's get back.'

I snatched up the basket and ran to join him.

'You didn't need to do that,' I said as we set off briskly for the village. 'Not for my sake. I know he's impossible, but so what if he took a picture of us?' I wanted to say kissing, but couldn't bring myself to utter the word. 'He would never use it. Not with Charles around.'

'Artists!' spat Benedict. 'You can never trust them.'

'We know the truth,' I said. 'Not them.'

'He shouldn't snoop.'

'But his camera, though. That's his livelihood.'

He wasn't mollified. 'His livelihood. Our lives.'

I felt timidly for his hand.

'Precisely so,' I said. 'Our lives. Ours and no one else's.'

He let my hand lie for a moment in his; then, disentangling it, said sadly: 'If you believe that, then you're not the person I thought you were.'

To which there didn't seem any reply, so side by side, but taking care not to touch, we walked the rest of the way in silence.

There were long shadows snaking across the lawn to greet us as we came in sight of the manor house, and standing at the head of them, on the steps leading up to the french windows, the figure of Charles, a glass of wine in his hand and an amused, almost speculative look on his face.

'Well, well!' he said, raising his glass as we approached. 'To travellers returned.'

Something in his tone made me uneasy, and I found myself snapping: 'We were hardly at risk. The sea was like glass.'

He was not put out by my acerbity. 'And did you view yourself therein?' he queried sweetly, before turning on Benedict: 'She handle well?'

Benedict met Charles' stare head-on and answered levelly: 'Like a dream.'

'You must take me out one day,' said Charles. 'When I'm totally over the hump.'

'What hump?' asked Benedict.

'The work,' said Charles. 'The everlasting work.'

'With pleasure,' said Benedict. 'Just name the day. Now if you'll excuse me, I need a shower.'

As he passed between Charles and me, his body came into brief, electric contact with mine. The subversive surge of it would have quite unnerved me, had not the contact been so fleeting: one minute he was palpably between us, the next he'd merged with the shadows in the living-room.

'A drink?' suggested Charles. 'I had something of a breakthrough today, in the work. I feel like celebrating.'

I shook my head. 'How nice for you,' I said tightly. 'But not for me. I'd better get the supper on.'

Though no sooner had I gone through to the kitchen, the celebratory Charles at my heels, than I realised the only way to get through the evening was with the help of alcohol; so thrusting a glass at him, I let him fill it, and refill it too, as often as he did his, with the result that by the time we were sitting down to the meal the room had begun, ever so subtly, to spin, Benedict and Charles to go disconcertingly in and out of focus.

'Lucy!' said Charles. 'Are you all right?'

I put down my glass with exaggerated care. 'A little seasick perhaps.' I grinned sheepishly. 'I think I'd better have a lie down.'

And stumbling to the door, I blundered upstairs and collapsed into bed.

The bed was instantly lifted by an unsettled sea and swept towards the horizon, passing, on its way, the coastguard, the man whose face I thought I knew, Jorgen with his camera. Then, thankfully, there were no other boats, no other distractions, only a healing emptiness and the endlessly rocking sea, carrying me towards oblivion.

The next morning I woke late, and with a splitting headache.

For a long while I lay without moving, staring dully at the ceiling and wishing the pain away. Even though I guessed it was late, I didn't have the energy to check my watch, push back the covers and swing my legs out of bed; besides which, I was scared that if I moved, I would make my headache worse.

Finally I sat up, acclimatised myself to being vertical, then made for my dressing-table. The face that met mine in the glass was puffy, creased and crazed with hair. I reached mechanically for my brush.

Emerging later from my room, I happened to glance along the corridor towards Benedict's – and saw, to my surprise, that his door was ajar. Without hesitating, I approached and pushed it open.

A flurry of movement greeted this action, except that it wasn't him, it was merely his curtains flapping at the open window against a day that was every bit as grey and windy as he'd said it would be. I took a step into the room. The bed was unmade; there was a pile of clothes on the floor. I stared from the one to the other, not quite believing that these twin points of reference, the ridges of sheet and blanket, geography of his night, and the tangled heap of clothes, evidence of his day, should have been left out like this for my inspection. Before I could stop myself, I'd scooped up the clothes and buried my face in them, drawing deeply on their sustaining smell – and almost immediately I felt my headache shift, the tight arrangement of pain in my forehead begin to loosen, relax its relentless hold. Whether Benedict was present in person or not was suddenly, gloriously immaterial: whatever happened next, after our day on the boat, and with what I – and I alone – now knew of him, the complication of Nick, he was more perfectly, more wholly mine than I'd ever imagined possible. I knew we'd never be lovers, but that wasn't, I realised, what I'd really wanted. There are other, more binding intimacies than the merely physical.

I might have stayed like that for hours, my face in his clothes, adrift in the second-hand smell of him, had not the window banged shut in the wind, startling me back to reality. I dropped the clothes onto the bed, took a last look round the room, then closed the door and continued downstairs.

Charles was at the far end of the kitchen table, huddled in his tattered dressing-gown over a cup of coffee.

'Good wife!' he said. 'Good morrow!'

'Don't!'

He pretended a frown. 'You mean it isn't?'

I made for the kettle. 'Benedict was right. He said the weather would change.'

'Ah!' said Charles. 'The all knowing Benedict.'

I held the kettle under the tap.

'Have you seen him this morning?'

'This not-so-good morning, you mean? No.'

I plugged in the kettle.

'But I imagine,' he continued, 'that's only because the two of us got rather smashed last night and he's sleeping it off.'

'No, he isn't.'

'Oh? And how would you know?'

I turned to face him. 'Because,' I said, 'the door to his room was open as I came downstairs.'

'And?'

'And I looked in to see if he wanted anything and he wasn't there.' I turned to the dresser to get myself a cup and saucer.

'That's funny,' said Charles. 'I've been up since six and I haven't seen him.'

'What time did you get to bed?'

'Oh,' he said. 'God knows. After three.'

'Perhaps he went for a walk?'

'Perhaps.'

I sat at the opposite end of the table to Charles, and the two of us regarded each other warily. Now that he'd told me how little sleep he'd had, I could see it in his face. He was abnormally pale and his skin looked as if it had been stretched too tightly across his bones.

'Do I really look that pitiful?'

'We drink too much,' I said. 'You more than me. It isn't good for us.'

He grinned. 'Well, it was quite a celebration last night.'

'Celebration?'

'The work.'

'Ah, yes,' I said, remembering. 'Of course. The work. You finished a canvas?'

'Perhaps.' His eyes didn't shift from mine, but that was all the answer he gave me. Instead, still intent on holding my gaze, he went on: 'And you. You had a breakthrough too. Going sailing.'

It was another of his gauntlets, and the decent thing, I suppose, would have been to dispel his fears, to indicate there was nothing to be feared any longer from Benedict. Or nothing physical, at any rate. But something about his smugness over his work, his refusal to divulge any details, made me feel that I needed to be armed with a secret too. So, smiling enigmatically, I said: 'Indeed. A breakthrough all of my own.'

Then, getting briskly to my feet, I continued: 'But I've got things to do. As, I imagine, have you.'

I hadn't a clue, when I said it, what things I meant. All I really wanted to do was study the jewel that was yesterday, pore over its every facet, hold it up to the light, decide where and how I'd keep it safe, whether tucked away in a drawer or on my person, so that others could share in its beauty. But having issued myself with instructions, and because there was a part of me that was frightened to examine the jewel too closely (there was a great deal about Benedict's story, about Nick and about Wendy, that I hadn't understood; there were things he'd said about me that I hadn't liked hearing), as soon as Charles had left the room to go to his studio, I set about cleaning the dresser, a task I'd been putting off for months.

It was mercifully involving work, and before I knew it, it was lunch-time. Whereupon, because I wanted to avoid another sparring match with Charles should he pop down for a sandwich and a beer, I fetched a cardigan and went for a walk. It wasn't welcoming out, it was wet still and windy, so I only went as far as the bunker before turning back and retreating to my room, where I fell onto my bed and into a deep and dreamless sleep, quite devoid of image or emotion, a calming, healing void from which, with a start, I woke to find it was eight o'clock.

I lay perfectly still for a moment, getting used to the sensation of being awake. Then, feeling fresh and light, quite cleansed and revivified, another person almost, I skipped out of bed, and, singing happily to myself, ran a bath, and when I'd bathed, took particular, pleasing care with my make-up, then let myself, still singing, out of my room.

The corridor was in total darkness: no strip of light from under Benedict's door, no spill of it from the stairs leading up to Charles' studio. My song died in my throat. Pausing at the head of the stairs, I called out: 'Charles? Charles?'

There was no reply.

I ran downstairs and into the living-room, which was also empty, then through to the kitchen, which was precisely as I'd left it when I'd gone for my walk, with this one, small exception, a note from Charles on the centre of the table: 'Regarding alcohol again. Gone with Norman to the pub. Back when the causeway opens.'

A sudden chill went down my spine. If he wasn't upstairs, and if, as was obvious, he hadn't been downstairs, then where the hell was Benedict?

Pochade

'**I** have a feeling,' Charles had said in the orchard, 'that our young friend may be about to desert us.' It was this remark more than anything else, I realised, that was fuelling my horror; except that the horror – and horror was the only word for what I felt – was directed less at the fact of Benedict's disappearance than at how vulnerable it left me. When I'd been in his room earlier, I'd thought his physical presence immaterial. Now I wasn't so sure.

Though all I did – doubtless because this was a thought too awesome to acknowledge consciously – was simply laugh at myself for being such an alarmist. After all, why shouldn't Benedict go off on his own if he wanted to? It didn't mean he'd left for ever. More likely he'd merely gone sailing and decided to stay over somewhere, in that inlet by Broadwake, or further up the coast. Anywhere to be alone. Which I, more than anyone, should have understood. By taking me into his confidence, by detailing his betrayal at the hand of love, Benedict had given himself permission to act in whatever way he chose, had made me a party, too, to his actions, including me, whether I liked it or not, even in those of them that seemed to exclude me.

So, stifling my fears, I made myself an omelette, helped myself to the last of the peaches, and when I'd washed up, took my coffee out onto the lawn. With the advent of night, the weather had changed, become limpid again, and summer-like. The sky was ostentatious with stars, the sea a lullaby in black. I sat on the steps, and, soothed by the sea's lapping song, ran over the last two months in my mind, from that very first morning when I'd seen him in the doorway, to the moment in the creek when we'd kissed. So compelling were the memories, so seductive in their ebb and flow, that it was gone eleven by the time I looked at my watch and decided it was time for bed.

The next morning I woke early, and going to my window, saw that weather-wise at least, the promise of last night was holding good. Benedict's low had turned out to be purely transitory. There wasn't a trace of cloud in the sky, nor a breath of wind. Dressed, I paused in my progress downstairs to gaze along the corridor at his door. It was closed, and he could, I supposed, have been on the other side of it, safely returned from whatever trip he'd taken. But I knew, in my heart of hearts, that he wasn't. And when, a little later, following my ritual of the night before, I took my coffee out onto the lawn, I was certain he was on the water still, sailing free. In which case, I thought, my preoccupation with him is nothing less than a grappling iron, thrown out against his wishes to pull him back. How much did I understand really of what had happened to him? I wasn't even sure I quite believed his story about Nick, the friend who'd crept into bed with him and then left. It seemed a little pat, more riddle than explanation – a key, certainly, but not necessarily to the door that was indicated.

'Is there any more where that came from, or do I make fresh?'

I came to with a start to see a somewhat battered-looking Charles swaying in the french windows, his eyes aggressively bloodshot, his hair awry.

'Don't say a word!' he begged. 'My head is splitting.'

'Serves you right,' I said, 'if you will go drinking.'

'So is there?' he asked again, nodding at my cup.

'In the pot.'

He followed me into the kitchen, where he sat heavily at the table.

'Was it just Norman and you?' I asked carelessly as I poured him his coffee. 'In the pub?'

'To start with. Then a whole lot of chaps from Meldwich. Here for some race or other.'

'I know. We saw them the other day. Benedict and I. When we were out.'

'Bloody sailors!' he continued, shaking his head. 'Why are they always more proud of their prowess in the pub than on the water? Made us rather competitive, I'm afraid. Alcohol-wise.'

'What time did you get back?'

'When the causeway opened. Andrew pulled down the blinds and kept the bar open. It must have been half one at least – and they were still at it when we left!'

'And Benedict?' I put the question as casually as I could. 'Did you take him with you?'

Charles didn't look up from his coffee. 'No. Just Norman and me.'

'And he wasn't in the pub at all? On his own, I mean?'

He shot me a look. 'Why? Is anything wrong?'

'No,' I said quickly. 'Just wondering.'

He slumped forward on the table.

'Any more coffee?'

I poured him a second cup, then leaving him to his hangover went in search of Norman, whom I found on the lawn behind his house, lying full length on the grass with a wet towel over his head.

I came as noisily as I could round the side of the house, so as not to startle him, and called out as I crossed the grass towards his prostrate form: 'So! Another sufferer!'

He didn't move. 'Ten minutes and I'll be fine.' The towel muffled and slurred his words, making it sound as if he were still drunk.

'I think it's going to take Charles all day.'

'Ah, well,' he mumbled, 'artists and alcohol. It's an old story. They can't really stop themselves.'

'Farm managers are more sensible?'

'With the odd exception.'

'Tell me,' I said. 'Did you see Benedict at all? In the pub?'

'Benedict? No.'

'Or on the way there?'

'No. Why? Did he say he'd be there?'

'No,' I said. 'Just wondering. Or yesterday?' I went on. 'During the day, I mean. Did you see him at all yesterday?'

'I can't remember. In the morning, maybe. But I'm not sure.'

I waited a moment, in case he would elaborate – and when he didn't, said reluctantly: 'Well, I'll leave you in peace then.'

'Much obliged.' He lifted the towel and squinted at me. 'Tell that piss artist husband of yours,' he said, grinning in pleased surprise at the neatness of his joke, 'that he owes me a fiver. For the last two rounds.'

'Will do.'

He let the towel drop back into place. 'You're an angel.'

After the incident in the creek with the camera, I wasn't sure I was ready, yet, to face Jorgen – but the longer I left it, the worse it would get, and he above all was the most likely to have seen Benedict. So, letting myself out of Norman's garden, I took a deep breath and marched over to the Lilacs.

My first two knocks brought no response, and I was on the point of turning away when the door was yanked unceremoniously open.

'Yes?'

'Jorgen!' He looked so sullen and angry it took me a moment to regain my composure. 'I was just . . .' I stopped, and because I sensed it was the only way to get him to talk, found myself apologising. 'First of all, I'd like to say how sorry I am for the other day, your camera.'

'It wasn't you,' he said stiffly.

'All the same, I feel partly responsible. Is it – is it ruined?'

'Pretty much.'

'You see, what it looked like, Benedict and I, it wasn't that at all, we were just . . . Well anyway, Benedict thought you might have got hold of the wrong end of the stick, so he . . .' I ground to a halt. Jorgen's anger was making it impossible for me to continue. 'I just wanted to say I was sorry, that's all.'

'Is that it?'

'Well,' I said, 'I also . . .' But it was useless. I couldn't ask Jorgen about Benedict, not whilst he was in this mood.

'Yes,' I said, 'that's it.' And turning, I fled in the direction of the creek.

On reaching it, I found the proof which, subconsciously, I'd been avoiding all morning: Andre's yacht wasn't on its mooring. Wherever Benedict was, he'd gone on Andre's yacht. Leaving me to cope unaided with his absence and all that it entailed: decisions to be reached, emotions unravelled, sense made of the senseless.

It was now mid-morning, and, as I'd known it would be, punishingly hot. I looked up at the sky. It had been bleached by the sun into a baleful, anaemic blue, harbinger of further punishment. No answer there, nor the hope of any.

Wanting to avoid the village, I retraced my footsteps to the house via the sea wall. At the bunker, I paused and gazed about me at the estuary. Silly, I thought, it's all so silly. Of what account were my petty concerns when put against the rhythms of the river? It was, as I'd realised on the yacht, all a matter of perspective. I frowned. Perspective and luck – because there on the horizon, made small by the distance, but large in actuality, not to say looming, sat Broadwake, squat symbol of an alternative, less pleasant reality. I shivered, and still shivering, turned away.

Back at the house, I wandered into the orchard and sat by the fish-pond. Too much to think about, too much to unravel. I giggled. Altogether too much for a girl. A silly, silly girl. I closed my eyes, and with my cheek against the rim of the pond, swam with my fish in the cool green water of my imagination. Best not to think about anything until he returns, I told myself. Go to the beach, swim, lie in the sun, carry on as if nothing has happened. For nothing has happened, not really, except in your imagination.

Common sense, though, is scant protection against obsession, and it came as no surprise to me that evening, after I'd gone to my room to change and was returning downstairs to prepare the supper, that on hearing a noise from Benedict's room, the sound of someone opening the cupboard or closing the window, a wave of such overwhelming joy should burst in me as to take my breath away. I pictured him in his room, changing for supper, pushing his pile of clothes to one side, extracting a sock, shaking out his jeans, puzzling over who had picked them off the floor – and skipping downstairs, I sang the supper into being, one song for the cooking, another for laying the table, and was still singing when Charles appeared, switching out the passage light behind him.

'Why three places?' he asked.

'Benedict, you and I,' I said. 'Silly!'

'But Benedict's not here.'

'What do you mean, not here?'

'Well,' said Charles. 'It was all in darkness when I came down.'

'It couldn't have been!' I was unable to hide my shock. 'I heard him. Quite distinctly.'

Charles came over to me and without saying anything, took me in his arms.

'I did though!' I insisted. 'Quite, quite distinctly.'

'There, there!' he said.

'Who could it have been, if it wasn't him?'

'Lucy, love!' He held me at arm's length, addressing me as a parent might a muddled child, a look of chiding concern in his troubled eyes. 'It was probably the wind, a beam of wood creaking, your imagination. I don't know. This whole thing . . .'

'Yes?' I said. 'This whole thing? What about this whole thing?'

'It's all in your imagination, and if you're not careful . . .' He stopped. 'Believe me!'

'I don't know what you're talking about.'

'Oh yes you do,' he said. 'Yes you do.'

Then, pulling me back into the curve of his arms, he held me tight.

'There, there!' he said again. 'There, there!'

'Oh, Charles,' I whispered. 'What's to become of us?'

I felt him shrug. 'Who knows? My paintings I can plan. Not the future.'

I pulled away.

'I'm sorry,' I said. 'I'm being ridiculous. Forget it. Please.' And crossing briskly to the table, I cleared away Benedict's place. 'Come! Otherwise it'll get cold.'

After supper, Charles took the last of the wine into the living-room. I switched on the radio and went through the motions of washing-up. The news was on. More heat was predicted, a Minister of Drought had been created, there was to be water rationing. Summer was waging war on us. I dried my hands, switched off the radio, and went outside.

The sky was studded with stars, the twin lights at the end

of the pier glowed their usual green, the water lapped darkly at the shore.

Not quite knowing where I was aiming at, or why, I started along the road to the village, and at the corner bumped into Norman. He had a chicken under his arm.

'Evening, Luce!' he grinned. 'Stinker of a day, eh?'

I nodded. 'Hangover gone?'

He looked rueful. 'More or less. You coming to return that fiver your old man owes me?'

I shook my head. 'Just going for a walk. And you?'

He held up the chicken. 'Have to bait the trap.'

'He got the other one?'

'No, it just needs replacing. Natural wastage, you know.'

I couldn't help but think of Benedict standing guard in the clearing, hoping to warn off the fox. That and how the chicken in its trap had reminded me of the baby I'd never had, the baby I'd allowed to be taken from me, and with it my womanhood.

'You have to keep trying,' said Norman. 'That's the secret. Perseverance. I'll get him in the end.'

'Tell me,' I said. 'You've spent time with him. What do you think? Of Benedict, I mean?'

He looked surprised. 'Why do you ask?'

I shrugged. 'He keeps so much to himself. Says so little. I just thought you, when you went out shooting, you know . . .'

'Still waters,' said Norman, 'don't always run deep.'

'Meaning?'

He laughed. 'Nothing sinister. He's very ordinary. Not entirely sure who he is, or what he wants. A typical youngster.'

'A youngster,' I echoed. 'Of course.'

Perhaps, I was thinking, since you want a child so badly, that was why Benedict was given you. To mother, and nothing more.

'And Andre?' I continued. 'What about him? How does he fit into the picture?'

Norman snorted. 'Don't talk to me about Andre.'

'No?'

'Well,' he said, 'as you know, it's harvest time. I'm

supposed to be doing the top field the week after next. But you know what Andre's done? He's gone away without letting me know, no warning at all, and he knows I need him to arrange the combine harvester. Unbelievable, eh?'

'Away?' I said. 'Andre's gone away?'

'The day before yesterday. Can you believe it?'

'Where to?'

'The gallery wouldn't say. Or couldn't. Business, they said. Whatever that means. And not a word to yours truly, not a bloody word.'

'So Andre's gone away!' It wasn't anything as defined as a thought, more a pulse of suspicion. Benedict and Andre, both away at the same time.

'Do you mind,' I said, 'if I use your phone?'

'No,' he replied, 'of course not. Go right ahead.'

'Thanks.'

'And tell that husband of yours I need my fiver.'

'Don't worry. I will.'

I'd already turned away.

'Apropos of which,' he continued unexpectedly, 'is he all right? Charles?'

I halted in my tracks.

'Yes,' I said uncertainly. 'Why?'

'He just seems rather distracted, that's all.'

'The work.' I said. 'He's very wrapped up in a painting.'

'Ah!' said Norman. 'Well, if that's all it is, that's all right then.'

I could tell from his tone of voice he didn't entirely believe me. But now wasn't the moment to be discussing Charles.

'Well,' I said. 'See you around.'

'See you around.'

I ran all the way to the old farmhouse, and ducking in at the door, burst into the long, low-ceilinged living-room with its open fireplace and beam-riven walls. A reading light was on behind the armchair opposite the fireplace, but otherwise the room was in darkness.

Feeling my way carefully round the huge and hideous furniture with which the room was cluttered (a great aunt of Norman's had died the year before, leaving him a small annuity and a surfeit of Victorian furniture) I inched my way towards the phone.

It rang for a good few minutes before it was answered.

'6023,' intoned an unfamiliar male voice.

'Andre?' I queried.

'I'm sorry,' said the voice. 'Andre's not in.'

'When will he be back?'

'I'm not sure.' The voice didn't sound as if it liked imparting information.

'Around eleven?'

'God no! Next week at the earliest.'

'Next week?'

'That's what I said.'

'You mean he's gone away?'

'Look,' said the voice, 'who is this?'

'Work?' I queried. 'Or business?'

'Who is this?' repeated the voice.

'Just a friend. I'm trying . . .' But before I could get any further, the line had gone dead.

I was tempted to dial again and try a different tack, ask for Benedict this time, and see what response that brought forth. But I knew the voice would recognise me. No, the only thing was to phone the gallery in the morning. Hilary, Andre's assistant, would give me his whereabouts.

Charles was still in the living-room reading when I got back to the house. Haloed by light from the lamp at his elbow, and with his book open on his lap, his horn-rimmed spectacles perched on the end of his nose, he looked disconcertingly domestic: at rest after a tiring day at the office. I hovered uncertainly in the doorway, guiltily absorbing his details, when he glanced up.

'Ah!' he said, smiling broadly. 'The wife.'

'Norman says you owe him a fiver.'

'So I do. So I do. I'll pay him tomorrow.'

'Good. Because he says he needs it.'

He folded down the page of his book, and shutting it with a snap, stood up.

'Fancy a whisky?'

'No thanks.'

He removed his glasses and slipped them into the pocket of his shirt.

'Nice, though,' he said, apparently apropos of nothing. 'Like this. Just the two of us. Don't you think?'

I thought back to Norman and what he had said: a typical youngster and a distracted husband. The twin poles of my being. And beyond that to what the youngster had said on the boat: I think you're bored. And to what I had said in reply: bored and silly and self-obsessed.

Though all I articulated was: 'Exactly so. For better or for worse. Just you and me.'

Staffage

The next morning I was at Norman's by ten o'clock, the hour the gallery opened. Norman was out and about already, or so I guessed since there was no reply from upstairs to my shouted 'Anyone home?' and downstairs was quite deserted, the living-room as silent and stiffly Victorian as ever, the kitchen a spectacular mess of unwashed saucepans and plates. I'd brought a fiver with me, which I put with a note on the mantelpiece before picking up the phone.

Hilary answered on the second ring in her usual harassed manner.

'Hilary,' I said. 'It's me, Lucy. I need to speak to Andre.'

'Lucy!' She switched instantly from harassment to pleasure. 'How are you?'

'Fine, fine.'

'We haven't spoken in ages! When are you coming up to London? You can't go on hiding away in the country for ever. It isn't fair. And Charles? How's the divine Charles?'

'Fine,' I said. 'We're both fine. Is Andre in?'

'Andre? Didn't he tell you?'

'Tell me what?'

Her voice took on an edge of exaggerated resignation. 'No, of course he didn't. It wouldn't occur to him to keep anyone even remotely in the picture.'

'What are you talking about?'

'He's had to go away.'

'Where to?'

'Ireland.'

'Ireland?'

'You know the writer Susan Wentworth?'

The name did ring a bell.

'Dreadful schlock she writes, but fantastically successful.

195

Well, it turns out she's also an art collector, quite discriminating, has the most wonderful collection, which she's asked us to sell. Quite a coup.'

'So Andre's . . .?'

'At castle Wentworth – madam lives in a castle, wouldn't you know – assessing the goods.' She paused. 'Is it urgent? Because if it is, I can give you the number.'

'No, no,' I said hurriedly. 'It can wait. It . . . It really wasn't urgent.'

'Well,' said Hilary, switching to her crisp, subtly dismissive 'I'd better be getting on' voice. 'I'll tell him you called.'

'There is another thing.'

'Yes?'

'Benedict.'

'Benedict?' She sounded puzzled.

'A friend of Andre's. I was wondering if he was in London earlier this week? Wednesday, to be precise.'

'What does he look like?'

'Tall, slim, sandy hair.'

'No,' said Hilary, 'no one like that. Short, squat and loaded with muscle, that sounds familiar, but tall and slim, not our scene, I'm afraid, not at present.'

'So no one called Benedict?'

'No one called Benedict.'

'Well,' I said. 'Thank you. I'm sorry to have bothered you.'

'No bother. I'll tell Andre you called. And give a thousand kisses to that man of yours.'

'Right,' I said. 'I will.'

I put down the phone and stared at the ornately carved sideboard that stood against the far wall. It was the sort of self-important piece designed to stand alone, in magnificent isolation; not, as here, wedged between a Regency commode and the dexion shelving which housed Norman's record collection.

I felt utterly confused, as fraught with thought as Norman's room with furniture. If, as Hilary's information suggested, there wasn't any connection between Andre's trip and Benedict's disappearance, then shouldn't I alert the coastguard? Phone the police? It was all very well putting Benedict's disappearance down to his desire to be alone, but what if I was wrong? What if I'd misread the signs? What if something awful had happened? Or was I, woman that I was, simply being hysterical? Looking for drama where none existed?

I got slowly to my feet, and fumbling for my handkerchief, blew sharply on my nose. Then, no nearer an answer, I went outside, where I caught sight of a movement behind one of the windows of the Institute. Without giving it a second thought, I darted across the road and in through the massive double door.

There was no one in the bicycle-cluttered hall, nor in what we called the playroom to the left, where, on occasion, Norman and I played table tennis, and where, the summer before, we'd painted a mural together on the one wall, a vivid and childish collage of the island, the village, the fields, the barn, a handful of boats and a bright orange sun, in which each object stood at an odd and arbitrary angle to its surroundings, the farmhouse next to the barn, the boats on a level with the sun. Now, as I skirted the ping-pong table, dust encrusted and spattered with pigeon droppings, on my way to the door in the opposite wall, I was chilled by how forlorn the room looked, how little-used. The archaeologists obviously did not squander time in play.

And it was at work that I found them in the room beyond, huddled over a line of trestle tables and sifting through miniature mountains of mud. They looked up in unison as I pushed open the door – then, as one again, and without so much as a murmur of greeting, returned to their work. There were seven of them in all, five men and two women, and they all wore glasses.

It was some moments before I plucked up the courage to clear my throat and say: 'Excuse me.'

The woman nearest me glanced up from her little mountain of mud.

'Yes?'

'Is Miss Kalberer about?'

'She should be.' She sounded neither surprised nor curious as to why I should want to see Miss Kalberer; nor did she volunteer any information as to where Miss Kalberer might be.

'Do you know where I might find her then?'

'At the back.'

It wasn't the woman who spoke, but the man to her right. The woman had already returned her attention to her mud.

I edged my way gingerly round the edge of the room, and, pushing open the door in the far wall, found myself in the old kitchen. Cracked and cobwebbed tiles lined the walls, and in the furthest corner, in the soot-blackened recess that used to house the Aga, there was a pile of clear plastic bags, all filled with more of the estuary mud. At a table in the centre of the room sat Miss Kalberer, her hair done neatly in a bun, her large, tortoise-shell spectacles obscuring the details of her face. She was writing in a little black book. She looked up as I came in and, unlike her fellow-workers, beamed a welcome: 'Good morning.'

I returned her smile. 'Isn't it just?'

'Quite glorious. It seems a pity to be cooped up inside. But the tides won't let us get at the site until this afternoon, and there's plenty to be doing here. We made a most important find on Wednesday.'

'Really?'

'It used to be a farm, you know, in Roman times.'

'The island?'

'The whole area. It wouldn't have been an island then. It would have been about two or three miles inland, maybe more. The sea is slowly encroaching, you see, on this part of the coast, eating it away.'

'You mean one day we'll be under water?'

'Precisely. But in Roman times, all this was farming land. Very rich. Good soil, and flat. And on the mud-flats, where we're digging, there used to be a settlement. A village, maybe, or just a farmhouse, we're not sure exactly. All we've found so far have been bits of pottery and the odd farm implement. But on Wednesday we uncovered what looks like a much earlier settlement, iron age I'd say, and it's absolutely crammed with artifacts. Some of them of a type I've never seen before.'

She removed her glasses, and getting up from the table, crossed to the window.

'To you it probably sounds dull,' she went on, 'but to me it's the essence of existence, being reminded that life has been here before. Sometimes we think we're the only ones. Or at least I do. When I get depressed, I think the world begins and ends with me. No one else. Just me. No past, and certainly no future. Whereas, in fact, it's endless. There have been people here for thousands of years, and, God willing, they'll be here for thousands more. We're just the tiniest speck, the merest blink of an eyelid. It didn't start with us, and it won't end with us. Unless of course,' and here she grinned crookedly, 'unless we blow ourselves up. Though even then, in time, life would probably reassert itself.'

She stood defiant and proud at the window, the sun radiant on her face, high priestess to the eternal.

'Still,' I said, 'that doesn't change the fact that all we have, you and I, any of us, really, is the here and now, today, this little bit of today.'

She turned from the window and replaced her glasses. 'You sound depressed. Are you all right?'

'Oh yes,' I said quickly. 'Just a little worried, that's all. You see, we had a young man staying with us at the manor, sandy hair, slim build . . .'

She nodded briskly. 'I know the one.'

'Well, he's . . .' I faltered.

'What?'

'Gone missing.'

'Gone missing?'

'Well, not missing, exactly, he . . . he tends to come and go . . . it's just that, well, he didn't say anything, and . . . I'm a little worried, that's all.'

'And you're wondering if I've seen him?'

There was no need for me to nod, for no sooner had she asked the question than she was supplying the answer.

'I'm afraid I haven't, not for a couple of days now. Not since Wednesday, I'd guess.'

'You saw him on Wednesday?'

She shrugged. 'Monday, Tuesday, Wednesday. Some time this week. I can't be more precise than that.' She smiled apologetically. 'Our little discovery has rather blotted out the present, I'm afraid.'

'Of course! And he'll be back, I know he will, I'm just being – well, silly, really.' I crossed to the door. 'Besides which, I'm taking up valuable time. I must let you get on.'

Miss Kalberer sighed. 'That's our problem, of course, lack of time. The tides are constantly against us. We never have long enough on the mud. And soon the summer will be over.'

Back at the manor house, and to still the confusion of ideas in my head, I ran down the lawn to the sea, and, stripping to my T-shirt and knickers, plunged into the sharp, cold water and struck out for the pier. There were a couple of boats on the water, and a glider overhead, but as with most weekdays the estuary had an abandoned look, like a playpool left forgotten at the bottom of a garden. I reached the pier, and rolling onto my back, allowed myself to drift with the tide whilst I stared at the pale and bleached expanse of sky, blown like a balloon around my forgotten playpool.

After about ten minutes, I became aware of how cold the water was and how quickly the tide was carrying me out past the pier towards the bunker, so I struck out for the shore, and emerging from the water, scooped up my jeans and ran up onto the grass, where I collapsed full out to dry. The heat wrapped itself around me like a lover, causing my muscles to relax and abandon themselves to its urgent sensuality. I closed my eyes, and, surrendering myself totally to the heat, fell asleep.

I don't know how long I slept, but when I woke I felt that a long time had passed; more than time, an entire period, an epoch, an era. Outwardly, the world I woke to was no different to the world in which I'd fallen asleep: the same pale sky, the same vituperative sun, the same grass and, at the corners of my vision, the same structures of pier and house. But intrinsically, it felt altered, as if things had happened behind the scenes whilst I'd been asleep, things hidden but crucial to the outward show, the composition and texture of the place. Decisions taken, as it were, by the artist.

In concert with which thought, very faintly, as if emanating from the sky, or issuing from the universe itself, I heard the familiar, lilting strains of the music to which Charles worked.

Anamorphosis

*T*hat night, thankfully, I slept very well, dreamlessly and deep, and I continued calm for most of the week that followed. The more I thought about Benedict's disappearance, the less I imagined he could have come to any harm. If something awful had happened, we would have heard. And the more accustomed I became to his not being around, the less I missed him in person. As I'd realised the day of his departure, when I'd stood alone in his room, my face in his clothes, there were other, more binding intimacies than the merely physical; other, more subtle gratifications than those of the senses.

So, ostensibly at peace with myself, I went shopping, swimming, walking, got waylaid by Geoff and Caroline, who inveigled me in for tea and left me with the distinct impression that all was not well between them, chatted once to Miss Kalberer on her way back from the mud-flats, and more than once to Norman, who dropped by a number of times, first to say that a depressed-sounding Ralph had phoned for Charles, then to check all was well with Ralph, then simply for a drink and a gossip – was it true that the Landies had had a fight; was there something wrong between Jorgen and me; did I think he, Norman, stood any chance with one of the archaeologists (who, he assured me, was quite a looker when she removed her glasses); and wasn't it exactly what one expected, that anyone whom Andre brought to the island would sooner or later drift off without explanation?

Then, on the Thursday, returning from a shopping trip to Meldwich, I happened to stop the car in the middle of the causeway to watch the archaeologists at their tables on the mud-flats, heads down, searching for proof of yesterday, when I was surprised by a tap on the passenger window. Turning, I found Jorgen peering at me through the glass, a conciliatory smile on his uncertain face.

I leant across and wound down the window.

'Jorgen!' I said. 'What on earth are you doing here?'

He gestured vaguely behind him. 'I was out on the mud-flats. Photographing them.' He brought his arm round to encompass the archaeologists.

'Good copy, eh?'

He grinned shamefacedly. 'Unusual, certainly.'

Then, dropping onto his heels so that his face was level with mine, he asked hesitantly: 'Could I have a lift to the village?'

'Well!' I said as we drove off. 'We speak again.'

He was fiddling nervously with his camera. 'I'm sorry. I feel very bad about the other day.'

I essayed a placatory smile. 'That's all right. I understand. Your camera. I'm sure I'd have been angry too.'

He shook his head. 'It wasn't only the camera.'

'No?'

He turned to look out over the mud-flats, and his voice, when next he spoke, was barely audible.

'Do I have to spell it out?'

'Oh, Jorgen,' I said. 'Surely not . . .'

But he didn't let me finish. 'I know nothing happened between us, you and me, I mean, and I believe you, really I do, when you say nothing happened with Benedict. But even so.' He brought his face round to stare into mine. 'I worry about you, Lucy. I know how difficult it is, living on the island, and Charles. I know how it is with Charles . . .' He tailed off.

'And so?'

'There's something I'd like to show you. Something I think you should see. Have you got a moment?'

Not knowing how to answer this, and feeling a need, suddenly, to make light of the encounter, I managed a laughing: 'You know how it is. All the time in the world.'

'Right,' he said. 'Good. I'm glad.'

We drove in silence after that, until we'd reached the village; whereupon, leaping out of the car before it had quite come to a halt, he ran round and opened my door.

'Some coffee?' he asked. 'It's Danish. Rather good.'

'Thanks.' I let him help me from my seat. 'Coffee would be great.'

Another silence accompanied his making of the coffee. Then, handing me my cup, he said decisively: 'Right. Let me show you.'

He ushered me into the spare bedroom, which was where he did his developing. By means of a blanket over the door and paint on the window, he'd cut out all natural light, transforming the room, in its wash of sickly red, into something quite sinister, almost malevolent.

'Mind how you go!' He steered me towards the centre of the room. 'I won't be a second.'

He let go my arm, and reaching for a box from the shelf in the corner, switched on the lamp that was clamped to the side of the table.

'Right,' he said. 'Come!'

He dealt the pictures like cards into the pool of light on the table. I put down my cup and took a step closer.

'Some of them you'll know,' he continued. 'Others I think not.'

It was a typically Jorgenian understatement, ill-preparing me for the revelation to come. On one level, of course, the pictures were all familiar, being of the island, the island that summer. And some of them I had indeed seen before, at the tea party. The one of Norman, for instance, with his gun, the one of me on the causeway. But what I hadn't seen, and what came as such a shock, were all the pictures of Andre and Benedict together. I knew Andre had been coming to the island all summer, but that he and Benedict should, on the evidence of Jorgen's photographs, have been quite so linked, that I hadn't seen till now; or hadn't wanted to see. But here they were, these two figures, the one an analogue of the other, in picture after picture, in the creek, on the yacht, in the fields; even those places I thought of as mine: by the fish-pond, in the orchard or on the bunker. And that wasn't all. More disturbing still was a series of long shots of the grain shed, taken the afternoon Jorgen and I had bumped into each other. There, in the grass, was Andre's car. There, by the door of the shed, was Andre himself, squinting into the sun.

And there, running between the car and the shed with what looked like a shoebox under his arm, was the unmistakable figure of Benedict.

'Things,' said Jorgen quietly, stepping back from the table, 'are not always what they seem.'

I turned to look at him. In the dim red light his face was oddly mask-like, totemic and frightening.

'You and Benedict,' he said. 'That's your affair. But do be aware of what's happening.'

'So what is it?' I challenged. 'What is it that's happening?'

He shrugged. 'That I can only guess. But something they don't want you to know about. Or me, for that matter.'

It wasn't enough of an answer, and it caused me, in my desperation, to turn my challenge on him. 'And you? Why take these photos? Do you intend to use them?'

That made him laugh. 'Use them? Good heavens, no. I just like to be in the picture, that's all. See behind the scenes. But use them . . .' He paused. 'Well, except that I'm using them now, of course. In a way.'

Having made his point, he was suddenly embarrassed, clearly fearful he might have overstepped the mark. Crossing briskly to the table, he began to gather up the photographs and stuff them back in their box. For a moment I didn't move; then, snapping out of my reverie, I came forward to help him, and picking up the shot of Andre's car in the field, was about to toss it on top of the others when something in the corn caught my eye.

'Good God!' I breathed. 'But that's Charles! What was he doing there?'

'Let me look.' Jorgen took the photograph and studied it. 'Oh,' he said, 'this! This isn't important. And anyway, surely he's shown you?'

'Who? Who would have shown me?'

'Charles, of course.'

'Charles?'

'He asked me, the other day, how it was going with the photography, so I . . .'

'Charles asked you how it was going with the photography?'

'So I gave him a couple. Not all of them, obviously. Not the ones I've shown you. But the unimportant ones. Let me see now. This one, and that one, and this one here, and this.' He indicated the one of Charles in the field, one of Benedict alone at the creek, one of me on the sea wall, and one of the archaeologists at their tables on the mud. 'He seemed to like them. In fact, I've never known him so complimentary. He even promised to show them to someone in London.'

'And you didn't wonder why he should suddenly be so interested in your photographs?'

'I told you,' he said dreamily. 'He likes them.'

I shook my head to clear it of the chilling question that had started to form in my mind.

'He's not all bad,' continued Jorgen, 'that husband of yours. He realises how hard it's been for me. How we all need help.'

But I wasn't listening to him, I was transfixed by the voice in my head – and backing out of the room, I ran outside and dived into the car, where I fell against the circle of scorching plastic that was the steering wheel. More searing, though, than the merely tactile, more insistently inflammatory, was the voice that was screaming in my head. Given that he'd never expressed the slightest surprise at Benedict's disappearance, nor even so much as commented on it, what had my shadowy husband been doing in the field? What was his role in the drama that was unfolding?

It was gone four by the time I got back home, to a silent house and a note from Charles on the kitchen table saying he was in the final stages of the new painting and wouldn't be down till at least nine o'clock.

I made myself a cup of tea and took it into the living-room, where I stood at the window and stared out across the estuary. I don't know how long I stood there, staring sightlessly into the middle distance, but a scum had formed on my tea and it was cold by the time I'd taken my last sip. I went upstairs to have a bath.

I lay numbly in the bath till, like my tea earlier, the water had turned cold and my hands and feet had crinkled, albino-like, into a parody of extreme old age. Then, throwing myself onto my bed, I tried to lose myself in a book. Later, much later, I got up and dressed. I looked at my watch. It was twenty past nine. I went downstairs.

I half-expected to find Charles in the living-room, in his favourite armchair, reading in the pool of light cast by the standard lamp. The chair, however, was empty; as was the room. I went through to the kitchen. Also empty. I came back into the hall and called his name. There was no reply. I returned to the living-room.

The sky was only just beginning to dim from a pale grey to its darker, midnight blue, but all the same, I was uncomfortably aware, in the silent room, of the encroachment of night, of darkness, darkness and a deeper silence. I went to the window and drew the curtains, then turned to face the room. It was, on the surface, reassuringly familiar: an untidy conglomeration of chintz-covered chairs, a sagging sofa, magazines on the coffee table, books by the door, prints on the wall. Ordinary, suburban, secure. But on the surface only. Underneath the surface, subtle forces were at work, inimical to security. Coming to a sudden decision, I marched into the hall and began to mount the stairs.

The first floor was in darkness, but on the second Charles had switched on a light; a single, naked bulb that cast a harsh and unlovely glare the length of the silent corridor. Now I moved more slowly, taking care not to make the floorboards creak, and when I came to the last flight of stairs, reached for the wall to steady myself and only put my weight on the very edge of each step.

Once I'd reached the studio landing, I paused to regain my breath. Then, my eyes fixed on the vivid strip of light that ruled off the door from the floor, I pressed my ear to the wood. At first I heard nothing, and was about to try the doorknob, when, faint and delicate as the scrabbling of mice, I heard the rasp of Charles' brush against the canvas, running now in a sweep, now in a series of short, sharp jabs: aural shorthand for creativity.

I took my hand away from the knob, and as I did so the scratching sounds stopped. I half-expected the door to be flung open, and for Charles to challenge me as to what the hell I was doing. But there was no movement from inside the studio, only a great and crushing silence. Until, unable to stand it any longer, I cleared my throat and managed a stuttered: 'Charles?'

'Lucy?'

It was only by a supreme effort that I was able to keep my voice level.

'I'm about to warm up some soup. Do you want some?'

There was another pause, then a mumbled: 'That would be lovely, yes. Don't worry. I'm almost finished. I'll be right down.'

I returned to the first floor to find I was trembling violently, and pausing on the landing, looked wildly about me for a means of escape – and saw, of course, at the end of its darkened corridor, the black rectangle that was Benedict's door. I was through it in a flash.

Like the rest of the house, Benedict's room was absolutely still; absolutely, too, as last I'd seen it. I crossed to the bed, and, pushing aside his clothes, lay out full length on the coverlet, waiting for the bed to lift up and carry me away, sail me out of the window and over the treetops, to that point on the horizon where the sky meets the sea, and Benedict, the only figure, the only point of reference in an infinity of sea and sky, would be patiently waiting. Then, when it didn't, and because I was due downstairs, I stood up, and picking up his shirt, folded it neatly and placed it on the chair, then did the same with his jeans and jumper. Charles was by the dresser opening a bottle of wine when I entered the kitchen.

'Ah!' he said, looking up. 'Good. I'm starving. Some wine?'

I shook my head. He looked surprised.

'Are you all right?'

'Absolutely fine. I just don't feel like wine, that's all.' I crossed to the stove. 'It's cream of tomato. Is that all right?'

'You really are splendid,' he said. 'Do you know that? Do I tell you often enough? You are a splendid and beautiful woman.' He raised his glass. 'To my wife!' he went on. 'To my one and only and entirely beautiful wife!'

I didn't make any response, and we didn't speak again

until I'd heated the soup and we were sitting at the table.

'So,' I said then, 'did you finish?'

'The painting, you mean?' He nodded.

'Pleased?'

Usually, if he went so far as to tell me he'd finished a canvas, he would also tell me a little about it: how long it had taken, say, or what had given him the idea for it. Now, however, and as if talking to himself, as if I hadn't asked my question, he simply sighed, and cutting himself a slice of bread, added quietly: 'Reserving judgement.'

'Will you show Andre?'

He shrugged. 'Perhaps. Next time he's down. Whenever that is. Though of course we can't count on such regular visits any more, can we?'

'What do you mean?'

He was in the process of lifting his spoon to his mouth, and he paused in mid-gesture. 'Now that we've lost our lodger.' His spoon continued its journey. 'Mm!' he said. 'Delicious!'

When he'd finished his second helping and picked out an apple from the bowl on the table, he pushed away his plate and announced: 'I think I'll go round to Norman's. For a nightcap. I haven't seen the old bugger in ages. What about you?'

'For me bed.'

'Tired?'

'For some reason.'

He stood up. 'See you in the morning, then.'

'Give Norman my love.'

'I will.'

He reached the door, then turned.

'Are you sure you're all right?'

I smiled brightly. 'Just a little tired. That's all.'

'Sleep well, then.'

'Don't worry. I intend to.'

I waited until I'd heard the front door close, then, pushing back my chair and getting slowly to my feet, I walked, automaton-like, into the hall. Climbing the stairs to the second floor, I passed along the corridor, mounted the final flight of stairs to the studio, placed a tentative hand on the studio door, and, like someone in a dream, gave it the merest push to find that, miraculously, it swung open, inviting me in.

'Now that we've lost our lodger.' His words still echoed in my head, I could still feel my horror at the unconcern with which, in between mouthfuls of soup and his reluctance to discuss his new painting, he'd relegated Benedict so carelessly – but oh! so emphatically – to the past.

I stepped cautiously across the threshold and sniffed appraisingly at the room's bouquet, a potent mix of dust and turpentine and paint. Then I felt along the wall for the light switch.

As the room flooded with light, I saw that stacked against every wall were what looked like empty canvases, five or six deep in places. Baffled that none of them seemed to have been used, I shuffled first through the ones immediately on my right, then, intrigued by what I found, through all the canvases along that wall. I discovered that the completed paintings were at the back; discovered, too, that Ralph had been right. They had changed. They were still of the wood, but whereas, albeit faceless, I had featured in at least half of the paintings from the last exhibition, in every one of these I was absent. The only figures to feature here were the men who in the past had hounded me through the wood, and who now, themselves faceless, simply lurked amongst the trees, sinister as ghosts.

I frowned. The last exhibition, which Charles had worked on for two years, had featured some twenty oils and twice that number of sketches and water-colours. This collection he'd been working on for almost three years, and yet there were only ten or twelve completed oils, and no sign at all of any water-colours.

I paused at his table. It was overflowing with strips of paint-spattered, turpentine-soaked cloth, jam jars crammed with brushes, a collection of palettes, and innumerable tubes of paint, some new and untouched, others squeezed into a variety of contorted shapes. On the wall above the table were an assortment of pictures torn out of newspapers and magazines (ideas, no doubt, for future paintings), and in the farthest corner I spied a board covered with snapshots, old and faded shots of me, of the island, the house, Andre, and in the centre, side by side, two of Jorgen's more recent pictures: the one of me on the sea wall and the one of Benedict in the creek. I approached the board, and putting out a hand, traced a line from my face to his. Then, turning my back on the photos, I surveyed the length of the room, my eyes coming to rest at last on the shrouded easel by the window: the painting, presumably, which Charles had been working on over the last few days.

I walked across to it, and pulling the sheet from the easel, took a step backwards before lifting my face to study it. The shock of what confronted me literally took my breath away.

It was a large canvas, five feet square at least, and it was of the goldfish-pond in the orchard, my goldfish-pond, looked at from above, so that almost the entire canvas was taken up with the pond. The pond wasn't, however, as I would have expected, empty. It was brimming with water, water of a particularly eerie hue, on the surface of which there were lilies, fat, glistening lilies, and beneath which – glimpsed, as it were, through the translucent veil of water – was the pale moon of Benedict's face, his skin beginning to bloat, his mouth open in a silent scream.

Letting out a cry, I managed to fling the sheet back over the painting, then ran for the door, switched off the light, and, closing the door behind me, tumbled downstairs and into my room, where I locked the door and threw myself, sobbing, onto the bed.

Contrapposto

I didn't sleep at all that night. I just lay there in the dark, staring at the ceiling, absolutely terrified that if I closed my eyes, my mind would give gallery space to Charles' painting. I purposefully didn't turn on the light – initially because I didn't want to attract Charles to my room when he returned from Norman's; but afterwards, after I'd heard his footsteps on the gravel outside, the rise and fall of their percussive tattoo up the stairs and down the corridor to his side of the house, because the awesome implications of the evening were easier to bear, somehow, in the dark.

Yet when, the next morning, a good few hours after the sun had begun to stream in hot abundance through my window and the day was already cheerfully under way, I got up and went to my mirror, I was surprised to discover my face didn't show too many signs of the night before, and it was an unremarkable-looking Lucy, a Lucy in keeping with the day, who half an hour later ventured downstairs to discover that her thoughtful husband had cleared the table of last night's dinner, done all the washing-up, and even left her some coffee in the pot on the stove.

I reheated the coffee and made myself a slice of toast, then – because I had to do something to get to the bottom of things – I instituted a search of the house. I didn't bother with Benedict's room, but I went through all the other rooms on the first floor, including Andre's, and all the rooms on the floor above, some of which I don't think I'd ever been in before. There were no clues, however, to be gleaned from Andre's bare and impersonal little cell, nor anything of the remotest interest on the floor above, unless one counted the fact that someone (probably Benedict) had been looking through the magazines from Andre's modelling days, which were kept in a box in a room overlooking the orchard.

Cheated of answers, then, by the house, I made my way out

217

onto the lawn and was crossing it to the pier when I had the
distinct sensation I was being observed. I swung round, but
there was no face I could see at any of the windows, nor any
suggestion of movement behind their many and gleaming
panes of glass. With monumental and pebble-dashed indif-
ference, the house was keeping its secrets hidden, safely
screened behind its façade of dilapidated grandeur.

And not just the house, I thought, but the entire island. A
breeding ground for secrets. Secrets from the distant past,
from previous owners, from Andre, from Benedict (whose
involvement with Nick, even though he'd pretended to share
it with me still – I felt – wasn't fully explained). And now, to
cap them all, the provenance of Charles' painting.

Shivering, I tore my gaze away from the house to the
frivolous gaiety of the estuary, the nimble and nifty wind-
surfers, the elegant yachts, the solitary and magnificent
Thames barge which, powered by an extravagance of burgundy sail, was progressing like a dowager through the water
– and breaking into a run, I set off along the beach in the
direction of the causeway.

A speedboat came roaring round the corner of the island,
throwing up an ostentatious wake across which, now this way,
now that, cut a confident skier. The boat headed for the
beach, then veered away, but not before the skier – blond,
trim, and proud of himself – had waved and shouted
something which sounded like: 'Come on, darlin'! Is he
worth it?'

I smiled, despite myself, and was still smiling as I rounded
the end of the island and noticed, across the rising water, on
the soon to be submerged mud-flats where the archaeologists
worked, a flurry of activity. The tiny, ant-like figures of the
archaeologists were not, as usual, crouched over their tables,
nor – as might also have been expected, given the state of the
tide – were they carrying their tables onto the sea wall to wait
until the water receded. Instead, they were milling about on
their patch of mud in a positive frenzy.

I reached the point where the causeway, already half-
submerged, joined the island, and clambered onto a rock to
get a better view. An ambulance crested the sea wall at the

opposite end of the causeway, and two men, carrying what looked like a stretcher, emerged from the rear end of it to run across the mud-flats towards the archaeologists.

I screwed up my eyes to decipher more precisely what was happening. At that distance, though, it was impossible to make out anything with any certainty. All I could see was that when the men from the ambulance reached the archaeologists, they formed a sort of scrum from which, a moment or two later, some five or six figures returned to the ambulance. The ambulance then reversed slowly over the sea wall and vanished from sight. I looked back to where the archaeologists had been. The area was empty. Those figures which hadn't followed the ambulance had climbed the sea wall, where, like me, they stood and watched as the tide slowly but inexorably crept in to cover the mud.

I'm not sure if panic is quite the right word – panic implies uncertainty, and there was little uncertainty about what I was feeling – but at that moment a wave of something very like panic subsumed me and sucked me under. Suddenly I knew that the answer to what had happened to Benedict no longer lay with Andre, or with Jorgen, or with me, but with the ambulance and the line of archaeologists on the sea wall across the mud-flats; knew, too, that thanks to the rising tide, there was no way now of getting that answer until evening, when the causeway reopened. Whereupon, unable to cope a second longer with bearing such impotent witness to the scene on the opposite bank, I turned and fled in the direction of the village.

'Morning, Lucy! Lovely day, what?'

Geoff Landie, as large and bluff as ever, was in his garden, mowing his lawn.

'Been for a walk?'

I managed a nod, then – before I could stop myself – found myself spilling the story of the ambulance.

'Good Lord!' he said. 'What do you think could have happened?'

But that, of course, I couldn't tell him.

'Maybe,' he suggested, 'one of them cut themselves. Or stood on something. They use a lot of dangerous implements. Axes and things.'

'Of course!' I grasped thankfully at the straw of his words. 'Why not? Of course!'

'Well,' he continued, 'Norman's just gone to the campsite shop. In the launch. Maybe he'll be able to tell us when he gets back.' He abandoned the mower and came to stand by the fence. 'Do you mind if I ask you something?'

His voice was oddly low and hesitant, and I noticed then, which I hadn't at first, that he didn't look quite himself. There were dark rings under his eyes and he hadn't shaved.

'If you were having an affair,' he went on, 'would you tell Charles?'

'I beg your pardon?' I was still having difficulty clearing my mind of the possibilities planted there by the ambulance.

He held up both hands. 'I'm not suggesting for a minute that you are, or ever would, but if you did . . .'

I forced myself to concentrate properly on what he was saying. 'Is it Caroline?'

The directness of my question caused his face to collapse inwards, and looking down at his feet, he nodded.

'Last night,' he said, 'as we were making supper, she told me she's been seeing Henry . . .'

'Henry?'

I could see it was only by a supreme act of will that he was holding back his tears.

'You remember,' he said. 'Henry and Margaret. The child psychologist. Old friend of Caroline's. They were down that weekend, to help us with Harriet.'

I remembered: a pale, overly serious man, a face made memorable only by its glasses.

'We've been seeing a lot of him, because of the trouble with Harriet, Caroline particularly, maybe three times a week. She had to let me know, she says, it would have been deceitful otherwise, and she wants to do the decent thing. She doesn't want to hurt me. But she won't stop seeing him. She can't. It's bigger, she says, than both of them.'

'Oh, Geoff! I am sorry.'

He'd lost his battle against the tears, and now he looked at me through brimming eyes. 'She says she doesn't want to leave me. She says she still loves me. But she can't, can she, not properly, not if she can behave like this?'

I found I couldn't meet his gaze. 'Love!' I muttered. 'It's not something you can control, not properly.'

'Obviously not.' Now his whole body was being shaken by sobs. 'I'm sorry. It's just that we've been together twenty years, and she's kicking them away, just kicking them away.'

'Where is she now?'

'In London. She wanted to be with him. They don't get enough time together, apparently, the two of them. Harriet's staying with a friend, so I said I'd come down here, leave them to it.' He fished a crumpled handkerchief from his pocket and wiped his eyes. 'Shall I tell you a secret? I hate this place. Always have. It was her who wanted it. A place in the country. "Everyone has one," she said. So we had to too.' He laughed. 'All I wanted was for us to live quietly together, grow old, have memories, die. Be normal.' He spat out the word. 'Normal! Like other people. You know. Ordinary. Run of the mill. Instead of which we always had to pretend, pretend we were richer than we are, that my job was better than it is, that we own this house in the country, that Harriet's our pride and joy. All to impress the neighbours. And for what? So she can up and off after twenty years with a child psychologist!'

'Geoff, please! You mustn't!' I reached out and made contact with the furry, yielding warmth of his arm. 'You don't know it'll last. You say it's love, and maybe it is, but even love, it's about all sorts of things – boredom, dissatisfaction, loneliness, getting old. Sometimes it's simply that the right person comes along at the right time. You know. Synchronicity, or whatever they call it. Chance.'

He blew his nose. 'That makes it less dangerous?'

'Of course not, but . . .'

'Well, then?'

I shrugged. 'I'm sorry. I was just trying to . . .'

'Look,' he said, 'maybe it's my own fault. All my life I've done what was expected of me. I've been the wage earner, the model husband, the doting father, I've rented the house in the country, mowed the lawn, I've done everything so fucking correctly, I don't know who the fuck I am any more.'

'But if we make our own worlds,' I said softly, 'then we can unmake them also.'

'No,' he said. 'That's where you're wrong. Making something, that's easy, but dismantling it . . .' He didn't finish the sentence. Then, drawing himself up to his full height, he stuffed his handkerchief back into his pocket. 'But listen to me! Rabbiting on like this, when I should be finishing the lawn.'

I touched him once more on the arm. 'You and your lawn!'

'Thank you,' he said. 'For listening.'

By now it was past midday. Heat enveloped the island, filming me in sweat and seeming to sound, fly-like, in my ears, buzzing there with an invidious, insect-insistent drone.

I reached the orchard, which was deserted and rendered pallid by the sun. I could sense the plants and the grass wilting under its attack, and when I came to the pond the noise of the heat grew so intense suddenly that I thought I would pass out. I put a hand on its burning rim to steady myself, and as I did so the buzz transmuted into the sound of Charles' voice.

'I've been looking for you.'

He was standing in the shade of an apple tree, one arm hooked casually over its lower branches, his shirt – the heat again – unbuttoned and hanging out of his jeans.

'I've been for a walk.'

'A bit hot for that, no?'

'I saw a funny thing. On the mud-flats. Where the archaeologists have been digging. There was an ambulance, and two men carrying what looked like a stretcher.'

He removed his arm from the tree.

'And?'

'You tell me.'

He held my gaze for a good few minutes before effecting an elaborate shrug. 'An accident, I suppose. Maybe one of them dropped a skull on his foot.'

'An accident,' I echoed. 'Yes, wouldn't that be convenient?'

He stepped out from under the tree.

'Last night,' he said, 'up at Norman's, I rang Ralph. They've taken him into hospital. I think I may have to go up.'

It was as if, to block my next move, a contrary god were bringing his biggest pieces into play.

'When?' I asked.

'I'm ringing again tonight, but maybe tomorrow. Or early next week.'

'Will you have to stay?'

'Who knows?' He was staring at the pond. 'If he wants me to.'

'Of course he'll want you to.'

'How long, do you think,' he said suddenly, 'since there's been water in this pond?'

I stiffened.

'And would it hold water still? Or would it just drain away through the cracks?'

His eyes came up to meet mine.

'How would I know?' I said slowly. 'I've never tried to fill it.'

'I wish,' he continued, in exactly the same tone of voice, as if still discussing the pond, 'I wish you'd come back. From wherever it is you've gone. I miss you, you know.'

He took a step towards me.

Without thinking, I pulled away.

'Don't!' I hissed. 'Don't you dare touch me!' And when he fell back, startled, added recklessly: 'I'm not that easy to get rid of, you know. Either in your paintings or anywhere else.'

Then, turning tail before he could defend or explain himself – and perhaps, more crucially, before I was called upon to explain my own enigmatic challenge – I ran out of the orchard and back up the road to the village.

As I approached the Institute, I saw to my relief that Norman had returned from his shopping trip. Bracketed by a pair of plastic bags, he was standing outside the old farmhouse, deep in conversation with an excited-looking Jorgen.

'But surely they have some idea?' Jorgen was saying as I came within earshot.

Norman shook his head and began patting his pockets to

locate his cigarettes. 'Apparently not. Hello, Lucy!' He had a knack of greeting you without turning to look at you or interrupting the flow of his conversation. 'They can only tell when they get to London, or get someone from London down here, I'm not sure which.' He found his cigarettes and tapped one out of the packet onto the back of his hand.

'What is it?' I asked. 'What's happened?'

'Well . . .' Norman paused to light his cigarette.

Jorgen spoke for him. 'They've found a body in the mud-flats.'

'A body?'

Jorgen nodded eagerly, his excitement at the prospect of a new assignment for his paper spilling over into delight. 'One of the archaeologists dug it up apparently. This morning.'

'A body?' I repeated the word, as if by repetition I could rob it of menace.

'That's right,' expounded Norman. 'The body of a man.'

So! I had been right. A match had been found for the body in Charles' painting. We now had a corpse, an actual corpse, its eyes, mouth, nostrils, all sealed by slimy, stinking mud.

'Lucy, are you all right?'

Jorgen's voice came to me long distance. I opened my eyes to discover I was lying on the strip of grass that bordered the old farmhouse.

'I'm sorry. I must have fainted.'

'You fainted all right,' said Norman. 'Dead away.'

'Are you all right?' repeated Jorgen anxiously.

I sat up, smiling wanly. 'It's probably the heat.'

'I'll get you some water.'

'Thank you,' I said. 'That would be nice.'

The moment he'd gone inside, I turned urgently to Norman. 'Do they know who it is?'

Norman shook his head. 'Apparently not. That's why they need this bloke from London.' He broke off. 'Why? You're not thinking . . .?'

'Of course not,' I said. 'I'm not thinking anything.'

'Because if you are,' he continued, 'you've been reading too many thrillers. He'll pitch up again, just when he's least expected. Or wanted. You'll see. You know what Andre's friends are like.'

'What's this about Andre?' Jorgen was back with the water.

'Ah!' said Norman. 'Water!' And relieving Jorgen of the glass, he held it to my lips. 'Here you go, my lovely, drink this.'

I took a couple of sips, then pushed the glass away and got to my feet.

'Careful how you go!' Norman reached for my arm.

'I'm fine,' I said, refusing his offer of support. I took a few steps. 'See! She walks. She talks.'

As I knew he would, Norman struck an obliging pose:

> I do my best to please her
> Just 'cause she's a
> Living doll!

'Would you like me to walk you home?' asked Jorgen.

I shook my head. 'No thanks. I'll be fine. Really.'

'Are you sure?'

'Quite sure. Honestly.'

And before either of them could insist on accompanying me, I set off briskly down the road, and didn't let my pace slacken until I'd turned the corner onto the lawn leading up to the manor house. Here I fell onto the grass, and staring up at the overblown balloon of sky (stretched so taut today, about the island, that its colour was a watered-down echo of its potential richness), found to my horror that this membrane of sky had become a canvas on which was painted Benedict's pale and bloated face.

I let out a cry, and as I did so the canvas tore, and through the rent in Benedict's face came swimming a shoal of fish, pink and golden, pretty as a sunset, and Charles was asking silkily: 'How long, do you think, since there's been water in this pond?'

Found Object

It was maybe an hour, maybe two hours later – after the sky had transmuted so terrifyingly into Charles' canvas, I lost all track of time – that Norman found me in the living-room, my mind numbed by the thoughts that had taken up residence there, my eyes fixed blankly on the meaningless serenity of the passing river pageant.

'Sorry to disturb you,' he said, 'but there was a message for you on my answerphone. Can you ring Andre?'

'Andre?'

'He must have rung whilst I was at the shop.'

'This morning, you mean?'

'This morning.'

It was like a hand reaching out to pull me back to sanity, the thought that perhaps Andre could still provide an alternative explanation to the chilling but inescapable deduction I'd made from the facts so far.

'Right,' I said, trying to keep my voice level. 'Andre. Right.' I stood up. 'Can I go up now?'

'Of course. Just let yourself in.' He beat a rapid tattoo on the tin of paint he was carrying under his arm. 'And tell that husband of yours he's got competition. Got this stuff in Meldwich last week. For the rats in the barn. You paint it along the beams, and their feet rot off.'

I shuddered. 'Don't!'

He grinned. 'Michelangelo, they'll be calling me. All that ceiling work, you know.'

'Horrible,' I said. 'Horrible.'

He shrugged. 'Little fuckers shouldn't eat my grain.'

I had joined him at the french windows, and now he peered worriedly at my face. 'You feeling better?'

'Of course I am. Why?'

'You and your lame ducks,' he said. 'Mother Teresa of the marshes.'

I laughed at that. 'Mother? Anything but mother.'

'I know I'm speaking out of turn,' he continued unperturbed, 'but I can't help watching you. And I know it's only natural, wanting to help people. Especially since most of us need all the help we can get. Some people, though, are a waste of time.' He shrugged. 'Well, not a waste of time, exactly, but beyond the help of others.'

'I don't know what you're talking about.'

'You're a good person, though.'

'Am I? I wouldn't be so sure.'

'Don't waste yourself. That's all.' He patted me clumsily on the arm, then stood back to let me past. 'Well, see you later.'

'Yes,' I said. 'See you later.'

Once I'd turned the corner and was no longer in his sights, I broke into a run, and when I reached the old farmhouse, collapsed panting onto the sofa and, without waiting to get my breath back, snatched up the phone.

Hilary answered it on the second ring.

'Charn Gallery. Can I help you?'

The words came tumbling out of me. 'Hilary! It's Lucy! Can you put me through to Andre?'

'Lucy! What a nice surprise. How are you?'

'Fine, fine!' I gabbled. 'Is he there?'

'Just a second.' There was a pause, a click, then I was through.

'Lucy?' Andre sounded wary.

'Andre! Thank God you're back.'

'Is everything all right? Hilary said you sounded upset.'

'It's Benedict.'

'What about him?' The wariness in Andre's voice became more pronounced.

'Where is he?'

'What do you mean, where is he?'

'He isn't here. He's vanished.'

'What do you mean, vanished?'

I took a deep breath. 'Are you telling me you don't know where he is?'

Andre's wariness gave way to impatience. 'Look, Lucy, I

don't know what the hell has happened, but you'd better explain.'

'What about your yacht, then? Where's your yacht?'

'What's my yacht got to do with it?'

'Tell me!' I cried. 'Tell me where your yacht is!'

'Lucy!' Andre began to speak very slowly, as if to child. 'My yacht is up the coast, at Long Creedon, having the ballast checked. And you still haven't told me what you mean about Benedict.'

'Who sailed her there?'

'The guy who's fixing her.'

'Not Benedict?'

'Lucy, you have to explain!'

'No!' I heard myself cry. 'No, no, no!'

'Lucy, what the fuck is going on?'

But now, of course, I couldn't answer him. I couldn't say well you see, last Wednesday Benedict vanished, I thought with you, or because of you, I thought in your yacht, but now I don't know, I don't know how he got off the island, or indeed whether he got off the island, because now there's this body, they've found this body in the mud-flats, and if you don't know where Benedict is . . .

'It's nothing,' I said. 'Nothing. I'm just being hysterical.' And I hung up.

Benedict's face hung before me, pale and silent as the moon, until, like paint, the mud welled up to cover it, to suck it into darkness.

I got slowly to my feet. The phone began to ring. Norman's answerphone clicked in with its crackled: 'Hello. I'm sorry I can't come to the phone, but leave a message and I'll get back to you as soon as I can. Speak after the tone.'

The tone sounded, followed immediately by an anxious and insistent Andre: 'Lucy? Are you there? Lucy? For Chrissakes, Lucy, pick up the fucking phone! Lucy?'

I didn't wait to hear more, but fled instead into the kitchen, slamming the door behind me. My eyes fell on Norman's tide timetable. The causeway opened at ten to six. I looked at my watch. Just after five. Almost an hour to go before the archaeologists arrived.

There was the usual clutter of dirty crockery on the table, and in the sink a saucepan into which Norman had emptied what looked like the remains of his last five meals. Without giving it a second thought, I rolled up my sleeves, and hoiking the saucepan out of the sink, turned on the tap. I hadn't got through a quarter of the dishes, though, before I saw swimming in the water a face, and attached to the face, a body: the face and body of Benedict.

I put out a hand to touch him; to stroke his face, just once, and to run my hands, just once, and gently, down the seductive length of his body; but as I put out my hand, it encountered not the subtlety that was Benedict, but something hard and unyielding. Bringing the world into focus with an effort, I saw that what I'd thought was Benedict was nothing more than a grease-encrusted glass.

I heard a sound in the living-room. Norman, having dealt new-fangled death to the rats, had obviously returned home. Abandoning the sink, I eased open the back door and slipped silently from the house.

The middle of the causeway was still under water when I got there, and I guessed it would be a good half an hour before it was passable. On the far bank, glinting in the sun, were the archaeologists' van, one of their cars, and a vehicle I didn't recognise at all, a sleek, white affair that looked altogether too flash for the island.

I clambered up the sea wall, and to take my mind off the cars on the other side and the answers they were bringing, plucked three strands of grass and began to plait them. As a child I had plaited grass endlessly, compulsively, storing the completed plaits in a box under my bed, and using them as adornment: necklaces, bracelets, even crowns. In those days I had been a queen, with Sue from across the road as convenient courtier.

I finished the plait, and, laying it carefully on the grass at my side, began another. The middle section of the causeway was still under water, but the white car, followed by the other two, had begun to inch its way across. Above the line of cars, seagulls wheeled, and in the mud below the sea wall a collection of waders picked their way fastidiously from rock to rock, pecking disdainfully at the mud. A couple of them had bright orange beaks, too vivid, I felt, to be real. It was as if they'd chosen the beaks from one of those baskets of cheap jewelry you find by the till in certain chemists, and were wearing orange today only because that was how the mood took them. Tomorrow it would be green, or red, depending on where they were going, and with whom.

I finished the second plait, and looking up found that the causeway was now clear, the white car on the final approach to the island. I stood up. The car drew nearer, and as it did so I saw to my amazement that huddled in the passenger seat – and wrapped, despite the heat, in a winter coat – was a nervous-looking Ralph!

Dropping my plait, I ran into the road. My voice, when I found it, was shrill with shock. 'Ralph! What on earth are you doing here? You're supposed to be in hospital!'

He rolled down his window. His face was more drawn than ever, and there was that smell coming off him, sickly sweet and faintly nauseating. He smiled sheepishly at me from between the wings of his coat collar.

'I'm sorry. I know I shouldn't, and you've every right to be angry, but I just had to get out of that hospital.'

'Why? Weren't they looking after you properly? And what did they say when you left?'

An improbably impish grin flitted across his face.

'They don't know yet.'

'You mean you ran away?'

He nodded. 'Like a naughty schoolboy.'

'But your medication?'

He held up a hand. 'Please!' He turned to the driver of the car – which, I now noticed, was a taxi – and said: 'I'm sorry about this.' Then he returned his attention to me. 'I had to see Charles again. There's something I have to tell him.' Then, before I could interrupt, he brought the conversation to a close with: 'But look, we're blocking the road.'

I became aware, out of the corner of my eye, of the archaeologists' van bumping up the last stretch of causeway.

Although it meant waiting to hear about the body, I didn't
see how I could avoid going back with Ralph.

'Hang on,' I said. 'I'll get in the back.'

'No!' Ralph's voice was surprisingly firm. 'I'd rather arrive
on my own.'

'But how will you manage? Charles is in the studio.'

'We can hoot, or else I'm sure this kind man won't mind
going in and calling him for me.'

I went round to the driver's door. 'My husband's studio is
at the top of the house. Go right to the top of the stairs. It's
the door facing you.'

'Don't you worry, lady.' The driver sounded remarkably
laconic, as if he spent his entire life ferrying dying men to
and from the island. 'We'll be all right.'

I straightened up. 'I'll be along shortly.'

'When you're ready,' I heard Ralph say. 'No need to
hurry.'

The driver slipped the car into gear, and off it moved. I
stepped back, resisting the impulse to wave, and as I did so,
the archaeologists' van shot past me. I was on the verge of
running after it when I saw that the driver of the car behind
was Miss Kalberer.

'Lovely day, what!' she called through her open window.

I stepped smartly into the road, forcing her to brake, and
not bothering to return her greeting, said: 'Norman tells me
you found a body in the mud?'

She beamed from ear to ear. 'Goodness, yes! What a day of
excitements!' She turned to her companion, one of the more
serious-looking archaeologists, a young man with wispy
blond hair and the inevitable spectacles. 'Eh, Martin?'

Martin nodded. 'I'll say.'

'It was Martin,' continued Miss Kalberer, 'who made the
discovery. He was working on the edge of the settlement,
where he'd found these jugs, rather good jugs too, complete
with handles. We thought there might be more. But instead
he found this hand.'

'A hand?'

'At first we didn't know what to do, whether to leave it and call the police, or go on digging. Martin thought we should call the police, but, as Adrian pointed out, we do have the tools, not to mention the expertise, so we all set to work, and . . .'

'We found this body,' said Martin. 'We found a whole body.'

'Then we called the police, and they sent an ambulance, and we had to go with them to the station where they asked us a mass of questions, like whether we'd seen anything else near the body, the exact position of the hand, and so on.' Miss Kalberer turned to Martin. 'There were moments I thought we'd never get away. Didn't you?'

'Very thorough,' agreed Martin. 'But then they have to be, don't they?'

I couldn't bear it any longer. 'And the body? Could it be identified?'

Miss Kalberer laughed. 'Well, this is the most amazing bit. Quite incredible. The name escapes me, but . . .'

'Benson,' supplied Martin.

'That's right,' said Miss Kalberer. 'Benson. Mr Benson. The man who used to own the island. You'd know the story, I'm sure. The one who crashed his plane into the estuary.'

'Mr Benson?' It took me a full few seconds to take in the name.

'Amazing, no? Quite, quite extraordinary! You do know the story?'

I nodded numbly.

'And?' She glanced at Martin. 'That sergeant was most unforthcoming, didn't you think? Not at all satisfactory.'

'Well, he was notorious for his parties, and his wife, she was awfully unpopular because she treated the locals like serfs, used to stop people on the causeway, apparently, if they were winkling, to ask them their business, as if she owned the whole river. People hated her. And they mistrusted the parties. People swimming naked in the sea, dancing on the lawn. That kind of thing. So when the crash happened, people took a kind of perverse satisfaction in it. The river had taken its revenge, they said. You know what locals are like.'

The relief of knowing the body wasn't Benedict's had made me overly voluble.

'How Sophoclean!' Miss Kalberer was staring at me fascinated. 'Mind you, what's equally intriguing is how perfectly the mud had preserved him. That's how he was identified. They'd rung some specialist from London, who was going to come and examine the body, when one of the sergeants who's been in the force since God knows when said: "But that's Mr Benson!" Incredible, huh?'

'Incredible.'

Miss Kalberer felt in her pocket, and pulling out a handkerchief, dabbed at her brow. 'But if we stay here any longer, we'll melt! Can we give you a lift?'

I would have preferred, in the aftermath of the news I'd just heard, to have returned home alone, but I wasn't to be given the choice.

'But of course we can! Only an idiot would walk in this heat.'

'Thank you,' I said dutifully. 'A lift would be lovely.'

Once in the village, after I'd extricated myself from Miss Kalberer's further entreaties to join the archaeologists for tea ('Tomorrow,' I promised. 'I'll come by tomorrow.') solitude – and the chance, therefore, to make sense of the events of the day – was once again denied me by the taxi-driver, returning from the manor house.

'Now you're not to worry,' he called, leaning out of his window as he drew level with me. 'I found your husband, no trouble at all, and he's putting the old man to bed.'

'You've been very good,' I said. 'Very good indeed. Thank you.'

He took a quick pull on the cigarette he was smoking, then stubbed it out in his overflowing ashtray. 'Well, to be honest with you, when he came up to me like that off the four thirty-five and asked if I'd take him to the island, I was going to say no. I don't like coming out here. That causeway is death to cars. But then I saw that under his coat he was wearing pyjamas, and, I don't know, there was something about him, I just couldn't.' He shrugged. 'The wife's always going on at me for being a softie, but life's not worth the candle, I don't think, unless we help each other. Know what I mean?'

'You've been very good,' I repeated. 'Very good indeed.'

He put the car into gear. 'Please! My pleasure entirely. As long as no one tells the wife, of course!' And with a cheery wave of the hand, he let in the clutch and accelerated away.

I watched the car until it was through the village and out of sight, then, alone at last, I turned and proceeded home.

Bodegón

ou would not have guessed from the empty living-room that a crisis had hit the house. The only pointers to Ralph's arrival were his coat, which had been thrown over the sofa, and a white plastic bag by the door, dropped there, presumably, as Charles had manoeuvred the old man upstairs. I collected both pieces of evidence and went into the hall, where I found space for the coat in the cluttered cupboard beneath the stairs. The bag I took into the kitchen. It contained an apple, a neatly folded banana skin, two bottles of pills, and that morning's *Daily Mail.* I dropped the banana skin in the bin, added the apple to our bowl of fruit on the table, put the pills on the sideboard, and threw the *Mail* onto the pile of yellowing papers we kept by the Aga. The plastic bag went into my stock of bags in the pantry. Then I made a pot of tea.

I wondered, of course, whether Charles could manage Ralph on his own, but if Ralph had something to tell Charles, then surely it was better to leave them to it? Besides which, I still needed to make sense of what had happened. Mr Benson was an answer only of sorts. If, as I now had to assume, the river hadn't claimed Benedict, then who had? Did Andre know more than he was letting on? And what about Charles? From where, and to what purpose, had he dredged up that painting?

So, taking my tea into the orchard, I settled under one of the apple trees to work things out – and it was there, half an hour later, that Charles found me.

As was only to be expected, he looked tense and upset.

'There's been a call for you,' he began. 'From Andre. Frantic, apparently. Can you ring him immediately?'

'Never mind about Andre,' I said. 'How's Ralph? Have you made him comfortable?'

Charles shrugged. 'I've put him to bed.'

'And?'

'I'll ring the hospital, let them know he's safe – and Doctor Cole, I suppose, ask him what to do.'

'What about Meldwich? Couldn't he go there?'

He shook his head. 'He doesn't want to move. I think . . .' He broke off.

'What?'

'I think he's come here to die.'

He began to cry, and, despite myself, I got up and went to him.

'Don't!' I commanded. 'Doctor Cole will know what to do. He'll find a nurse for us. He's very good like that. We'll cope, I know we will. You'll see.'

I pulled his head onto my shoulder and put my arms about him, cradled him as a mother might cradle her child, and he accommodated himself to my embrace, let himself be held, and powered by sobs, pulsed gently in my arms until, after a couple of minutes, he came to a sort of rest.

'There, there!' I whispered. 'There, there!'

He didn't pull away, and after another couple of minutes I asked softly: 'What was it he came to say? Ralph, I mean. Why couldn't he have written? Or phoned? Was it that important?'

He didn't answer my question. Instead, gently disengaging himself, he returned to practicalities: 'I'd better phone the hospital, tell them he's here, and Doctor Cole, see if he can come out tomorrow morning.'

'It's a good tide,' I said. 'Opens just after eight, closes at twelve thirty.'

'I won't be long.'

'I'll look in on Ralph, see he's all right.'

'And some wine,' he said. 'Open a bottle of wine. I could do with a drink.'

'Me too,' I replied. 'And not just one.'

He smiled – a sudden, jaunty smile, as of old. 'Alcoholic!' he jeered. Then he ran away through the trees.

Although it was early still, it was gloomy on the stairs, and when I turned down the corridor leading to Ralph's room, I had to switch on the lights.

Ralph was sitting bolt upright in the bed, his hands plucking fretfully at the sheet, his eyes fixed on the wall opposite. He looked very old and very frail.

'Ralph?' I approached the bed cautiously. 'How are you feeling? Are you comfortable?'

His eyes flicked in my direction, then returned to the wall. Almost imperceptibly, he nodded.

'Is there anything you need?'

He shook his head, and this time he spoke: 'No thank you.'

'I'm about to make supper. Are you hungry?'

Again he shook his head.

'But you must have something!'

'I'm not hungry.'

'I'm sorry,' I said, 'but I insist.' I switched on the bedside lamp, then went to the window and drew the curtains. I was about to return to the door when he spoke.

'You don't have to worry,' he said. 'I won't stay long. I promise.'

I turned to look at him. 'You'll stay,' I told him, 'just as long as you want to.'

'Be gentle with him, though,' he went on, as if he hadn't heard me. 'Do be gentle.'

It sounded, from the timbre of his voice, as if he were crying, but when I stepped forward to check, he turned his face to the wall.

'You must go now,' he said. 'Talking tires me.'

'Of course,' I said. 'You try and sleep. I'll be up later with supper. Some soup and a little fruit. You'll be able to manage a little soup.'

At the head of the stairs, I paused to glance down the corridor in the direction of Benedict's room. That corridor, that side of the house, was in darkness: no guest there, nor any likelihood of one; and the memory, when I tried to conjure him up in my mind, not of him, but of Charles, fitting so easily into my arms in the orchard. I continued downstairs.

Back in the kitchen, I opened a bottle of wine, helped myself to a glass, poured one for Charles, then began to prepare the supper. I put the large saucepan on the Aga, sliced two onions, and set them frying, then looked out a selection of vegetables: potatoes, parsnips, leeks. I had just finished peeling the potatoes when Charles appeared.

'Your wine,' I said, pointing to his glass.

He took it and leant against the dresser.

'Any success?'

He nodded. 'Doctor Cole is coming over first thing tomorrow, and the hospital, well, they were just very relieved to hear he's safe. I gave them Doctor Cole's number so they can ring him with anything he needs to know.' He shook his head bemusedly. 'It's all happening at once, isn't it?'

'And I'm still in the dark,' I added. 'You haven't told me what it is he came to tell you.'

He crossed to the table, pulled out a chair, sat down slowly and took a sip or two of his wine. 'A diary,' he said eventually. 'A diary my father kept, in the year before the crash. It seems my mother was having an affair with her boss, wanted to leave my father, in fact, for this other man, and when they had the car crash they were on their way to his house, her boss's house, to discuss a divorce.'

I sank into a chair opposite him.

'You mean your father may have crashed the car on purpose?'

He met my horrified gaze head-on. 'Perhaps. Or else, which is what Ralph thinks, he was so upset he wasn't concentrating. Normally, Ralph says, he was very careful on the road.'

'And why hasn't he told you this before? Why wait until now?'

Charles swirled his wine round his glass. 'He thought I'd be upset. He didn't want to tell me when I was little, obviously, and then later, well by then he knew how important the memory of my parents was to me, and he didn't want to come between us. Now, of course, he knows I'll find the diary in his papers.'

The light fell at an angle across Charles' face, highlighting his hair and the wine in his glass. Like a painting, I couldn't help thinking, a study in light and shade – and I thought of that other picture, the one Charles kept by his bedside, of his parents the week before they died, standing arm in arm on the steps of their home, smiling into the camera: another study in light and shade, the real and the unreal, comfort and deception.

'It's funny!' said Charles. 'All my life I've painted the wood where we had that picnic, that clearing, because I remember Ralph in his deckchair, and Mother and Father, the three of us together – and do you know, when he gave me the diary and told me what was in it, I suddenly remembered there'd been another person at the picnic, a man I didn't know, but who'd pinched my cheek, I suppose in greeting, meaning to be friendly, but so hard it hurt, so hard it frightened me. And when I told Ralph, he nodded and said: "Yes, that was him. He was there that day."' He looked at me. 'It explains something else, you know. He was from Kent, my mother's boss, a real toff, Ralph says, a typical southerner. Which is where he gets his mistrust of them. Funny, huh? Neat and pathetic. Like him.'

'Oh, Charles,' I said, 'I am sorry.'

He shrugged. 'We only see what we want to see.'

'But it doesn't change how you feel about your parents. It doesn't change how they felt about you. They both loved you. Just because your mother . . .'

'She would have gone away, though, wouldn't she? With her man? Maybe taking me with her. Maybe not. I was really an irrelevance.'

Like me, I was thinking, like I've been away. And not only from Charles, but just as crucially, from my father before him: running from responsibility because love is too difficult.

Charles was smiling crookedly to himself. 'I used to think children were a way of redeeming yourself. A second chance. My paintings are also my children, of course, in their way, except they're inflexible, without any life of their own – any proper life, I mean. But maybe I'm fooling myself. Maybe with children – real children, I mean – I would have been as clumsy as everyone else.'

There were a million and one things I could have replied to that, but somehow now wasn't the moment.

'You're too hard on your parents,' I said. 'Not to mention your paintings. Just because your parents lived their own lives, had their own loves, doesn't mean they excluded you. And as for your paintings, well . . . If it wasn't for your paintings, then what would you be?'

'So I should forgive them, should I?' he asked. 'My parents?'

I nodded. 'Of course.'

'And us? Who's going to forgive us, when we go? For the things we've done?'

'You,' I said, 'and me. We'll have to forgive each other.' I became aware of a burning smell. 'Oh my God! The onions!' I leapt to my feet and snatched the saucepan from the stove. It was too late, though. The onions were ruined. 'Damn! I'll have to start again.'

Charles had also got to his feet. 'First Arthur and his cakes,' he laughed. 'Now Lucy and her onions.' He threw back the remains of his wine, then refilled his glass and thrust the bottle at me. 'Can I help redeem the meal?'

'You mustn't fret,' I said, 'about your parents. Or whether they loved you. I really . . .'

He held up a hand. 'Food!' he commanded. 'Let's concentrate on supper.'

Whereupon we did something I don't think we'd ever done before: we prepared the meal together. He helped me chop the vegetables, kept an eye on the new lot of onions, and, when the rest of the vegetables had been added to the pot, stayed by the saucepan stirring it. We didn't talk much, and when we did it was mainly to do with our preparations: 'Shall I chop them finer?' – 'Does this look all right?' – 'More salt?'

Eventually the soup was ready, and Charles took Ralph's up to him on a tray, together with a banana and his two bottles of pills, whilst I set the table and opened a second bottle of wine, a burgundy this time, richer than the claret we had been drinking. When Charles returned, we sat opposite each other at the table, raised our glasses in a silent, smiling toast, then fell hungrily upon the meal we'd prepared together.

I was the first to finish eating. I pushed aside my plate.

'I'll go up, shall I?'

Charles didn't demur. 'See he's had his pills.'

I went upstairs.

Ralph hadn't moved. He was still bolt upright in the bed, still staring straight ahead. His supper tray was on the bedside table, untouched.

'Ralph!' I said reprovingly. 'You haven't eaten a thing.'

He smiled at me weakly. 'I said I wasn't hungry.'

'But you must eat. If you don't eat . . .'

He gestured feebly at the tray. 'Please take it away.'

'How about if . . .?'

But again he cut me short. 'Please!'

I had no alternative but to capitulate. 'All right. But tomorrow you'll have to make up for this. Promise?'

As I went to pick up the tray, he shot out an arm and caught me below the elbow. His grip was surprisingly strong, almost painful.

'I owe you an apology,' he said.

'Whatever for?'

'I never gave you a chance. From the moment Charles brought you up to Hull to meet me, I mistrusted you. It . . .' He paused, and his grip on my arm slackened.

'It was very wrong of me,' he concluded. 'Very wrong.'

I took his hand and laid it on the coverlet.

'Am I all right now?' I asked lightly.

He didn't look at me. 'I lied,' he said. 'I told a terrible lie. One should never lie. It never helps to lie.'

'It's all right,' I said. 'It's over now. Forgotten. And you were only doing what you thought was right. You were only doing your duty.'

'Duty!' Screwing his face into a grimace, he literally spat out the word. 'It's a terrible thing, duty. Duty kills.'

The grimace seemed to tighten on his face, and suddenly his whole body went rigid.

'Ralph!' I cried. 'What's wrong? Are you in pain?'

He managed to force a feeble smile through the grimace. 'Just a little uncomfortable, that's all.'

'Have you had your pills?'

He shook his head. I looked in desperation at the two bottles on the tray. 'Which ones?'

'Two of the white,' he hissed through clenched teeth, 'and one of the pink.'

I fumbled with the lids of the bottles, then handed him his pills and held the glass of water to his lips whilst he swallowed them.

'Thank you,' he said, and as he said the words, his body began, very slowly, to relax.

I hovered over the bed a moment longer, watching until he'd relaxed completely, then took the bottles off the tray and put them at the back of the bedside table alongside the glass of water.

'Now are you sure there's nothing else you want?'

He shook his head.

I picked up the tray. 'Well, just call if you need anything.'

'I will.'

'Charles will be up later.'

'I'll probably be asleep,' he said. 'All that travelling. It's worn me out.'

At the door, I turned to take a last worried look at him. His head had fallen forward on his chest, and his eyes were closed: asleep already, or feigning it.

'Duty,' he'd said. 'Duty kills.' And he was right, of course. Except that duty wasn't the same as responsibility. And here, as a back-handed gift from the gods, decades after the death that had started it all, here in the pitiful shape of Ralph, I was being offered the opportunity to redeem myself, to prove myself worthy, at last, of another's need; and in the process, the chance to lesson my guilt about my father, my guilt at all the deaths and betrayals that littered my life.

Back in the kitchen, I put the tray thoughtfully onto the dresser, then fell onto my chair and reached for my glass.

'How is he?' asked Charles.

'In pain.'

'Did you find his pills?' I nodded.

'Two white, one pink. And I told him you'd look in on him later.'

Charles reached for the bottle of wine and emptied the last of it into his glass.

'I'll go in a minute. First, though, I'd like to hear about Andre.'

'Andre?'

'Why he was ringing.'

'Oh,' I said, returning with difficulty to the present. 'That! Well . . .'

He didn't let me get any further. 'It's that boy again, no?'

There was a long silence in which we regarded each other solemnly. Then, speaking very slowly, quietly too, I said: 'Yes. I'm afraid it is.'

'And Andre – dear, ubiquitous Andre – has all the answers?'

'Can you suggest anyone else?'

'I don't expect you to believe me immediately.' He too was speaking slowly, choosing each word with care, placing it precisely in its sentence, and stepping from that word to the next, coming a fraction closer each time, as if it were only by means of words that he could bridge the distance between us. 'But I can tell you one thing.'

'What's that?'

'He isn't coming back. He's gone, Lucy, gone for good.'

'Oh,' I said quickly. 'That I know.' I smiled. 'For good. For better or for worse. Gone without ever being here. Not really. Over before it began.'

'Shouldn't you just leave it, then?'

I shrugged. 'There are still things I need to know. Answers to certain questions. Did he ever tell you about a friend of his called Nick?'

'Nick?' The name obviously meant nothing to Charles. 'Who's Nick?'

I paused, then, tossing back my head, came straight out with it: 'Nick was Benedict's oldest friend. Nick was in love with Benedict. He even tricked Benedict's girlfriend into leaving him so he could have Benedict to himself.'

Charles was shaking his head. 'But what's that to you?'

'I'm sorry,' I said. 'I know it isn't fair of me. Or nice. But I need an answer.' I transferred my attention to my glass. 'And if you're angry – well all I can say is, I'm sorry.'

'Angry?' He sounded genuinely surprised. 'Good heavens,

no! Confused, maybe, and sad, but not angry.'

I looked at him then, long and hard, and saw he was telling the truth. 'You know what I thought for a while?' I said finally. 'After he'd vanished, and there was no sign of him? That you'd had something to do with his disappearance.'

Charles let out a quick, incredulous laugh. 'Me! Goodness no! Me? Good heavens!'

'And yet you painted him,' I concluded softly.

There was silence.

'You've been in the studio?'

I nodded, and again there was silence, no words to aid us, until he whispered, so softly I could hardly hear: 'Wish fulfilment, Lucy. Nothing more. Wish fulfilment. And a little hurt, I suppose. Nothing more.'

'I see.'

'What you have to understand,' he went on quietly, 'is that what I paint, the people I paint, it's never them. Not really you. Not really Benedict. I reinvent you every time.'

'I know,' I said, standing up. 'In a way, that's what this is all about. Always has been.' I crossed to the dresser. 'Coffee?'

'No, thanks,' he said, then: 'On second thoughts, yes.' And then, after a further pause: 'So what are you going to do?'

'Find some answers, that's all. If I can. I've been very worried about him, these last few days.'

I had my back to him, so I couldn't see the expression on his face when, speaking very softly still, he said: 'I want you to know, Lucy, that anything I've ever said or done to hurt you, it was never intentional. That time you went to London . . .'

I interrupted him. 'The abortion, you mean?'

He caught his breath at that, but only for a second.

'The abortion, yes. My anger then – it was myself I blamed, not you.'

I should have turned to him then, I suppose, and said what I'd said to Ralph: 'It's over now. Forgotten.' Because in speaking of it, in hearing him speak of it, it had been ended, put behind us, buried. But I was scared that if I did look at him, if I did say anything, I would simply break down. I heard him push back his chair.

'Well,' he said. 'I'd better check on Ralph.'

'Yes,' I said. 'You better had.'

I was aware of him crossing to the door.

'When will you go?' he asked.

'Tomorrow.'

'That soon?'

'But only after the doctor's been,' I added quickly. 'I want to know what he says, and I won't go at all if Ralph . . .'

'No, no! Ralph and I can look after ourselves.'

Now I did turn to face him, and saw, glistening on his cheeks, the tell-tale trace of tears.

'I'm sorry,' I said finally. 'I don't understand this any more than you.'

'You mustn't worry about Ralph,' he repeated, running a hand through his greying curls. 'I can look after Ralph.'

And then, with a funny little flourish (almost, but not quite, a bow), he was gone.

For a moment I didn't move; then, abandoning any pretence at preparing coffee, I ran through the hallway into the living-room and out onto the lawn. It was completely dark by now, the only traces of light being the stars, the lights at the end of the pier, and Meldwich's faint, orange glow low on the horizon.

I walked towards the pier. I knew that no matter what happened, no matter what Doctor Cole had to say in the morning, I would go to London. It had become imperative that I reach the end of this story, this narrative, this fairy tale that was Benedict. I smiled grimly. That was exactly it: a fairy tale. Ever since I'd first set eyes on him, he'd run through my days like a fairy tale, leading me out of one day and into the next, providing impetus. A fairy tale: strong, wily, muscular, surprising. Something that took unexpected turns, was passionate one minute, perplexing the next, now meaningful, now trite. But which always moved on, charting itself as it went. A salutary fairy tale, to which one person, and one person only, could supply the key. Andre.

Immersed as I was in these thoughts, I took little notice of my surroundings, and was almost at the beach when some sixth sense made me stop in my tracks and glance to my right

– where, just beyond the lawn, I saw a shadow, a certain deepening of the darkness. I screwed up my eyes in order to bring it into focus, and as I did so, it assumed the shape of a fox. I could make out the unmistakable outline of its poised and cautious head, the elegant sweep of its body, the thick, proud bush of its tail. Then, as I let out a sigh of wonder at this sighting, the shape or shadow dematerialised, the darkness became just darkness again, and what had been the fox returned to being merely air.

I stared for a long time at the spot where the fox had been – wondered, even, whether I should follow the beach in the hope of a second sighting. Then, acknowledging the fact that I was more than blessed to have been granted the one, I turned towards the house – where, a shadow himself against the light spilling gaudily from the french windows, stood my husband Charles, awaiting my return.

Sfumato

By the next afternoon my need to speak to Andre had passed beyond being a need and become an obsession. The comparative peace of my illicit first-class compartment on the one fifteen from Meldwich to Liverpool Street was all very well, but not only was its tranquillity temporary, liable to interruption at any moment from a fellow traveller, it was also spurious: lasting peace could only come when the questions that were haunting me had been resolved.

I'd woken that morning as fluttery as a schoolgirl on her first date – in a tizzy because I couldn't decide whether to return Andre's call before catching the train to London, or whether it was simply best to arrive on his doorstep and take him by surprise – when I'd been side-tracked by a knock at my door, and Charles had appeared, bearing a tray.

'Would madam care for some tea?' he'd grinned. 'Lapsang Souchong. The very best.'

He'd put the tray on my dressing-table and set about pouring. I'd pushed myself upright.

'What's the time?'

'Seven o'clock.'

'Have you been up long?'

'A while.'

'And how is he?'

'Not in pain, I don't think, at least not at the moment, but he didn't sleep well.'

He finished pouring, and now he handed me my cup before settling with his on the foot of the bed.

'And you?' I asked.

'I got up once to check on him, but otherwise I slept like a log.' He smiled, a deft, ironic little smile. 'It's obviously a great weight off my shoulders, realising my parents weren't perfect. Gives me some leeway at last. Allows me my own little failures. And to cope with yours. Talking of which . . .' He

255

took a sip of his tea. 'Must you still go to London?'

'You know I must.'

He frowned. 'After last night, silly of me maybe, but I sort of thought . . .'

'But only when the doctor's been,' I added hastily.

'Oh, that!' he said. 'I told you not to worry about that.'

'I know. But I'd feel happier waiting. And anyway, I can ask him to give me a lift to the station.'

Charles chuckled wryly. 'So it's thank God for merry old Doctor Cole, is it? What would we do without him?'

There was a silence, in which we both sipped our tea.

'I'm sorry if last night made you think otherwise,' I said eventually. 'I didn't mean it to.'

'No, no!' he replied. 'My fault entirely. I shouldn't have mentioned it. Last night was last night. I quite understand.'

He got up and returned his cup to the tray. I saw his eyes go to the painting that hung above the dressing-table: the young girl lying laughing on a patch of grass in a bluebell wood, her secretarial books forgotten by her side.

'Isn't it silly?' he said. 'You live all your life thinking something is so, is true, and then you discover it wasn't so at all, and nothing in your life has actually changed, you're still the person you always were, and you've done all the things you've done, and yet somehow, suddenly, subtly, it's all totally different. You view it from a different perspective.'

He turned away from the painting. 'You know why I started painting you? Because of your beauty and because I loved you and because I wanted to capture those two things, your beauty and my love for you, and share them with the rest of the world.' He frowned. 'I never meant to make you only mine.'

'Charles, please! There's really no need . . .'

He held up a hand, and crossing to the bed, very lightly brushed my forehead with the tips of his fingers.

'Go well,' he said. 'Journey well.'

Then, turning sharply on his heels, he left the room.

I went back in my mind to the night before, to how he'd taken my hand as I returned to the house, and without saying a word, had led me upstairs and down the corridor to my room, and turning on the light, had searched my eyes for permission to stay; and finding it, had led me to the bed, undressed us both, and then very slowly, with infinite tenderness, sadness almost, and regret, proceeded to make love to me, kissing my neck and scooping up my body in his hands like water. Except that unlike water, I didn't run through his fingers, but stayed there, held in his palm like a reading, the lines of my desire miraculously matching his, the might-have-been merging with the real, the left with the right, me with him.

I pushed back the covers. How ironic, I thought, that contrary to what the tabloids would have us believe – that family scandals are sparked by an excess of love, or love wrongly placed (the husband running off with his mistress, the uncle taking advantage of his niece) – the real scandal is invariably the paucity of love, how meagrely it is parcelled out.

I went to the window. Impervious to family dramas, supremely indifferent to the merely human, the day was preparing for another display of summer perfection. The air was cool, still, and gentle, but already it contained both hint and promise of the heat to come, of the bleached sky, the relentless sun, the wasps and droning bees, the roses and the fields of burgeoning wheat, the familiar, sensual trappings of high summer.

I crossed to the wardrobe and fetched out my Laura Ashley. Dressed, I reached down a suitcase from the top of the wardrobe and packed as if for a weekend away: a change of underclothes, another dress, my toiletries.

I didn't feel I could go downstairs without looking in on Ralph, but when I knocked on his door, there was no reply, and when I inched it open I found he was asleep. Carefully, thankfully, I shut the door behind me and continued downstairs.

The kitchen was empty. I made myself a slice of toast, then let myself out the back door and made off along the beach in the direction of the bunker. The less I had to be with anyone before Doctor Cole arrived the better, and it was with some relief that, at the end of my circuit of the island, I saw

his figure emerging from his sleek grey Volvo, as sleek
himself, with his layered, lacquered hair and his smartly
tailored suit, as the car in which he drove: a visiting financial
advisor, one would have said, rather than a country doctor,
come to discuss Ralph's investment portfolio.

'Mrs Hamilton!' He raised his hand in a business-like wave.
'Good morning!'

'Good morning!'

'Lovely day, what?'

'Lovely!'

Then Charles appeared to usher him inside, and I went up
to my bedroom to fetch my case.

I waited for them on the lawn.

'So?' I asked when, some ten minutes later, they reappeared, Doctor Cole to make a beeline for his car, Charles
to cross the grass towards me.

'He'll tell you,' Charles said, 'on the way to the station.'

'And will you cope?'

'He's getting a nurse.'

'I don't want to say goodbye to him,' I said. 'Do you think
that's all right?'

'It's better.'

'I'll ring Norman to let you know where I am.'

'Right.' He took a step backwards, as if to distance himself
from what I was doing. 'Well, look after yourself.'

'And you.'

'Come on, you two!' It was Doctor Cole, calling from his
car. 'I've got other patients to see you know.'

Charles ran over to where my case stood on the steps. I
approached the car and put my head through the passenger
window.

'Are you sure he'll be able to manage?' I asked. 'On his
own?'

'I don't see why not.'

'You don't think . . .?'

But before I could get any further, Charles appeared with
my case. I opened the car door and got in. Charles put my
case in the boot, slammed it shut, then came round to my
window.

'Give my best to Andre,' he said. 'Tell him I'll be in touch.'

Then we were speeding down the drive in a swirl of dust and Doctor Cole was saying: 'The roads seem to have improved since the last time I was on the island. Is that possible?'

'They were graded in the spring.'

'Like chalk and cheese,' he said. 'Chalk and cheese.'

We didn't slow down until we'd reached the causeway.

'Magical place,' said Doctor Cole, rolling down his window and relaxing in his seat. 'Magical place.'

The water was still right out, and the mud lay gleaming in the sun like something glazed, its sheen reflecting the birds pecking there for food.

'Hard on cars, though,' he continued. 'My father knew Mr Benson, used to treat him, in fact, and he went through a car every three years, so Father said. And they built them better in those days.'

'They found his body yesterday.'

'They what?'

'Mr Benson. They found his body. Over there. In the mud.' I gestured to where, seemingly unruffled by the excitements of yesterday, the archaeologists were once again at work, huddled over their tables like figures in a piece of surrealist performance art.

'Good God!' said Doctor Cole. 'Really?'

'Apparently the mud had preserved him perfectly. A sergeant at the station recognised the body.'

'Good God! I met him once, you know, when I was a boy. He used to throw the most fabulous parties, and I went to one. Heaven knows how I came to be there. Perhaps Mother and Father didn't have anyone to look after me. Anyway, I remember being at a window quite high up in the house, the nursery, I suppose, looking down on all these fairy lanterns in the trees. There was a band on the pier, and people were dancing on the lawn, and as I watched, a woman suddenly tore off all her clothes, absolutely everything, and ran into the sea.' He paused. 'It was one of the oddest and most disturbing things I'd ever seen. Beautiful, though.'

We had reached the end of the causeway, and as we crested

the sea wall I twisted round in my seat for one last look at the archaeologists, and – beyond them – the island. Then, as we dipped down to join the caravans, I rolled up my window.

'I can still see her,' said Doctor Cole, 'running across the lawn into the sea. Quite magical.'

'Nowadays it's Charles' studio,' I said. 'What you call the nursery. The room at the top of the house.'

'Quite magical,' he repeated.

We had reached the main road, and he looked carefully to the left and the right before turning onto it.

'How long?' I asked. 'Can you say at all? For Ralph, I mean?'

He shrugged. 'Not with any accuracy. A month. Three months. Maybe a matter of weeks.'

'And shouldn't he be in hospital?'

'Ideally, yes. But I've left your husband plenty of pain-killers. That's all one can do, really, at this stage. Control the pain. And I'll make arrangements for a nurse. There's no need to worry. Really there isn't.'

Now we were driving through the housing developments on the outskirts of Meldwich, developments with fanciful names like The Saltings and Ocean View, romantic names quite at odds with the regimented meanness of the dwellings. We reached the one way system that led up the hill to the station.

'It's very good of you to be going out of your way like this.'

He smiled. '*Pas de problème.*'

He pulled up with a flourish in front of the station, and without switching off the engine, leapt out, fetched my suitcase from the boot and carried it to the ticket office, where he deposited it against the wall.

'So!' he said. 'Have a good trip. Shopping?'

I nodded – and then, because it must have seemed odd to have an overnight bag for a shopping trip, added quickly: 'And visiting Mother.'

'Not poorly also?'

I shook my head. 'As fit as a fiddle, thank God.'

He grinned. 'Not always a blessing.' He proffered his hand. 'Well, duty calls. Successful shopping.'

'Let's hope,' I said. 'And thanks again for the lift.'

'A tip. They never have inspectors on this line on a Saturday, so sit in first-class. It's always empty. Much more civilised.'

And so it was that I came to be in sole possession of a first-class compartment on the one fifteen from Meldwich to London, sitting with my face to the glass, registering in a purely subliminal way the shift in scenery from an occasional village surrounded by an infinity of fields, some a conventional green, others fluorescent with rape, to an absence of colour: a drab succession of suburbs enlivened only by the sporadic flash of a park, a glimpse of children on swings, a game of cricket, the odd line of washing.

It was almost a year since I'd been off the island, and as the landscape diminished from country to suburb to rise again in the makeshift Manhattan of the city, I found myself unnerved by its unfamiliarity, its vastness and complexity.

At Liverpool Street I was similarly thrown by the crowd, a surging, determined mass of shoppers and youngsters with backpacks who, if I'd let them, would have tricked me off course. But I put my head down and fought my way to the taxi rank, where, surprisingly, there was hardly any queue, and it was only a matter of minutes before I was giving my driver Andre's address.

Still Life

*T*he taxi-driver (not your standard cockney, but a laconic Jamaican whose musical taste, judging by the symphony flooding his cab, tended towards the classical) knew and relished the back routes. In the course of our drive from Liverpool Street to Earls Court, we passed only one landmark I knew: Hyde Park Corner. For the rest, we turned from anonymous sidestreet into anonymous sidestreet, occasionally crossing a main road that might have been familiar, except that in every case, before I could register the road's name, we had turned down another sidestreet.

It had the effect, this drive, of making me feel smuggled towards my destination, of being rushed to Andre's incognito, and of arriving not only unheralded at his towering slab of a house, but also unprepared. There had been a worrying absence of markers on our route against which to measure my progress.

I paid off the taxi-driver, and leaving him with reluctance to the balm of his Sibelius, stood nervously regarding the sheer white façade before me. Its opulent symmetry seemed, in my present frame of mind, more daunting than I remembered. Then, picking up my suitcase with all the resolution I could muster, I mounted the steps and put my finger to the large brass bell.

There was no reply at first, and I was beginning to wonder if anyone was home, and to curse myself for not ringing ahead, when the door was yanked open by an aggressive young man in tattered jeans and large black boots. His face, beneath its spikes of bleached hair, was fixed in a suspicious scowl.

'Upstairs,' he muttered, then shouldered past me down the steps.

I was rendered speechless by the young man's belligerence, and it was a moment before I managed to call out after him: 'Who?'

The young man had reached the pavement. He turned, the scowl on his face deepening.

'You've come to see Andre, right?'

I nodded.

'So I told you, he's upstairs.'

'Right,' I said. 'I see.'

But the young man was already half a block away, striding out with a determination that would have been commendable had it not been so ferocious.

I pushed open the door with my suitcase, and once I'd entered the hallway, kicked it closed behind me. I dropped my suitcase by the Victorian coatrack that dominated the hallway, took stock of myself in the mirror on the wall, then went to the foot of the stairs.

'Andre?' I ventured.

There was no reply, so I mounted the stairs to the first landing and tried again: 'Andre?'

This time he heard me, and following the direction of his muted and irritable 'Who is it?', I came, on the second landing, to a door through which, very faintly, could be heard music. I pushed it open.

Wearing, of all things, a filmy, black and white burnouse with a large cowl that hung down the back, he was sitting cross-legged on the floor in the middle of the room. He looked neither surprised nor pleased to see me.

'So!' he said. 'I wondered when you'd come.'

'I would have rung,' I began, 'only . . .'

He waved away my explanation. 'It's better like this. The phone leaves a lot to be desired.' He got to his feet. 'You must excuse me. I was meditating.' He crossed to a cabinet in the corner of the room and turned down the music, then gestured me towards the black leather couch that ran the length of the far wall. 'Please,' he said. 'Sit.'

Not having visited Andre's house since the evening five years previously when he'd offered us the island, I'd forgotten how idiosyncratic it was, graduating from the Victorian pomposity of the hallway to the high-tech iciness of the room we were in now, and which, with its pale grey walls, its black leather furniture and aluminium spotlights, would have seemed

utterly soulless had it not been for the three early Bacons,
whose splashes of purple provided the room with a certain
tortured colour. The rest of the house, if I remembered right,
was an equal mix of surprise and contradiction: a kitchen out
of the 1950s, a spartan turn of the century bathroom, entirely
bare except for an enormous bath and a towel rail, and a
dining-room whose walls and ceiling were painted panels
depicting, in licentious detail, a Roman orgy.

'So,' said Andre, sinking onto the opposite end of the sofa,
'where were we when you hung up on me?'

The words came out in a rush: 'I'm worried about him,
Andre, that's all. Ten days ago he vanished, without saying a
word.'

'And you think he might have come to some harm?'

'Well, couldn't he?'

There were tassels on the sleeves of Andre's burnouse, and
he began to fiddle with them as he talked.

'What did he tell you, exactly, about himself?'

'What do you mean?'

'I know he's secretive. But how long did he stay with you?
Three months? He must have let the odd thing slip?'

'And so what if he did? What's that got to do with his
disappearing?'

'Tell me what he told you,' said Andre. 'Everything.'

I hesitated.

'Everything,' repeated Andre.

So I told him. I told him all that Benedict had told me: that
he came from Cornwall, that he played the drums in a band
called The Unknowns, that he'd had a girlfriend called
Wendy, that he'd shared a flat in Kentish Town with a friend
called Nick.

'But you know this Nick,' I said. 'He works at the gallery.
Some sort of messenger.'

'Anything else about Nick?'

Again I hesitated.

'Don't worry,' said Andre. 'I won't tell anyone. And maybe
I know anyway.'

So I told him how Nick had got rid of Wendy, and how he'd
tried to seduce Benedict, and how Benedict had let him, and

how, the next morning, when Benedict had told Nick it couldn't happen again, Nick had run away.

'Nick?' said Andre, sounding surprised. 'Where to?'

I stared at him. 'I think you know.'

'I do?'

'Don't you?'

Here he smiled. 'Let me guess. I had some friends. They needed something doing. I suggested Nick. My suggestion was taken up.'

'Something like that.'

He stood up and went to the window. The outline of his body was thrown into stark relief against his burnouse.

'The other day,' he said, 'when you hung up, you'd rung to find out about Benedict. But suddenly you didn't want to talk about him any more. Why?'

'Oh,' I said quickly, 'it was just . . .'

'What?' he demanded. 'What was it just?'

'Well,' I said, 'it seemed that maybe I was overreacting, maybe there was nothing to worry about. We women, we get carried away, hysterical, you know how it is.'

He turned to face me. 'But you're worried again now?'

I met his gaze. 'I'm sorry. I can't help it. He did, after all, stay with us. We were looking after him.'

'And is that all?'

He said it ever so lightly, a feint not a thrust, but there was no avoiding what he meant. It was, after all, he who'd first asked me if I'd always been so vulnerable to men.

'Of course. What else would there be?'

He stared at me a moment longer. Then, shrugging, he turned away. 'No,' he said. 'Of course. Nothing else.'

'And so?' I pursued. 'What has happened to him? Do you know?'

'Well,' he said, speaking very softly, almost as if to himself, 'this Benedict you tell me about, what he told you is absolutely accurate, and yet – well, I'm not entirely sure I know him. Or not as he would want to be known.'

'What do you mean?'

He held up a hand. 'We've talked enough for now.' He came away from the window, his legs as sharp as scissors within their filmy casing. 'You weren't planning on going back today I hope?'

'Well, I . . .'

'Good! Then you'll stay the night, and over dinner we can talk properly. At leisure, as they say. Where are your things?'

'In the hall.'

'I won't be a moment.'

He vanished through the door. I got up and crossed to the window, staring without really seeing them at the houses opposite. So, I was thinking, you're here at last, at the point of no return, where the story of Benedict can be told by another, and where – if you're lucky – the facts won't be twisted to suit the teller.

My thoughts were interrupted by Andre putting his head round the door, my case in his hand.

'Come on then, let me show you your room.'

I followed him up the stairs to the next landing.

'I would put you here,' he said, gesturing at one of the three doors that led off the landing, 'opposite me, but I already have someone in there.'

So we continued upwards, to the very top of the house, where the stairs gave out at a minute door made of dark, gnarled wood. At its centre, for a handle, hung a black metal ring.

'Goodness!' I said, unable to restrain a giggle.

Andre shrugged. 'I know. Somewhat fairy-like. But then this is Earls Court. Now mind your head!'

He opened the door and we ducked through it.

The room was built into the eaves. One could stand, just, by the door, but then the roof sloped sharply to the floor, and against the far wall, where the bed was, one had to crouch. There was a window built into the eaves at the foot of the bed, and a tiny dressing-table to the right of the door. The floor had been covered by a carpet featuring a hunting scene: a proud stag at bay in a wood, surrounded by a circle of colourful hunters.

Tucked as it was under the eaves, and with everything in it on a miniature scale, like a doll's house, the room made me feel as if a giant hand might reach through the window at any minute and pluck us into another dimension.

'It's on the tiny side, I know,' said Andre, 'but at least no one can disturb you up here.' He put my suitcase on the dressing-table, then returned to the door. 'There's a bathroom on the landing opposite my room. Dinner at eight?'

'Perfect,' I said. 'Dinner at eight.'

It was, as he had said, quiet in the little room. It was also stiflingly hot. I opened the window. A faint wash of noise came through it, followed, limply, by something pretending to be fresh air. Summer was starving London of oxygen.

I crossed to the dressing-table, and, unzipping my case, slipped out of my dress, wrapped myself in my dressing-gown and ventured down to the bathroom.

It was not the room I remembered; either that, or it had been changed. It seemed smaller, for a start, and its bath, a circular, green affair, was let into the floor. In addition, it boasted a bidet, a washbasin, a shower attachment in the shape of a mermaid, and a forest of plants. And on the walls there was a sequence of black and white prints, all of half-naked men, their bodies seeming to burst not just out of their jeans, but out of their very skins, as if mere membrane were not enough to restrain the play of their muscles.

I turned on the bath, took off my dressing-gown, and ruefully studied my own body in the mirror that ran the length of the wall behind the bath. Despite the advantages of colour and the artful masking of a plant or two, it was no longer in the league of bodies one could photograph. It couldn't have withstood a camera. It cried out for a paint-brush: interpretation rather than objectivity.

I stepped into the bath, and, closing my eyes, gave myself over to the sensuousness of the water, tried to forget the bodies on the wall, my own body, Charles, Ralph, Andre and Benedict, the mosaic of bodies that constituted my universe.

It was exactly eight when I left my room to go downstairs. Andre was waiting for me in the hallway. He'd slicked back his hair and changed into a pair of black jeans and a black polo neck. The effect was formal, severe and slightly sinister.

'Dear Lucy!' he said, extending an arm. 'As ravishing as ever.'

'You're not doing too badly yourself.'

He grinned, and taking my arm in his, ushered me into the dining-room, where he sat me at the far end of the table.

'Excuse me a minute!' Crossing to the mural on my left, in which a young gladiator was having his toga removed by an ample matron, he opened a door in it, tearing the gladiator from the matron's embrace, and vanished down some stairs to the kitchen. I looked about me at the other murals. They all depicted a second dining-room, in which the naked men and women reclining round their table seemed more interested in sampling each other than the food. Our table, by contrast, was formidably correct: a daunting display of gleaming silver, crockery and glass.

Andre reappeared with a steaming bowl of pasta, and, kicking the door shut behind him, reunited the gladiator with the matron. He placed the bowl in the centre of the table.

'I'll serve, shall I?' He took my plate. 'It's very simple. Just pasta and salad. Say when.'

'When!'

He handed me my plate, then took his place at the head of the table.

'Help yourself to salad.'

'In a moment.'

He raised his glass. '*Bon appetit!*'

'*Bon appetit.*'

We started our meal in silence, and it was a good few minutes before Andre paused and said: 'I had lunch the other day in this club in town, some guy I'm trying to buy some paintings from, and do you know, we weren't allowed to talk business until the end of the meal? So many rules!'

He shrugged wryly as he said it, but I got the message: I was not to talk about Benedict until we had finished eating.

'Now tell me,' he went on. 'Your husband. How's the painting?'

'Fine, I think.'

'I liked what I saw the last time I was down.'

'So you said.'

'Different.'

I smiled. 'No me.'

'Indeed. No you.' He savoured a mouthful of wine. 'But he needed to move on. Continuity is all very well, but there has to be development.'

'Jorgen has something to show you,' I said. 'You know he photographs the island? Well, he's put together quite a collection by now, and I think they're rather good.'

Andre frowned. 'Not my scene, I'm afraid, photographs.'

'These are good.'

'Very good?'

'Very good.'

He dipped his head in acquiescence. 'Okay. I'll take a look at them.'

'It would mean a lot to him.'

'Next time I'm down. I promise. I like to look after my own.' He stood up. 'Some more?'

I shook my head. 'That was delicious.'

'Right, then, I have something to show you.' He came round the table and pulled out my chair. 'Follow me.'

He reopened the door in the mural, and I followed him down the stairs – and forward in time – into the dated futurism of the kitchen, all angular Formica and tubular stools and, in the corner, the garish afterthought of an original 1950s juke-box.

'This way.' He led me through the kitchen and down a narrow, poorly lit corridor to a door at the back of the house. 'After you.'

He stood back as he opened the door. I found myself in a large, whitewashed room, the centre-piece of which, indeed its only furniture, was a drum kit: four drums of varying sizes flanked by a pair of cymbals. On the largest of the drums, in Gothic script, was emblazoned 'The Unknowns'.

I turned to look enquiringly at Andre. 'And so? Benedict told me about the band. Remember?'

Andre's eyes were fixed on mine in dark, unfathomable contemplation. 'You misunderstand.'

'Misunderstand what?'

'Remember the young man you met when you arrived? These are his. These drums belong to Nick.' He took a step backwards. 'Now if you'll excuse me, I'll go and stack the dishwasher. You'll find me on the first floor.'

I turned to look again at the drums, and slowly, very slowly, like an incoming tide, the full implications of what he'd said washed over me. If the drums belonged to Nick, then it was Nick, not Benedict, who played in the band, it was Nick, not Benedict, who had a girlfriend called Wendy, and it was Benedict who'd worked for Andre, Benedict who'd been besotted, Benedict who'd made the advances, been rejected and decided to run away.

Punctuating which realisation came another: the man I'd seen on the yacht alongside ours had looked familiar because I'd seen him with Andre in Meldwich, going into the estate agents.

I remembered our exchange on the yacht.

'And have you heard from him since?'
'What do you think?'
'You have to tell me what happened.'
'Well, through the gallery, through Andre, he met these people, they wanted him to do some job for them, and because he was desperate, because he had nothing to lose, he agreed.'

I found Andre, as he'd said I would, in the art deco living-room on the first floor, the last piece of the jigsaw puzzle, a room for cocktails and laughter, who cares what comes after?

He was standing by the drinks cabinet, pouring two brandies. He turned as he heard me come through the door and thrust a glass into my hand.

'We met,' he said, 'Benedict and I, in a little club I sometimes visit in Kentish Town. His flat was just round the corner, he used to visit the club a lot, to drink, to dance, to find someone, maybe, to take him home for the night. He was sitting by the bar, and I bought him a vodka, and a little later we danced, and later still I bought him back here. Like you, I also have my phantoms. Like you, I was besotted. Who could fail to be? He's a special boy. But our Benedict, I'm afraid, had eyes only for Nick. He persuaded me to give Nick rehearsal space, he even got me to give him a job. I realised I was up against something I couldn't control. So I bowed out. I gave Nick what Benedict wanted, and when things didn't work out between them, I gave Benedict what he wanted: a method of escape.'

'How? How did he escape? And where?'

Andre shrugged. 'There are two possibilities. He is either doing a job for some friends of mine, the sort of job it doesn't do to enquire into too closely, which is why I don't have details, or else he's cataloguing china.'

'China?'

He laughed. 'Porcelain, not the country. A collection I'm thinking of acquiring, the cataloguing of which, since it's rather a famous collection, requires absolute secrecy. Which is why no one can say anything.' He shrugged. 'It's up to you to decide.'

'All right,' I said finally. 'But tell me this at least. Is he safe?'

'Safe?' He took a sip of his brandy. 'What is safe? How can any of us be safe if we want to live?'

'Your yacht then?'

'I told you. In Long Creedon. You can check if you like. I can even give you the number of the man who's fixing it.'

'No,' I said softly. 'It doesn't matter.'

'Poor Lucy!' He savoured another sip of his brandy. 'What you have to remember is that you are you. Wholly you. Not Charles'. Not Benedict's. You.' He paused, a wry smile playing about his lips. 'Less vulnerable than you think. Certainly less vulnerable than you led me to believe.' He cleared his throat. 'Now do drink your brandy. It's rather good.'

I handed him my glass. 'I'm sorry. I can't. Not now. In fact, I think I'll go to bed. If you don't mind.'

He put the two glasses on the drinks cabinet and took my face in his hands. 'You ought to smile more,' he said. 'You have a lovely smile.' Then he released me, and turning to the drinks cabinet, refilled his glass. 'Well if you won't, I will.'

'Good-night,' I said. 'See you in the morning.'

Upstairs, in my little room under the eaves, I sat on my bed and stared at the wall. I could, it occurred to me, tell Jorgen about the yacht and the man I'd seen with Andre in Meldwich, it would be quite a scoop for him – and then I thought: no, so what if Andre had set me up, relying on my vulnerability to provide Benedict with cover? So what if he wanted people to think, when they saw the two of us together, that that was why Benedict had come to the island? So what, even, if Benedict had simply been following instructions when he made himself available to me? He had, in the end, tried to protect me from himself by telling his story obscurely, casting Nick in the Benedict role, so that I wouldn't be tempted to comfort him.

I remembered Norman's comment about lame ducks. Benedict had known what I was doing, and to prevent me reinventing him utterly had reinvented himself, putting sufficient distance between us to allow for safe passage.

I took off my dress and hung it behind the door, then sat on the bed again and continued to stare at the wall. Later, after maybe an hour, I stood up, put on my dressing-gown, took up my toilet bag, and went to the door.

As I opened it, I heard a sound on the landing below. The bathroom door was open, spilling a golden wedge of light onto the landing, and I heard the toilet being flushed. I stayed where I was, just inside my doorway, and after a minute the light in the bathroom was extinguished and Nick, naked except for a pair of boxer shorts, appeared in the doorway. He looked, in that instant, like one of the prints from the bathroom wall. Then he moved, breaking the composition, and padded across the landing to Andre's room. He glanced over his shoulder, as if sensing he'd been observed, then opened the door and slipped silently through it.

I was reminded of another door, another young man framed, caught like Nick in that moment between rooms, that gap between one space and another, one world and another. Then, unable suddenly to move myself, I turned back into my little room, shut the door behind me, and threw myself onto the bed – where, miraculously, I fell more or less instantly asleep.

And so we come full circle, to the beginning of the fairy tale, to me in the attic, dreaming about Benedict, Benedict in the creek, Benedict kissing me, Benedict running the back of his hand down my cheek: the point from which we departed, approached from a different angle.

The dream woke me, impelling me to the window, where, Rapunzel-like, I sat gazing over the rooftops until the liverish glow of the night sky paled into the subtler tones of morning: delicate pinks and greys underscored by the merest hint of blue.

I stood up and stretched. I was tired and stiff and in need of tea. I took my dress off its hanger, and slipping into it, went downstairs to the kitchen.

Nick was there before me, sitting at the table surrounded by the Sunday papers, his spiked hair made crazier by sleep. He put down the paper he'd been reading, and without bothering to greet me or to introduce himself, got to his feet, fetched a cup and saucer from the cupboard and demanded: 'How do you like it? Milk and sugar?'

I nodded, and pulling out a chair, sat opposite him at the table.

He handed me my cup and returned to his seat.

'You're Nick,' I said. 'Is that right?'

'That's right.'

'And you work for Andre?'

A brief smile flickered across his features. 'Sometimes. The odd job here and there.'

'At the gallery?'

'Sometimes.' He finished his tea and stood up. 'I've seen you there,' he said.

'Me? No. I haven't been to the gallery in ages.'

'In those paintings,' he said. 'Those landscapes. That's where I know you from.' He crossed to the door. 'He does you well,' he continued, 'whoever paints them.'

'My husband,' I said. 'They're my husband's.'

'You're lucky,' he said. 'To have such a keen observer.'

And with that he was gone. I looked at my watch. It was eight o'clock. Time to be moving on.

On the landing outside his bedroom, I encountered

Andre. He was dressed in a suit, the very image of a businessman.

'Sleep well?' he queried.

I nodded. 'Well enough. And you? Where are you off to so early on a Sunday morning?'

He smiled. 'No rest for the wicked, I'm afraid. Now do you need a key?'

I shook my head. 'No thanks. You've been very kind, but it's time for me to go.'

'Well,' he said, 'give that husband of yours my best. And don't let out my room. I'll be down at the weekend. Might bring Nick, even. I think he'd like the island, don't you?'

'Everyone likes the island,' I said. 'You know that.'

'So!' he said. 'Until the weekend.'

'Until the weekend.'

He started down the stairs.

'And don't forget about Jorgen,' I called after him.

He turned. 'Don't worry. I won't. As I told you, I like to look after my own.' He raised a hand in farewell, then vanished round the turn of the stairs. I continued up to my room. Although it was a Sunday, I knew I wouldn't have any trouble picking up a cab in the Earls Court Road, and as there wouldn't be much traffic I reckoned I could reach Liverpool Street in time for the ten twenty.

When I got to Meldwich, there was only one taxi at the rank in the station forecourt, and although the driver wasn't prepared to take me onto the island I decided not to risk waiting for another in case I missed the tide.

The driver dropped me below the sea wall. The caravan park was abuzz with children on bikes, their whoops and yells drowning out the more subdued drone of their parents gossiping across the fences that separated the plots. Taking firm hold of my suitcase, I marched over the sea wall and onto the causeway.

It was nearing the end of the tide, and in the central depression in the mud-flats grey fingers of water were already reaching out to pull the causeway under. On the flats to my left, I could see the marks made in the mud by the archaeologists, but of the archaeologists themselves there was no sign. They'd obviously packed up for the tide – which meant that if I wanted to get across safely, I'd better be brisk.

By the time I reached the middle of the causeway, which was also its lowest point, the water was lapping at the stones by the side of the road. I stopped to rest, and as I watched saw the water, gingerly at first, then with growing determination, reach onto the road and run for the potholes.

I picked up my suitcase and, stepping round the puddles, proceeded onwards.

I didn't stop until I'd reached the island, when the weight of my suitcase forced me to rest again. Balancing it on a rock by the side of the road, I turned to look back at the causeway. The middle section of the road had been covered, and that part of the mud-flats was a rising expanse of water; water which, according to Miss Kalberer, would over the years rise ever more inexorably until our makeshift island, home before us to a chain of people stretching back in time to the iron age, perhaps beyond, would – finally – be claimed by the open sea.

I became aware of a noise behind me, and turning back to the present, saw, at the far end of the field to my right, a combine harvester, inching like an ungainly dinosaur through the wheat. In the future, maybe, our island might yield to the sea, but for the moment, as Norman trundled from field to field in his mechanical monstrosity, so a contrary tide, the summer tide of wheat, would gradually recede to uncover the bare red earth. Then would come the burning of the stubble, and with that autumn, the island pared by the onset of winter to its bare essentials. The sky would change then, too, darkening from blue to grey, and the birds that now formed a plethora of notes on the overhead wires and sang, ceaselessly, the songs they measured out with their bodies on the wire, would gather in ever larger numbers until, abruptly, they would fly south, ceding the estuary to the Canada geese.

And through this landscape, of it, as in a painting, would move myself. And although – as would be inevitable – I would sometimes think of Benedict, the pain of his memory – like all pains – would pass, and in time, when I went to the creek, I would cease to see his form and face in the shadow of

Norman's *Sprite*, would see instead just the mud and the miniature, almost invisible flowers that for some reason flourish there.

And I would return from my walks around the island, my tracings of its boundaries, to the manor house where, in the attic, Charles would be working, and from which, at six, he would emerge to tell me how, that day, he had created me, which aspect of me he had used – and I would put out my hand to touch him, not for confirmation, simply reassurance. And he would take my hand and put it to his lips and it wouldn't matter that one only exists as others see one, it would matter only that one had been blessed with existence, that still lives were still lives.

I smiled. It wasn't a good joke, but it was a joke Charles would appreciate, and I was glad to be somewhere I could share it with him.

I picked up my suitcase and, barely aware of the weight of it, made off down the road to the village and along the tree-lined road, striated by shadow, to the seafront, where, on turning the corner, I saw that Ralph, with a blanket over his knees, was taking tea on the lawn with Charles. I stopped, and putting down my suitcase, watched for a moment the picture they made. Then Charles looked up and saw me, and as he did so his face lit up in a welcoming smile and he waved. Picking up my suitcase, I stepped into the picture.

Osea and London 1992

THE MOON RISING

Steven Kelly

Having avoided all responsibility during his National
Service in the Italian army, Andreas Weissman returns
home to the realities of life as an apprentice to his uncle,
the hotel night porter. As a storm rages and batters the
hotel one night, Andreas has time to reflect on his love for
the beautiful but turbulent prostitute, Elisa. Her lust for
life and the knife-edge of her every self-destructive move
have cut him to the core. While he pieces together the
fragments of his past, the calm of his new routine is
shattered by the arrival of a pugnacious businessman and
his entourage of bodyguards and whores. And as the
moon rises and the night gets longer, it is clear that the
lines of stress between the characters must fracture . . .

With extraordinary assurance and skill, Steven Kelly
demonstrates again the qualities of precision, elegance and
originality which mark his stories. *The Moon Rising* is a
powerful and unsettling novel from one of the most
outstanding young writers at work in Britain today.

Praise for *Invisible Architecture:*

'Striking . . . impressive . . . polished' INDEPENDENT

'Stark, economical and elegant' SUNDAY TIMES

'Brilliant and disturbing . . . These extravagant stories of
love and death are told in the quietest, most economical
manner' *Penelope Fitzgerald*, EVENING STANDARD

FICTION
0 349 10595 2

CHARMS FOR THE EASY LIFE

Kaye Gibbons

'[Her writing] is filled with lively humour, compassion and intimacy' Alice Hoffman

Women of grace and gumption bloom in the pages of Kaye Gibbons' fiction and in *Charms for the Easy Life* she has created her most passionate and tough-minded heroines yet:

Charlie Kate, out of nineteenth-century rural North Carolina, a self-proclaimed doctor who treats everything – leprosy, malaria, even lovesick blues – with her roots and herbs, and advises the adolescent girls she 'caught' at birth that 'kissing's fine, nothing more than uptown shopping on downtown business'.

Sophia, her daughter, who has inherited her mother's singular wisdom and will, putting them in service to her desire to control the world around her and land the man of her choice.

Margaret, the narrator, Charlie Kate's granddaughter, whose struggle towards adulthood is complicated by the homefront demands of World War II and whose longing to defy heredity leads her to the happy discovery that for her, too, passion is the natural and most blessed gift.

Here, in *Charms for the Easy Life*, a timeless story of three generations of fiery women, Kaye Gibbons proves once again that, as Walker Percy has said, her writing is 'lovely, breathtaking, sometimes heart-wrenching'.

FICTION
0 349 10557 X

☐	The Moon Rising	Steven Kelly	£5.99
☐	Charms for the Easy Life	Kaye Gibbons	£8.99
☐	White Boy Running	Christopher Hope	£4.99
☐	The Beautiful Screaming of Pigs	Damon Galgut	£5.99
☐	Small Circle of Beings	Damon Galgut	£4.50
☐	Invitation to the Married Life	Angela Huth	£5.99
☐	South of the Lights	Angela Huth	£5.99
☐	A Bowl of Cherries	Shena Mackay	£5.99
☐	Loving and Giving	Molly Keane	£5.99
☐	The Quiet Woman	Christopher Priest	£4.99
☐	The Scissor Man	Jean Arnold	£5.99

Abacus now offers an exciting range of quality titles by both established and new authors. All of the books in this series are available from:

Little, Brown and Company (UK) Limited,
P.O. Box 11,
Falmouth,
Cornwall TR10 9EN.

Alternatively you may fax your order to the above address.
Fax No. 0326 376423.

Payments can be made as follows: cheque, postal order (payable to Little, Brown and Company) or by credit cards, Visa/Access. Do not send cash or currency. UK customers and B.F.P.O. please allow £1.00 for postage and packing for the first book, plus 50p for the second book, plus 30p for each additional book up to a maximum charge of £3.00 (7 books plus).

Overseas customers including Ireland, please allow £2.00 for the first book plus £1.00 for the second book, plus 50p for each additional book.

NAME (Block Letters) ....

....

ADDRESS ....

....

....

☐ I enclose my remittance for _____

☐ I wish to pay by Access/Visa Card

Number ☐☐☐☐☐☐☐☐☐☐☐☐☐☐☐☐

Card Expiry Date ☐☐☐☐